ONIMONOGATARI

DEMON TALE

NISIOISIN

VERTICAL.

ONIMONOGATARI
Demon Tale

NISIOISIN

Art by VOFAN

Translated by Ko Ransom

VERTICAL.

ONIMONOGATARI

© 2011 NISIOISIN
All rights reserved.

First published in Japan in 2011 by
Kodansha Ltd., Tokyo.
Publication rights for this English
edition arranged through Kodansha Ltd.,
Tokyo.

Published by Vertical, an imprint of
Kodansha USA Publishing, LLC., 2018

ISBN 978-1-947194-31-1

Manufactured in the United States
of America

First Edition

Third Printing

Kodansha USA Publishing, LLC.
451 Park Avenue South, 7th Floor
New York, NY 10016

www.vertical-inc.com

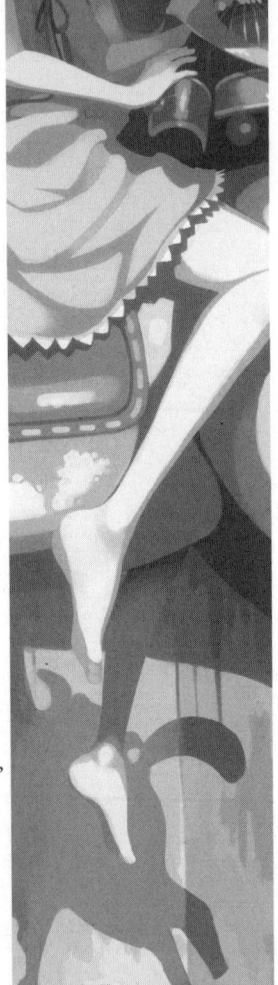

CHAPTER SNEAK

SHINOBU TIME

CHAPTER SNEAK
SHINOBU TIME

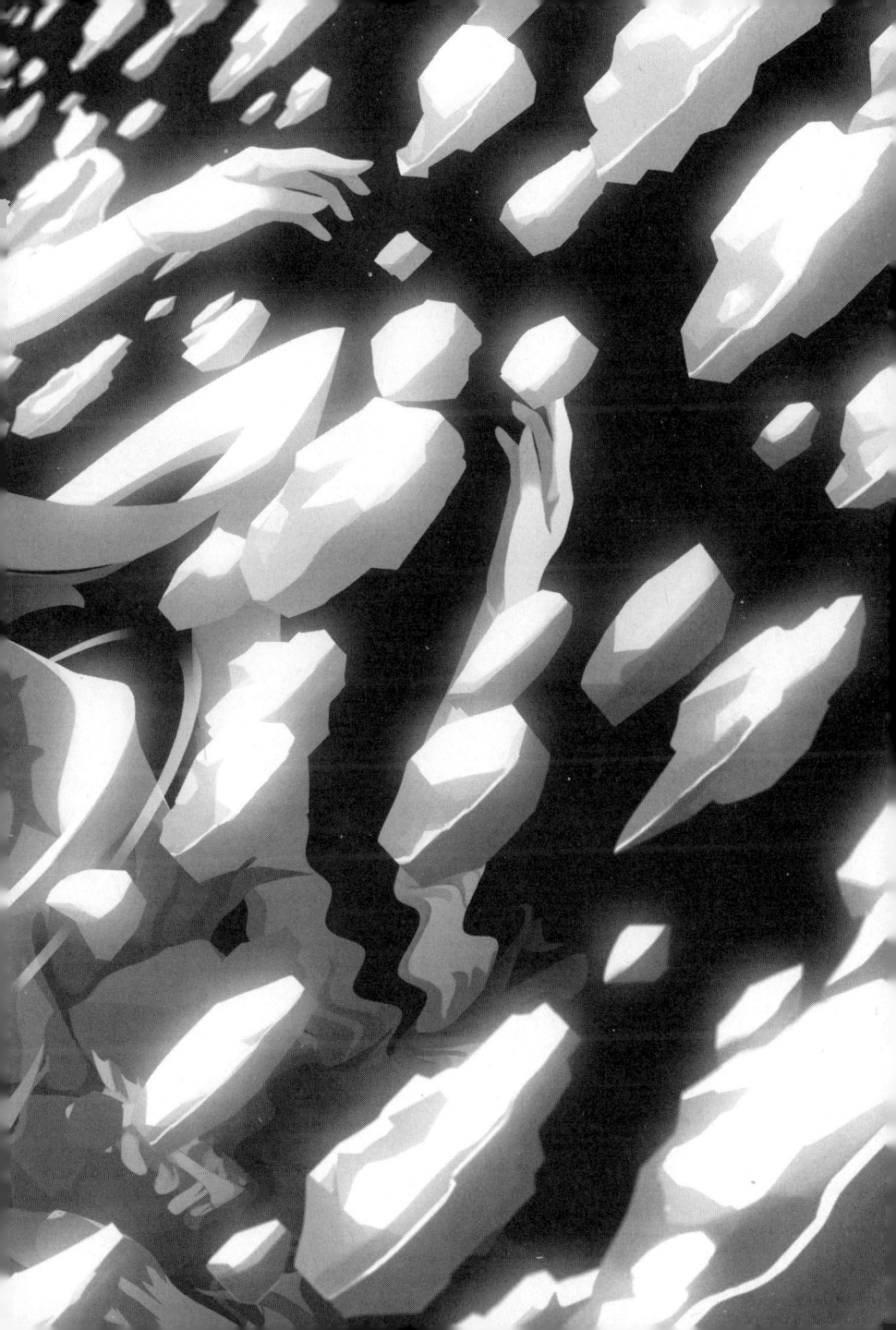

001

We're already quite familiar with the name Shinobu Oshino. Hearing it doesn't make me particularly happy, but I don't find it odd, either. It feels just right. The name she once had, Kissshot Acerolaorion Heartunderblade, must already be a thing of the past, even to her.

The past.

What came before.

What's ended.

Or perhaps—what never happened.

What's uncertain if it ever happened.

That's what it is to her. Something spoken alongside her memories, or maybe even something with no relation to who she is now.

Unrelated.

I think it goes without saying that a past self is far more of a stranger than the average stranger and is subject to a kind of hatred completely different from self-hatred—if you take me, for example, me during spring break, me during Golden Week, me climbing the stairs, me on Mother's Day, me on my bike, and me in class are all someone else.

Someone else. Strangers. People I don't know.

This isn't an attempt to shift responsibility.

I'm certainly not trying to disavow who I was back then, either—me back then did a very good job of things back then. I think I did everything I could with everything I had.

But my everything was different from my everything now—I think in each instance, based on each conviction, the person I am today would have behaved differently.

Nevertheless, I'd have saved a vampire in the end.

Nevertheless, I'd have been attacked by a cat in the end.

Nevertheless, I'd have caught Senjogahara in the end—taking those actions in each instance, based on each notion.

Whether they are right or wrong, there are something like an infinite number of other paths I could have taken—and choosing from that infinitude is ultimately something decided in the moment. You could even say that it's up to whimsy.

That Shinobu is the Shinobu she is now.

That she's the Shinobu she is now and not a different one.

That she's willing to throw away the name and form of a legendary vampire, the iron-blooded, hot-blooded, yet cold-blooded vampire Kissshot Acerolaorion Heartunderblade, and be the Shinobu she is now—this fact that is my greatest saving grace of all could be called the product of her momentary whims.

What joyous whims.

Despite appearing like a little girl, she's far older than me, an eighteen-year-old kid, and has lived a long life that's gone on for more than five centuries, so maybe, rather unexpectedly, she can be considerate in these matters—no, not considerate, I know it's nothing more than caprice.

So this time, let's talk about how these whims of hers played out four hundred years ago. About what she went through in this country four hundred years ago, and what she did—that's our story.

Shinobu Oshino.

A story that goes back through her timeline.

We'll rewind Shinobu's clock.

That's not all we'll be doing, of course, because that past relates and doesn't relate to the present day—as always, I'll save, be saved, do things, be unable to. Please entertain your own thoughts on that as you read.

I, Koyomi Araragi, am going to be thinking, too.

About her—as I tell it.

002

Previously in the series:

I, Koyomi Araragi, traveled through time with my vampire partner, Shinobu Oshino, a dime-a-dozen experience during which we failed to change history and returned dejected to the modern day, the end.

If you wanted details, I'd ask you to consult *Kabuki*, the work before the work before last, but you don't really need to. "I'd ask you" to do it, but I'm actually not. To be honest, I wish you wouldn't consult that tale of failure. Do you think I like showing off my faults or something?

But I will go so far as to say that there was a moving reason behind our time travel, namely an attempt to revive Mayoi Hachikuji, my friend who died eleven years ago and has since been wandering this town. For the sake of my honor, I'd like to divulge (stingily) that I was trying to prevent her from ever losing her life in a traffic accident at the too-young age of ten—though when I asked her directly after coming back defeated and disappointed...

"It's not as if I particularly want to revive. How pointless and self-serving, Mister Araragi, tee-hee!"

That's what she said (she didn't actually go that far), so my grand midsummer adventure, on which I spent the last day of my last, precious high school summer break (technically the day of the start-of-school ceremony for second term) was totally meaningless, as in why bother wasting an entire book's worth of space on that, are you stupid or what, why don't you just die, oh, being half-vampire and immortal you can't even do that, hopeless bastard.

So don't read Kabuki, okay?

Promise me you won't!

This isn't just an act!

...But anyway, I was plodding back home with this problematic ghost girl, or really just the problem child known as Mayoi Hachikuji.

Our start-of-school ceremony had already begun when I'd failed to change history via time travel and came back to the present (the exact time being an hour past noon on August twenty-first, a Monday). I was already feeling excited on the inside, as in look at what I've done, absent on the very first day of the new term, never having managed to start on my summer break homework in the end, Senjogahara and Hanekawa are gonna kill me two times each, I can't wait (hooray), but all of that aside I needed to return Hachikuji's backpack to her.

As far as the details regarding that one, they're not really worth discussing here, and to someone who'd just slipped into the past and future and whatnot in a "pointless" use of time as Hachikuji put it (she didn't actually), it felt like old news, but chronologically speaking, the ghost girl Mayoi had come to play in my room and forgotten her backpack there only yesterday, on August twentieth.

If you wanted details, what was it you could consult? Uh, the *BAKEMONOGATARI Anime Complete Guidebook*, if I'm not mistaken?

There might be a short piece in there about that episode...but wait, that would mean it happened in the anime adaptation, so for us, does the event belong to a parallel world?

Parallel world.

A grating term...

Well, in any case, I suppose that book isn't in distribution anymore... Gosh, the anime world is so rough.

Just when it seemed to be a hit, it got weeded out in the blink of an eye.

You could say such a quick turnover rate is in fact healthy for an industry... Actually, never mind.

While I'd been hustling to alter the past, Hachikuji had been roaming the streets trying to retrieve her backpack from my house.

If she was going to meander around for nearly half a day looking for me, then she could have just waited in front of my house around the time I usually got back from school, but when I put the question to her...

"I don't want you searching my backpack! Searching it would be one thing, but the idea of you doing this and that to the fabric makes me want to vomit! What, you'd never? True, you might not. But the simple fact that you had the time is already inexcusable!"

So went her reply.

She didn't trust me at all.

In fact, she plain hated me.

Of course, a girl of such a young and tender age treating you like the plague might be a rare and welcome experience, so I wasn't at all opposed to partaking in it, but either way, Hachikuji still needed to reclaim her backpack.

Hence, with her walking by my side, I was pushing my bicycle from Kita-Shirahebi Shrine, the site of my time warp, and heading home.

"I do have to say, Hachikuji, you somehow feel weaker as a character without your backpack."

"How rude of you, Mister Araragi. These pigtails should be more than enough to establish who I am."

"Pigtails, huh. They aren't up to defining you on their own, though... I heard good characters need to have designs that are identifiable just from their silhouette."

"That's a very dated way of thinking… I believe it's been a long time since we've entered an age where templates like characters being identifiable by their silhouette and stories needing a traditional dramatic structure don't hold anymore."

"I see you're as skeptical of pre-existing values as ever…"

"What I think determines a character design's quality isn't the silhouette, it's whether they're recognizable even if someone with no artistic talent draws them. Like Goku, or Pikachu. A child could draw them and you'd still recognize who they are, right?"

"Good point."

"Though without my backpack, I'm more like a slug than a snail."

"Was it Oshino who said it, or did Hanekawa, I forget… But yeah, snails and slugs are basically the same. Slugs are snails whose shells retrogressed, or something…"

"But it feels weird when there's something left after their shells de-evolve—like a bird that can't fly, or with humans, isn't it like saying, 'I lost all my bones but I'm still alive, I'm doing fine'?"

"Hmm. If you considered the shell an exoskeleton, I guess, but in terms of its role, isn't it more like their skin? Not that I'm sure a human could survive without any."

"Yes, it's hard to say for sure. But you've proven it's possible to lose all your bones and survive, Mister Araragi…"

"Right, as a boneless chicken, I've proven…no such thing, damn you."

"Because the hermit crab is so unforgettable, we assume a snail's shell could be removed. If you actually did that, the snail dies. Pretty important innards seem to be stuffed in there."

"Like with your backpack."

"No, there's nothing that important in mine… It wouldn't trouble me not to have them, it's just that you holding onto my belongings sickens me, Mister Araragi."

"…"

"It would only mean Mayoi Hachikuji turning into Mayoi Muckyoozy... Wait, did we already make this joke before?"

"I'm not too sure because I wasn't there, but didn't you, for the anime's alternate voice track?"

"Dear I. I did reuse it, oh dear."

"I think recycling is fair game as long as it's across different media... And that's a parallel world, anyway. I do think you might want to avoid that joke so people don't start associating you with slugs..."

"I am based on a snail, though. Not much of a difference. It being a cat for Miss Hanekawa makes me jealous."

"Uh huh."

"The same goes for your demon."

"...Uh huh."

"Is something the matter?"

"No, well... Kids love snails, don't they? While slugs creep them out... Having or not having that shell makes a big difference."

"Maybe not so much these days. And snails do have a lot of parasites."

"Parasites?"

"In my case, you, Mister Araragi."

"I see, I see, in your case, me—hold on a sec, who're you calling your parasite?"

"You've been doing that a lot today, going along with it. I personally feel that kind of humor is embarrassing in writing."

"I've heard of that before, though. What was that snail parasite called, again? The really scary type that takes over the brain...the leucochloridium."

"How very much like you that we find a scrambled 'loli' in there."

"Oh god. Did I throw a perfect alley-oop for you to dunk on me with?"

"You've got it, Mister Araragi. If you kind of try, you can also mishear a 'lewd' in there. What a nasty parasite."

"Just the worst. No, why are we trying at all?"

"Can we discuss how we might make the 'dium' part interesting too?"

"I'm not helping you brainstorm names to call me... But really, the leucochloridium is a real scary kind of parasite, isn't it? Just hearing about what it does gives you the chills. It attaches to a snail, makes it move to a place where it's more easily eaten by a bird, and even transforms the eyestalks so it stands out... Sure, you might think I'm worthless, but I wish you wouldn't lump me in with those things."

"I'm only joking."

"I know that, but still."

Hachikuji and I chattered on the way in this fashion until we arrived at the Araragi residence, or in other words, my house. We go on endlessly any time we start bantering, but it never amounted to much—though this one case may have been an exception.

That is, when I think back on it now.

The talk about the evolution, retrogression, and so on of snails and slugs and the stuff regarding the leucochloridium parasite might have actually foreshadowed things about this story to a rather ironic extent—but really, calling it foreshadowing is just an example of the so-called Barnum effect. You can say anything you want after the fact.

"When I think back on it."

Considering how humanity has been jerked around by those convenient, convincing words, my view sounds like a plain delusion—thinking back is the only way you can think about things, and even if you wanted to dispute that, people should only bother thinking about the future anyway.

I should have learned that more than well enough.

After my time travel.

"Okay, Hachikuji. Come on in."

"Hunh?"

I tried nonchalantly to invite her in, but she replied with a face that said, *What the hell did he just say?*

"Mister Araragi, you know the only time I'll ever enter your house is for your wake."

"While I'm hurt by your shocking language, some part of me also feels happy that you'd come to my wake…"

"You've become an oddly positive person in the short time since we last met."

"Well, I did go through a handful of inconceivable life experiences…"

"In any case, I won't enter your house. For as long as you live, I'll never cross the Araragi residence's threshold… Yesterday was the last occasion, or actually, wouldn't you say even yesterday was half like an abduction?"

"An abduction? Don't make it sound so scandalous."

"But it's the truth. Please don't feel like you can say whatever you want just because the original text isn't available anymore."

"I'm not denying that it happened. I'm just asking you not to make it sound so scandalous."

"How selfish… Anyway," Hachikuji said, caution crackling in her eyes. There was no feeling or relationship of trust in them. They were suspicion itself.

Makes my body tingle to have such eyes on me.

"Mister Araragi, I haven't lost my girlish sense of caution to the point that I'd enter into your home when both your parents and your little sisters must be absent."

"Cut it out, you're ten years old."

"I'd be twenty-one if I were alive."

"See, now you're killing my buzz."

"Don't let my actual age kill it."

"You used to shy away from smashing my dreams with that sort of line. Why would you suddenly go and let me down?"

"Well, you know, things have gotten a lot stricter after Tokyo implemented those youth ordinances. Going forward, this girl is going to have to state that she's over eighteen and legal, or else we may be subject to damaging rumors."

"Legal... I thought that ordinance didn't take actual ages into account?"

"Did it not? I dunno, I'm just a kid!"

"What's your positioning here, dammit? Are you a child or an adult?"

"I'm legally an adult but physically a child."

"Not that you have a physical body..."

"To be serious for a moment, it doesn't matter if there's an ordinance. The manga and anime industries were busy censoring themselves before it ever passed. They say it'll impede creative freedom, but it's been that way for some time now, in fact. Moaning about government regulations when you're already sucking up to whoever is paying you is pretty pathetic."

"Don't get serious like that with zero warning..."

"We, at least, ought to remain free among it all! I'm Mayoi Hachikuji, ten years old! I'll show you my panties!"

"That's a little too free!"

"Oh, but was just showing panties all right? I heard that the ordinance wouldn't affect my friend Shizuka from *Doraemon*."

"Well, I doubt they can regulate *Doraemon*."

And wait, why "my friend" Shizuka? Who are you anyway, are you important?

"Yes," Hachikuji agreed, "*Doraemon* is something of a national manga... Worst case, you'd even alienate international opinion. Still, if I may, *Doraemon* simply is erotic."

"No weird readings of that historic masterpiece!"

But sure, all of its secret tools are true to human desire and can easily be abused all day long...

"I believe, Mister Araragi, that four out of five elementary school boys owe their sexual awakening to *Doraemon*. How long is the Agency of Cultural Affairs going to turn a blind eye to this state of affairs?"

"I'm curious about the fifth boy..."

"Wakame from *Sazae-san*."

"..."

Our conversation gave me a lot to think about the legacy, both positive and negative, of nationally acclaimed manga; I also felt that the fifth boy was kinda kinky.

Wait, that had to be fake data.

Stop making things up.

"In that case...just wait here for a minute. I'll run and grab your backpack."

"You have ten seconds. Sprint."

"A haughty tone?!"

For some reason, I was now a ten-year-old girl's gofer.

No, a twenty-one-year-old woman's?

Makes my body tingle either way.

Well, since her eleven years as a ghost weren't any that "accumulated," Hachikuji would never turn twenty-one...

That, too—my time traveling had made painfully clear.

A historical fact.

Leaving Hachikuji to wait at our freshly built gate, I went in and climbed the stairs to get her backpack from my room.

I felt like swapping out her backpack's contents and filling it with stones in a pang of goatish mischief, but no stones were to be found in my room, naturally, so I gave up on the idea.

Now, let me swear to all the gods above while I'm narrating that I really didn't mess with the backpack after Hachikuji left it in my room the day before.

I may be a nasty parasite, but I'm not so criminal that I'd put my hands on a girl's personal belongings.

I'm chivalrous.

A gentleman.

I didn't want to make Hachikuji wait for too long, so I shouldered her backpack and headed outside again, not stopping to sit down or enjoy a cup of coffee.

"Ahh! Hey, don't be touching my property!"

"That's asking for too much…"

"Yikes, I'll have to take it to the cleaner's."

"Um… Haven't you been hating me a little too hard today?"

"I don't want it anymore. Go ahead and throw it out."

"Weren't we saying you'd turn into Mayoi Muckyoozy without this?"

"The way you're forcing it onto me is creepy. You've bugged it, haven't you? Ugh, you scum!"

"Why be that suspicious of me… What a hassle, just read *Kabuki*. It'll prove my innocence."

"I'm not buying such an expensive book."

"Don't call it expensive…"

"Sixteen dollars?! Imagine how many eight-dollar pocket-sized books I could buy with that kind of money!"

"Just two. Can't you at least call it bulky instead of expensive? The total word count should be about even."

Give me a break. Why the negative promotion when she's in its chapter title?

"Of course," she said, "fixed retail prices for books could become a thing of the past in Japan, too. The current resale system seems to be reaching its limits, and we're getting closer and closer to the age of electronic books. I don't know if they're a black ship, a rescue boat, or a privateer vessel."

"E-books, huh? You know, they're surprisingly good for reading manga. It's shocking how well the color black shows up on them."

"Yes, that's true. The ink can sometimes be too light in magazines. It could be that the better the art, the more you want to see it as digital data."

"If there's a problem with the format, it's the two-page spreads. Phones will show you one panel at a time, but manga's strength is its free control of the display size… Still, we might end up getting used to it."

"After all, panel layouts were incredibly straightforward until just a couple of dozen years ago. Like four long, horizontal panels in a row. The art was simple, too. It could be that we're experiencing a Renaissance in many ways."

"Calling it a Renaissance implies that we're learning from the past, though…"

Maybe that was the case for the panel layouts… Yet while I did bring it up, I'm not too knowledgeable on the topic. How do cellular phones deal with the complicated paneling you typically find in girls' comics?

Spreads might be the least of our problems…

"And more manga is getting serialized on the internet," Hachikuji noted.

"Right, online magazines. In that sense the manga industry's gates have widened for rookies. Not to mention the new print magazines that keep getting launched." Closing our eyes, for the moment, to the fact that existing ones are going under—sorry, "on hiatus"—one after the other. "In light of those developments, manga might actually be a super-stable line of work. Lots of long-running series nowadays, and the skills are pretty transferable."

"That's an awfully optimistic view… But like you were saying about the paneling, and how manga's strength is adjusting the display size, I think another strength is being able to continue one story for as long as its popularity and its creator's stamina lasts."

"Well, culturally, novels are a bit different in that regard."

I think it's a matter of different release formats.

The magazine serialization is the main thing for comics, but it's the book for fiction. A novel's nature is that of a "one-shot" in terms of comics. It's very discrete, whether you like it or not.

"Don't forget the fiction franchise that repeatedly pretends the series is over but comes back to life like a zombie each time and chooses to drag on forever!"

"Stop it," I begged. "Stop with the masochism."

"That aside, I think electronic books will become prevalent all at once if they can solve the pricing issue. Just as long as they set it at a point that won't see anyone starving."

"Starving... In this slump, that feels like it's easier said than done."

"Considering the bother of turning them into convenient electronic data, I think they could be sold for more than real books, in fact."

"How patronizing." As if it were a seller's market.

"There just needs to be more added value. Like search functions, or links to foreshadowing that let you come right back to it, or the ability to revisit the character intro at any moment, or voice actors reading the lines."

"All of those are pretty far from our image of a book..."

I could feel myself being left behind by the times.

And I'm only in high school.

Still, it's not something you can readily accept without an elite education in it, so to speak, from your earliest days. I don't even feel comfortable with cell phones, not having gotten one until I was a high school student.

Text messages? They make me panic a little even now.

"It's fine, Mister Araragi, be glad that you're present for the genesis of a new culture and aware of the fact."

"I wonder. I'd have preferred to take my sweet time enjoying it after it's become the norm."

Also, a ghost telling me how I should feel over being "present"? Not that a half-vampire could say it better.

"I envy people who were there for the emergence of cell phones," remarked Hachikuji. "They composed their own incoming call notifications with chords!"

"Is that so enviable?"

"Now you can download a ringtone by pressing a button... But either way, isn't it a good opportunity? The publishing industry could use a revolution."

"A revolution... I just hope it doesn't implode in the process."

Brooding over the future of publishing with an elementary schooler,

I started to get hungry.

It was getting to be about that time.

As a vampire I don't need to adhere to that strict of a meal schedule, but habits, not to harken back to what we were saying, are hard to shake, and it wasn't every day that I ran into Hachikuji.

Why not treat ourselves to lunch?

"Is there anything you want to eat, Hachikuji?"

"I could name many dishes, but no, nothing, if it has to be with you."

"Hey, hey…"

Weird. Did Hachikuji always hate me this much?

It's been so long, I couldn't even guess why…

Come to think of it, was the last time we talked at this much length actually *Nise*?

That, indeed, would be quite a while ago.

"Well, Miss Hanekawa and Miss Kanbaru and Miss Sengoku did organize coups d'état and hijack your role as narrator."

"Hold on a second. Chronologically, it wouldn't make sense for us to know about Kanbaru and Sengoku."

"I never thought that Miss Sengoku would turn out that way. How frightening."

"Stop it, it really would cause a time paradox if I knew about that now. Sengoku is just my cute little junior."

"I want to say that was the problem…"

"By the way, aren't you ever going to narrate?"

"The rule is that beings that are nothing but aberrations can't become narrators."

"So there was a rule about that…"

I looked down at my shadow.

Ah.

Right, so this time, too…

"All joking aside, isn't there anything you want to eat? My treat."

"Oh… As you are aware, though, I'm a ghost. If you lunched with me, Mister Araragi, you'd be looked at like parents who order food for their deceased daughter too."

"I don't mind."

Hm.

While that didn't matter, if Hachikuji ate real food, how would that eaten food be treated in reality?

Normal people couldn't see her, but they could see her food... Would the food in her organs look like it's floating in space?

That couldn't be it.

It's not like things look like they're floating just because Hachikuji is holding them... Maybe it all gets patched over by the brain of whoever sees it happening.

Of course, if anyone's brain is patching things over, it could be mine, "recognizing" a human who died eleven years ago.

But that's just a hypothetical ghost story.

"It's my treat, but I'm a penniless student getting ready for his college exams. We'd only be able to go to a fast food place."

"Fast food..."

"Not enough for you?"

"It makes you want to fast? That would be more than enough."

"Give me a break."

Wrong sense of the English word.

As a student studying for exams, I at least know that much.

"Well, get on my bike. Let's ride together."

"No way, Mister Araragi. Riding behind you..."

And then.

Just as Hachikuji started to give another one of her answers in the "I hate Mister Araragi session" that seemed to be all the rage with her.

It already had its hooks in me, and I was on the edge of my seat waiting for her answer but wasn't able to hear it to the end—because.

That's when we spotted something.

It.

003

If you asked me what *it* was, it's a mystery.

A mystery.

That's the only answer I could give.

But not because I…or Hachikuji was lacking in knowledge about aberrations. Well, of course it was partly that, too…but not the only reason.

I say this because we—or at least I—couldn't really tell if *it* was even an aberration.

I couldn't identify what *it* was.

Since I couldn't see *it*.

While it does feel like a bit of a contradiction to say that I spotted something that I couldn't see, in this instance it'd be the most suitable expression.

Although I couldn't see it, it wasn't at all transparent—meanwhile, with the ghost girl known as Mayoi Hachikuji, whom regular people couldn't witness as we discussed earlier (I'm not going to make a "given up on the ghost" joke here. It would be unfunny and inappropriate), it's not necessarily that she "can't be seen"—because not witnessing means rejecting even the recognition that it can't be seen.

Not noticing that you can't see it.

In other words, it's *not there*.

What can't be recognized doesn't exist. That logic stands in the confines of the human brain, at least.

And in this case—I was able to recognize *it*, which I couldn't see. *I recognized that it couldn't be seen*—because after all.

There was a Darkness there.

A darkness—a blackness, if you want.

Or just plain black.

To repeat myself, it was the middle of the day—the middle of a midsummer day, at that, with sunlight pouring down on us from the sky.

Weather that could make you start sweating just standing still—it was in an environment with simply excellent visibility that it appeared out of nowhere.

That Darkness.

"…"

I could…try to interpret this phenomenon.

Vision amounts to reflections and wavelengths of light, so if something doesn't reflect it, the area is "displayed" as black—for example, coal looks so black because it has a high rate of light absorption, or better, black holes can't ever be observed by the eye because they bend and suck everything into them, including light—it seems like there's just a Darkness there.

Only, we weren't in space.

There's no way a black hole could have emerged. No way I'd be fine if a black hole did this close to me, for one thing—well, no.

Actually, no.

Even if *it*—even if this Darkness wasn't a black hole, if it was just a lump of coal, there was no guarantee that I, or we, would be fine—*szzt*.

It felt like the Darkness moved.

Just barely.

"...nkk!"

It was instinct.

Intuition.

A bad feeling.

If you insist, it was experience.

I immediately straddled my bike—and Hachikuji wasn't any slower to act, because despite her earlier firm refusal in the making to ride together with me, she leapt onto the cargo rack.

"Step on it, please!"

"I know!"

Directed by Hachikuji for some reason, I began pedaling—as hard as I could, at top speed from the first down-stroke.

I wanted to exploit my leg strength as a vampire, but unfortunately it wasn't good for much in the middle of the day.

True, subjected to a vampire's full leg strength, no mere granny bike could hold itself together (probably the chain would blow off), so pedaling in a standing stance like a dead-serious human might have been just about right.

I felt like ever since Kanbaru destroyed my mountain bike, I was really abusing this granny bike—yeah, it really deserved some maintenance work already.

"Raaaaaaaaaaaaaaagh!"

Of course, that was only if we had any future to upkeep.

In any case, I pedaled as hard as I could.

Apparently, bicycles can break the speed limit under Japan's Road Traffic Act too, but I ignored that fact as hard as I could.

To me, some things are worth protecting more than the law. I count my own life among them.

I might run over a pedestrian if I barreled down the sidewalk at that speed, so I descended onto the road and began going even faster.

"Hachikuji!"

"Yes!"

"Check behind us! Is that thing following us?!"

"Um!" Hachikuji seemed to turn her head. After a moment or two, she cried, "Something is!"

Come to think of it, while I'd known Hachikuji for a pretty long time, I'd only ever chatted with her on the roadside for the most part and never seen her so flustered before.

Maybe the only other times were, well, when I assaulted her.

"Which is to say, every time we meet!" she quipped dutifully even on this occasion.

What a nice kid.

We could be lifelong friends.

"When you say something is—like how?!"

"Um, well, like it's there when you notice. Like it's not close, but not far…"

"?"

The phrasing was pretty ambiguous by Hachikuji's standards. But I couldn't blame her.

After all, that Darkness couldn't be seen—in which case, its distance wasn't to be fathomed accurately, either.

No, not just its distance.

Its size…its scope and scale, so to speak, were also an enigma.

We only knew it lurked there…or rather, "existed" there—and had to judge based on the surrounding scenery, but that could change in an instant if you shifted your angle.

Plus, we were moving at a high speed on a bicycle.

Of course her phrasing was ambiguous—but in any case, that it *seemed* to be coming after us was enough.

"Okay, got it! No need to check anymore!"

Instead of pedaling in a standing stance, I sat down. I was faster when I stood in terms of pure speed, but the cargo behind me, a young girl, made it a different story.

"Hachikuji! Grab onto my back!"

"No way!"

"Don't refuse, you idiot! I'm off balance!"

"Tch!"

With a very unbecoming tongue click for a young girl, Hachikuji complied in what was probably a reluctant manner.

This combined our centers of gravity, letting me go even faster—not to mention, I risked flinging off Hachikuji if I pedaled at full speed while standing.

"Would it be better if I also threw away my backpack?!"

"Nah…"

To be honest, I'd have been grateful if she had. I wasn't sure if the ghost girl had any weight or if I was just feeling it on my own, but real or not, heavier meant heavier.

In other words, like Hachikuji herself, the backpack felt as heavy as it looked. If she chucked it, I could expect to go even faster—still. That was a big still.

"You don't have to throw it away!"

"But…I can come back for it later!"

"I said it's fine!"

It was her own suggestion, and she was right that she could just pick it up later. Hachikuji's idea was absolutely sensible, but it somehow felt wrong.

Our speed might actually fall if she did.

Or so I imagined.

It was just my imagination, after all, but I've lived my whole life faithful to whatever I imagined.

"Instead, Hachikuji, hug me tighter, like you're trying to merge with me!"

"Okay!"

"Push your chest even harder into me!"

"L-Like this?!"

Perhaps because it was an emergency, once Hachikuji made up her mind, she docilely obeyed me.

Her body, ripe for a fifth grader's, pressed unsparingly against my own—converting this joy into energy, I pedaled even harder.

"Hachikuji! With more of a grinding motion!"

"O-Okay!"

Hachikuji, probably a bit confused, was at my beck and call.

You never knew what life had in store for you, whether it was feeling Hachikuji all across your back or being chased by an inexplicable Darkness.

I may need to offer an excuse at this point.

Sure, it's understandable to be frightened by a mysterious Darkness appearing out of nowhere, but why commit so thoroughly to flight? some of you may be wondering. *Why desperately pedal away from something that, while unknown, might not be dangerous?*

Allow me to reply.

Yes!

I thoroughly needed to take flight!

If you think that's pathetic, then go ahead and think it all you want, but how often I've had to go through hell because I didn't run when I should have like I was now!

I'm a veteran!

Having witnessed all kinds of "suspicious" since spring break and fought them, I can state that I was utterly, undoubtedly, one-hundred-percent following the correct course of action at that moment!

Now was the time to run!

By no means was I going to let myself face off against that Darkness!

It'd be one thing if only my person was on the line, but right now I had to protect my dear little friend Mayoi Hachikuji!

...Hm?

What's my excuse for taking advantage of the chaos to savor that little friend with my back?

Well, I haven't got any for you.

I'm not ashamed, at all.

"Mister Araragi!"

"What is it, pig-boobies?!"
"It's coming after us!"
"!"

I'd told her she didn't have to look behind anymore, but it seemed like she had—since there was no particular change in the sensation on my back, she must have contorted herself.

Like twisted her neck 180 degrees.

It was pretty scary to visualize.

"It might be getting closer!" she warned.

"I thought we couldn't tell!"

"W-Well... I can't, not the distance, but it feels oppressive..."

"!"

Hachikuji's testimony made even less sense now—at this rate, maybe I had to turn around myself to check out the Darkness... But no, that might be a bad idea...

Recognition.

If the Darkness was an aberration, it needed to be recognized, but there were also risks to recognizing an aberration.

Quite big ones.

Some aberrations curse you simply for observing them—they "emerge" by being seen. Which is to say, the Darkness might be an aberration that activates when it's spotted.

True, in that case, I'd already seen *it*, so maybe there wasn't any point in averting my eyes now.

Maybe there wasn't any point in ghosting a ghost.

"Hachikuji! Just stop looking at it!"

"B-But, but!"

"Be a good girl and kiss my back!"

"O-Okay!"

It was hard to say if my mysterious request was romantic or humiliating, but Hachikuji complied anyway.

It only got my shirt soaked with saliva, though, and felt yucky.

"Fshh, fshh, fshh. Lick, lick, lick... Mrrgh, mrrgh."

"…"

Make that scary.

Don't be eating my back.

I remembered hearing that snails have over ten thousand teeth, in fact… Was my back going to be all right?

My will isn't so unbreakable that I have the right to criticize others, but it seemed like Mayoi Hachikuji was lacking in mental toughness.

Being this weak in the face of adversity was rare.

Actually, wasn't it rare for any story character to be weak in the face of adversity? I mean, you wouldn't have any stories to tell then.

Come on, show your brilliance.

Was your usual unflappable attitude all for show?

"!"

And then.

I carelessly saw it.

The Darkness—it's not as if I turned around.

But towns are funny, they have mirrors all over the place—whether or not that's for Kamen Rider Ryuki's ease of transformation, at traffic crossings for instance.

And it was in the mirror.

That I accidentally saw the Darkness.

It seemed to grow the moment I did—though it might've been my imagination.

My imagination?

Then—that was everything.

Gwip.

I turned the handlebars of my bike as if to escape not just from the Darkness but the mirror it was reflected in.

I was basically sliding on my tires and nearly fell over but somehow maintained my balance—leaning almost far enough to scrape my cheek on the asphalt.

It felt like I was at about a 170-degree angle.

I'm amazed I made it back up.

"Hachikuji! Are you okay?!"
"I snapped one of my feelers!"
"Isn't that really bad?!"
And wait, did humans have feelers?
I guess that'd be the skin, but can you snap your skin?
"I misspoke! One of my pigtails came undone!"
"Oh..."
She'd frightened me for nothing.
"Also," she said, "my blouse shoulder tore just a bit!"
"Are we okay?!"
"Yes, it's just my clothes... But with part of my hair undone and my blouse torn, I look like I'm in the middle of being assaulted and abducted by you! That's the picture!"
"That's not okay at all!"
It was bad news for my future.
What was going to happen to me?
"...ck."
But then another, more imminent danger approached me.
To be precise, I was approaching it.
At the end of our hard turn was a traffic light, of all things.
You know, one of those red, yellow, and green things.
No.
Not red, yellow, and green—it was red.
"...nkk!"
I had, well, two options.
It was ridiculous to be thinking about it, but two.
Either blow through the light, or don't.
Looking around me as I flew forward, I saw neither pedestrians nor cars. Even if I ignored the signal, didn't hit the brakes, and cut straight across the light, it probably wouldn't cause any kind of accident.
It wouldn't, but.
"Tsk!"

Once again—I turned the handlebars.

A red light.

Feeling Hachikuji against my back—I couldn't ignore the light. Even if it wouldn't lead to an accident, I couldn't possibly—not while carrying Hachikuji, who'd died eleven years ago in a traffic accident, behind me.

But this is where I failed.

No, it's hard to call part of it a mistake—since I couldn't have made the turn, in any case, without hitting the brakes and slowing down.

The problem was my other failure.

Yes, I'd forgotten.

I was riding on the road—so the signals meant something different. If the light in front of me was red, any turn, whether right or left, was just as prohibited as going straight.

Stop on red.

Unable to uphold that rule—failing to do so with Hachikuji on my back, there was no room for mercy and heaven would punish me for it.

004

We turned and it was right in front of us.
The Darkness.
Almost like it was a pit—a trap waiting for us there this whole time.
"...nkk!"
I couldn't tell our distance from it.
Or maybe there wasn't any from the start—with this phenomenon.
As if it was always right there, and far or close didn't matter—crap!
I couldn't change directions now, I'd just turned my handlebars as far as they could go. Believing that I was fleeing single-mindedly, unwaveringly, I ended up putting a period to the game of tag by plunging straight into the Darkness.
Self-ruin. Autodestruct.
A completely pointless escapade.
Running, confounded, from a confounding thing, caught up to in confounding fashion—it was confoundedly over.
"Urrg."
But.

But Hachikuji, at least—

"Mrrgh, mrrgh, mrrgh."

Was still munching on my back.

I might have made her, but what a thing to be doing at the end of the line.

She was wrecking the serious mood.

But I somehow had to peel off Hachikuji, who literally had her teeth in me, and let her escape—escape!

This girl, at least—

"—*Unlimited Rulebook.*"

And then.

I heard a quiet, droning voice from somewhere—and was blasted away.

Not the Darkness lying in wait.

Me.

Us.

It felt like a giant hammer had sent us flying—and maybe that described the actual phenomenon.

A brutally physical aberration far more defined than the Darkness.

By the time I realized it, Hachikuji and I had been blown into the opposite lane. *Some sort of thing* had happened—and rescued us.

Only our wheels didn't make it, and my granny bike seemed to be swallowed up by the Darkness—disappearing without a trace.

"…!"

After all this time…

Having survived one crisis after another alongside me, my granny bike finally exited this world… It was quite a shock.

I was so depressed that I could die.

What was I supposed to ride to school the next day?

"Kind monster sir—over this way."

And there, suddenly—was Ononoki.

Yotsugi Ononoki.

An expressionless tween girl—whose terribly frilly, cute, and visually quite striking outfit was all thrown out of balance by her expressionlessness.

Like a doll trying too hard to act human.

She can't help it, though.

While she isn't a doll, she isn't human, either.

She, too, is an aberration.

An aberration known as Yotsugi Ononoki.

A certain violent *onmyoji* sorcerer's familiar—

"Huh? Wait, Ononoki… Why are you here?"

"What do you mean. I met you just yesterday."

Did she?

She did.

Thanks to my time travel, those memories were out of sync with reality—was it like jet lag?

Ononoki had appeared just as abruptly as the Darkness—but judging by the situation, she seemed to have saved Hachikuji and me.

"Th-Thank—"

"It might be a little early to be thanking me," Ononoki practically whispered.

She was absolutely right.

The menacing Darkness was still on the street—not having vanished or anything, it continued to exist right there.

A Darkness we couldn't see continuing to exist is a pretty weird formulation—but then it was that kind of phenomenon.

"Kind monster sir, what…is that?"

"Huh?" I was the baffled one at her question. "Really, Ononoki? Isn't your role to appear out of nowhere, save me, and explain everything?"

"I'm not sure I can handle your spoiled expectations…"

Expressionless as she was, Ononoki sounded overwhelmed.

Well, no wonder.

Just saving us deserved our thanks.

Though Oshino might say that people just go and get saved on their own.

"Hachikuji…"

As for Hachikuji—

Her arms around my torso, still clutching my body and even biting into the flesh of my back, the ghost girl Mayoi Hachikuji had passed out, as far as I could tell.

How mentally weak was she, anyway?

I'm so let down by you.

"…"

I ripped her off me.

Regardless of what we were going to do next, about the only activity that suited her posture was riding together on a bicycle. Loosening her grip was one thing, but getting her teeth out of my back was pretty rough.

Maybe she did have ten thousand of them.

"Good grief…" Ononoki said.

It was hard to read her emotions from her toneless voice—she was like the old Senjogahara in a way. Which is why I feel some affinity for Ononoki.

"I carelessly saved you, but at this rate maybe I should've left you alone… Did I get caught up in some confounding business? Talk about hard luck, give a guy a break."

That's right, I thought about the kid, whom I'd chronologically met just yesterday but internally felt like I hadn't seen in a good, long while, *Ononoki applies male identifiers to herself.*

"Don't say you should've left us alone… Life is a valuable thing."

"Says an immortal vampire?" shot back Ononoki. "And is that girl the ghost you mentioned yesterday? She sure is wearing a backpack… So you managed to return it. Good."

"Yesterday…"

Did I mention Hachikuji?

It was so far back that I didn't remember.

Well, in addition to being an aberration, Ononoki frequently worked alongside an expert, if only as a familiar, so I guess it was natural...but she could see.

Ononoki could see Hachikuji.

And just as naturally—the Darkness, too.

"Kind monster sir."

"Yeah."

"What do you want to do?"

"What do I want to do?"

"With that," Ononoki pointed.

With her index finger, at the Darkness on the street.

She pointed at the unmoving Darkness, which seemed to be observing us as though it was the one "witnessing" us.

Pointing.

For Ononoki, already an offensive maneuver.

Unlimited Rulebook.

She only needed to point to activate it.

Its power—was something my body knew first-hand.

Not my body, technically, so much as half of my body.

"Fight?" she asked, "Or flight?"

"Flight," I answered immediately. "That's not the kind of thing you try to fight."

"Yes. I agree."

I thought she might mock me for being a coward, but she lowered her finger right away. Almost as if that was her plan from the beginning—seriously, there was no reading this kid.

Inscrutable, just like the old Senjogahara.

"We're running away. Hold that child, kind monster sir."

"Got it."

"As gently as you can, slowly, not making any noise. That thing might react to it and attack."

"..."

Was it a beast or what? Well, true, aberrations might be animalistic, primitively speaking—and they do tend to have a creature motif.

Not that any beast could be darkness itself...

In any case, I did as Ononoki said and slowly picked up Hachikuji's body. Without making a sound, I slipped a hand under her neck, checked inside her skirt, held her legs, and cradled her against my chest.

"I feel like you added an unnecessary action there."

"Excuse me? What if there was an aberration inside her skirt?"

"Fat chance, bastard," scolded Ononoki, somewhat abrasively.

I assumed it was her onmyoji's influence on her, but the kid's character traits could be pretty inconsistent.

"Okay."

And then.

Almost the moment I stood up with Hachikuji in a so-called bridal carry—Ononoki grabbed me by the collar.

"Unlimited Rulebook: The Disengagement Edition."

005

Honestly, Ononoki's, what, special move? She uses it quite a lot so I don't think it's a secret technique... Anyway, I don't really understand her Unlimited Rulebook ability or skill and how it works.

I've heard that she's a *tsukumogami*, or an artifact spirit, and what's more, the tsukumogami of a corpse, but that, too (or being a tsukumogami in the first place), is something I don't really understand.

Her offensive power, I'm well acquainted with.

The Araragi residence's front entrance ended up needing to be rebuilt thanks to her offensive, or even destructive power, so I don't need to take anyone's word for that. It's the reason I vaguely assumed that Ononoki was a *shikigami*, or familiar, specializing in offense—but now.

Now that we'd safely escaped, I have no choice but to say, to my surprise, that I was mistaken.

Come to think of it, the onmyoji she serves, namely Yozuru Kagenui, is a ridiculously offensive fighter—so why would her partner, Ononoki, be specialized entirely in offense? Who would put together a team that lopsided?

43

If anything, the Unlimited Rulebook might be a skill for escaping—I couldn't get away from that Darkness for all I'd pedaled my bike, but she made a perfect getaway literally burdened by the two of us.

To explain what she actually did, though, she just seemed to jump as hard as she could using both of her legs…

"No, kind monster sir, that's correct. While I gave it a cool name like the Disengagement Edition, we simply ran away."

"Simply…"

"However, we did so vertically. Since you'd proved that horizontal flight was meaningless…I thought it might have trouble dealing with up-and-down movements… Looks like I nailed it."

"…"

I felt somehow bamboozled, but at the end of the day, we'd gotten away and that's all that mattered.

So—if you're wondering where we escaped to, we were now in a place with a lot of memories for me ever since spring break, a hidden base of sorts where I once staged a lethal battle with Ononoki and her master, Kagenui. In other words, the abandoned cram school.

We were on the ruins' fourth floor.

One of its three classrooms was serving as our resting spot. Finding rest in ruins might sound strange…but having gotten away from that Darkness, there was no reason for us not to feel relieved.

Hachikuji was still passed out.

Placing her on the floor would be crude even under the circumstances, so I put some nearby desks together to make a bed just like Oshino used to and laid her there.

While Hachikuji was grown for a fifth grader, she was still an elementary schooler. Three desks put together was enough.

Having put my shirt over her in place of a blanket then balled up my jeans for her to use as a pillow, I was in nothing but my underpants now.

Hmm.

It was out of consideration for Hachikuji's wellbeing, so why did I just look like a pervert?

Frankly, I could live without being branded an exhibitionist on top of everything else…

"You're quite muscular, kind monster sir," Ononoki said.

Once we'd settled down.

"Yep, those are good muscles."

"…"

"Good muscles. You must work out, because those are good muscles. It was hard to tell from over your clothes, but those are some good muscles."

"…"

She was praising my muscles… But it's not like I worked out, it was just one of the effects of turning into a vampire over spring break…

"How about staying undressed from now on? You should show off your muscles more, kind monster sir. I think you have a fine ottermode physique."

"Can we, uh, talk about something other than muscles?"

"Come on, don't be like that, how about some poses? As a way to thank me for saving you."

"Little girl's trying to guilt-trip me, huh?"

"If you showed me an abs and thighs pose, I might not mind sharing the secret of my Unlimited Rulebook."

"Isn't that a pretty important secret?!"

The kid was a mess.

Though again, it reminded me of Senjogahara.

…Except she never reacted to my muscles. Someone getting this into them was troubling, but no reaction at all was, in its own way, sad.

"Yeah, I can't deny that I'm interested in the Unlimited Rulebook…"

Given Kagenui's specialty, there was no guarantee that we would never fight again… Though it did seem like she wasn't in town at the moment.

"But what I really want to know about right now is that Darkness. Do you really not have any idea, Ononoki?"

"I said I don't know…"

She came to touch my abs as she spoke. She did it so casually that I nearly overlooked it, but this was outright groping.

"Your muscles are the only thing I know about, kind monster sir."

"What do you know about my muscles…"

"What don't I know?"

When Ononoki asserted this with her blank look, she was surprisingly convincing.

Maybe she did find out, somehow.

It could even be that… Wait, find what out?

Geez, there's no secret to my muscles.

"Well, what about you, kind monster sir? Do you have any idea… Do *you* have any *I*-dea?"

"Emphasize it as you might, that's not a very good pun or play on words… No, no idea."

Maybe I did, though.

I had too good of an idea.

You could even say my whole life was the idea.

That said…if you were to ask what it might be in particular, I'd have to throw up my hands.

Every aberration has its reasons, sure, but was that unreasonable, unidentifiable Darkness even describable as an aberration?

Unreasonable, unidentifiable—and of unknown cause.

"I dunno," I said. "It's not like I'm an expert on aberrations… I'm just a dime-a-dozen pseudo-vampiric high schooler."

"I don't think there are even a dozen of those…"

"In fact, thinking back on all the aberrations I've dealt with—"

A vampire.

A cat.

A crab.

A snail.

A monkey.

A snake.

A bee—and a bird.

Also, a corpse.

"—There's something different about it. I've never seen an aberration as abstract as darkness itself. What kind of aberrational phenomenon is it supposed to be?"

That there was any in the middle of the day already felt odd. Well, aberrations appearing only at night, during the witching hour and so on, might just be a preconception, but for it to be that clear?

No, *clear* it wasn't...not when it couldn't be seen.

"Darkness," Ononoki mumbled, like she was talking to herself. "True, *it* must be Darkness..."

"Hm? What?"

"Well... How do I put this? I hope what we're up against really is Darkness. That it's just Darkness..."

Ononoki remained expressionless, like she felt nothing, but also like she might be finding our situation simply tedious.

"What do you mean?" I asked. "That thing is Darkness, no matter how you look at it."

"But you *can't* look at it, can you? That black mass is much more likely to be just a phenomenon accompanying an aberration."

"Oh, okay..."

"If we start saying that, though, we can't be sure if we're even 'up against' it. Maybe it wasn't in order to come after you that it appeared, kind monster sir...just as a typhoon or a storm or any other meteorological phenomenon isn't going after a person."

"But then, that thing was obviously after me and Hachikuji."

"Right..."

Ononoki sounded so indecisive.

"No good," she said, seeming to realize this herself. "I'm just too captivated by your muscles to get my thoughts straight."

"It's fine that you're having trouble getting your thoughts straight, but could you go find a different reason?"

"My sister might know something…but I can't get in contact with her right now."

It goes without saying that by "sister" Ononoki meant Yozuru Kagenui—the violent onmyoji.

Indeed, being an expert, and also an old acquaintance of Oshino, she might possess some knowledge about that object (if it even was one).

She might…but actually, I was more relieved than anything to hear that Ononoki couldn't contact her.

Kagenui is one of those types I'd rather not deal with for the rest of my life, although things probably won't go that way.

"Where is she, by the way, and what's she doing? It must be work, right?"

"Yes, it's work, and of course the details are a secret. Why are you being so nosy? The nerve."

"I wasn't asking to be nosy…" I was only trying to be polite, but the onmyoji community took confidentiality much more seriously than I'd expected.

"If you really want to know, you could offer me those muscles."

"Yikes, offer them like how?"

"Gouge some out and feed it to me."

"Talk about scarring." It seemed like we were on the same page, but we weren't. "Whatever, it's not like it's a problem if we can't get in touch with her. We'll figure it out once night falls, anyway."

"Why is that? Do you suddenly become bright after dark?"

"No, I don't come with such a useful function… It's just when Shinobu wakes up."

Ononoki visibly grimaced when she heard the name. A normally expressionless face twisting into a grimace really underscored the level of disgust.

It was hard to blame her, though.

Once upon a time, in this very abandoned cram school, Ononoki nearly got murdered by Shinobu—no, that's not a good way to put it.

Shinobu was clearly playing around then.

She just toyed with Ononoki—of course it'd make her resentful, of course she'd hate her.

In any case, I pretended not to notice her reaction and continued. "Appearances aside, she's the king of aberrations—she'd be well-versed on the subject even if it weren't for a months-long elite education at the hands of Mèmè Oshino, a pro just like Kagenui. Shinobu's an even greater expert than the experts, in other words. She has to know something about that Darkness. Which is why we're bound to learn what it really is once she wakes up."

"...Keh," spat Ononoki, not hiding her displeasure.

She had a lot to learn as a human being, I thought—no wonder, she was an aberration. Since she used to be human, maybe it was more accurate to say she'd learned to be too aberrational.

"I'm not buying the knowledge of a geriatric like her."

"Don't call Shinobu geriatric," I scolded.

"And 'once she wakes up'? Are you saying that wicked woman is asleep right now? Unbelievable... To think she'd be napping while her master is fighting for his life."

"I'm not really her master..."

But when it came to that part of our relationship, things got hard to explain. At the very least, it was extremely difficult to convince someone like Ononoki who had a perfect, or a logically consistent master-servant relationship... Maybe the smart choice was to give up on trying from the start.

"What, are you not that vampire's master, kind monster sir?"

"No, no, I am. I'm so much her master that it's almost like I'm not. She's constantly there, waiting upon me."

"..."

Ononoki looked at me like I was some sort of dangerous character. Yeah, I could see why.

"It's not like I can stop her from napping... Something tiring happened to her the other day. She's probably sound asleep right now."

"Hm. So even a vampire like her gets tired... That's surprising."

Well, Shinobu, too, would get tired after traveling through time again and again. It might've been a different story had it been her at her peak...

"I don't think a half day's worth of sleep will be enough to recover from all of that fatigue..." I said. "But either way, all that needs to happen is for her to wake up and then everything will be solved. No matter what that Darkness is."

"I wouldn't be overconfident if I were you. Whatever elite schooling that vampire received, there's no one in the world who knows everything about every aberration."

That also goes for my sister and Mèmè Oshino—added Ononoki. While it sounded like her opinion owed in part to her dislike for Shinobu, I could see some sense in it.

If aberrations are something birthed by human cognition, then an infinite number of them could be born into eternity.

"True," I conceded, "there's no guarantee that Shinobu knows what the Darkness is... But Ononoki, it doesn't matter even if she doesn't."

"Why not?"

"Because she eats aberrations—regardless of the identity of that unidentifiable thing, she can just gulp it down. We'll take emergency measures to escape this crisis for now, and we'll ask Hanekawa or someone later about the mystery behind the Darkness."

"Hane-kawa? Who's that?"

"Someone who knows everything."

In fact, I might have called Hanekawa right then and there, but having skipped our start-of-school ceremony made me reluctant.

I could almost hear her reply: *Okay, I'll tell you, and you can even touch my breasts as much as you want, but could you please never talk to me again?*

"I don't know about that," Ononoki said. I thought she was talking about my fantasy, but I was wrong. "I don't know about relying on someone for everything like that."

"I don't think I rely on her for everything."

"You mean you're supporting each other? They say no man is an island—but you're no man at all, are you, kind monster sir?"

"..."

"Nor is that vampire, of course... I ought to warn you, the only person you can count on when it really matters is yourself."

Though it's not for me to say when I went and saved you, qualified Ononoki.

True, I had no idea know what would've happened to me if it weren't for her, so it did feel like a ridiculous self-contradiction.

"By the by, I, Yotsugi Ononoki, shouldn't be here doing this," her tone suddenly turned expository as she stood up. "I told you yesterday that I'm in this town for work, remember?"

"Did you?"

Yeah, I didn't remember.

So much happened afterwards... I'm not exaggerating, it was so much. You could even say my current situation wasn't too bad compared to that experience...

Seeing how I found myself in this situation immediately after resolving that one, I did seem to be living a jam-packed life.

What did I ever do?

Well, a lot, I guess.

And as far as the time travel, that was entirely me sticking my own head into it.

"You're busy, huh, Ononoki?"

"Of course I am. Unlike you, I'm no happy-go-lucky fellow who needs to do nothing more than go to school and have fun. I have to work to live."

"I wouldn't say that all I need to do is go to school and have fun..."

"You didn't even go to school today, did you?"

"Well... Stuff happened."

"Stuff happens to everyone. Don't make it sound like you're some special victim."

"...Okay."

I got scolded by a tween girl.

And I didn't have any excuse or retort, either.

Moreover, I was sitting there in just my underpants as a tween girl stood above me and took me to task.

Not bad at all. Scold me, scold me!

"I feel disgusted for some reason." Seeming to sense something, Ononoki began to walk off.

When she passed by my side, she ground her feet in my shadow in an obviously intentional way. She did this, of course, knowing that Shinobu was snoring away inside of it.

This went deep...

"I'll be going, then."

"Then... What? Back home?"

"Not home, really... Back to work."

"You're not staying by my side for the rest of my life to protect me?"

"Where would you get that idea?"

"I'm joking. I do appreciate your protecting me even once. Actually, I haven't thanked you, have I? Thanks. I promise to repay this favor to you somehow."

"Muscles?"

"No, with something other than muscles..."

If she insisted, maybe I could gouge one pack out from my six and give it to her... It'd heal later, given my vampirism... But such an exchange seemed to run afoul of ethical and humanitarian considerations in various ways.

You know, like we couldn't come back from crossing that line.

And anyway, wouldn't my gift of muscles disappear once I healed?

"I've never actually been repaid by anyone promising to 'return this favor somehow' or 'repay this debt without fail'... In fact, for someone like me, who might disappear from the world at any given moment, the standard for favors and debts is immediate repayment."

"Immediate repayment... Then is there something I can do right now?"

I really did feel indebted to her.

Now that I thought about it, bragging to her about Shinobu, whom she disliked, after being saved like that might've been rude.

Could it have spoiled her mood and made her suddenly say she was leaving? Even if that wasn't it and she really was leaving because she had work (asking what it might be certainly wouldn't get me an answer), I still wanted to do what I could.

"Something you can do right now? Hmm. Well..."

"There's only so much I can do, but tell me what you want. At least tell me."

"Hm."

Ononoki took a step back toward me for some reason.

She came back and stepped on my shadow.

...Could she stop doing that on purpose?

"Kind monster sir."

"?"

"Look this way, *smooch*."

She stole a kiss from me.

Out of nowhere.

It couldn't be described with a cute expression like "she kissed me" and really felt like she'd stolen something. A surprise attack, like your wallet being taken without you even noticing—I'd been shown a brilliant magic trick.

Wait, I was the victim!

A victim!

"Wh-Whuddryuh..."

What're you doing, I tried to ask, but I was tongue-tied.

I was just impressed that I didn't manage to bite my tongue. Who knew, she might have even stolen that, too.

"Wuhddidih," Ononoki played dumb, with no sign of guilt or shame. "Uh oh. Cheater, cheater! Kind monster sir, you're scum."

"?! ?!"

What was this kid saying?!

What was she saying with her expressionless face?!

I wasn't positive, but it felt like she was saying something really scary!

"Trusting relationships, that sort of thing? Well, I just wanted to teach you how easily they can crumble. I guess I've done you another favor instead of being repaid... Why, with all those favors, you could hold a party. But I suppose I do feel a little better," Ononoki said, turning her back on me as if I was a toy she'd lost interest in and tossed aside and not even bothered to put away.

It seemed like her "cheater" bit wasn't about my relationship with Senjogahara, but rather, my ties with Shinobu.

So she was getting back at Shinobu...

Young girls are scary!

"Well," said Ononoki, "do your best to survive this game you don't know the rules to."

"This isn't a game."

"Then what is it?"

With that, Yotsugi Ononoki left the ruins, and I wouldn't say reluctantly. She'd gone back to work.

006

I'm offering no excuses for kissing a tween girl.

It was my fault for letting my guard down, that's all.

While the "cheater" stuff Ononoki went on about was almost entirely a false accusation whether you looked at it from Senjogahara's point of view or Shinobu's, I wasn't sure I wanted to report it to them.

It seemed like the faithful thing to do between lovers, between partners, but also like I only wanted to in order to make myself feel better... If confessing my crime (?) was going to force the burden of forgiveness on them, maybe it was better to keep it locked in my heart.

There's no proof! And I'm the victim here!

...Putting it that way made me sound so shameless. Gosh, I had to deal with a fresh volatile situation now, of all times?

Ugh, I wished I could die.

The Darkness could swallow me and I could die.

Just kidding, but still.

"Hm?"

That's when I noticed my new predicament.

Yet another, arising from Ononoki having left—spine-chilling!
Dammit, Hachikuji and I were all alone!
In a dim room in an abandoned building, at that!
Plus Hachikuji was unconscious!
"…"
Oh no, things were starting to get exciting!
Hushing my breath, I glanced at the girl on the bed of desks who had yet to show any sign of waking up, who'd been revealed to be weak in the face of adversity, Mayoi Hachikuji.
"If she's asleep, doesn't that mean it's okay for me to do anything?"
I approached her as I made this precarious remark.
Umm, what was my rationale here?
Why would I be touching Hachikuji?
I was saving her life? Yes! Of course.
Being unconscious for a long time could be risky, she could be in danger, and I needed to do something to wake her up!
I was obviously the one in need of a wake-up call, but the absence of a straight man made this a sealed room, not a single factor existed to restrain me—
"'Tis thee who needs the wake-up call, dunce!"
I had a straight man, after all.
Actually, I'd been hit.
By a blond girl who came flying out of my shadow, and her fist.
"Vampire Punch!"
Treated to a solid punch with my guard all the way down, I went into a tailspin and flew through the air before crashing right into the wall.
"Hmph!"
Once I crashed into it, she followed up with a low kick.
A barefoot preteen girl's low kick.
While it felt good, I also felt like I might die.
"Wh-What're you doing, Shinobu?!"
"I ought to be asking thee that, fool! Why must I be forced to play

the role of thy conscience? I can't even take a nap! And sheesh, 'while it felt good'?"

Her criticism couldn't have been more sensible.

I never thought I'd be lectured in a sound manner by a vampire, who lived in a domain far removed from human ethics and morality...

"I'm sorry, it was just an impulse..." I apologized quite pathetically. "But I haven't done anything yet!"

"Of course ye have not. Had ye, that low kick would've targeted thy family jewels."

Shinobu looked around as she spoke those terrifying words—and confirming the precarious situation, whereby Hachikuji and I had been alone in the classroom of an abandoned cram school, she sighed.

"Agh. 'Twas a close shave, indeed. It seems I chose the right time to wake up."

"The right time, huh?" I looked out the window. It was far from dusk on the other side of the broken glass, and it seemed that the sun was still beating down. "Have you actually only slept for two hours?"

"And 'twas a restless sleep. I couldn't slumber soundly, at all. I am as tired as when I went to bed," Shinobu grouched, cracking her neck. I couldn't tell if she was grouchy because she couldn't sleep well or because she was appalled by my stupid behavior... Well, it was probably just both. She asked, "What happened?"

"Hm?"

"As I have told thee—since thou and I are mentally paired, thine agitation is communicated to me. Whether I hide in thy shadow or slumber, it makes no difference. I can only assume that my sleep was so restless because something happened to thee..."

"Oh... Well."

The Darkness.

It was because I was chased by it—no doubt.

Our senses were shared (technically they weren't, it was a one-way street running from me to Shinobu), but not our memories, so it wasn't as if she already knew about all of that.

Hm?

Wait, really?

Given her present demeanor, Shinobu certainly hadn't witnessed the Darkness—but what about after that?

Specifically, the act Ononoki and I engaged in—was Shinobu still asleep then? Or was she already awake… Which?

Just as Ononoki hated Shinobu, Shinobu wasn't partial to Ononoki, and if she'd been awake at that point, she'd likely have interfered… But then, maybe she was only half-awake and in a haze.

"By the way," Shinobu said.

"Uh… What is it?"

"Is there not something ye ought to say to me?"

…

Um. Why was I feeling this pressure?

Could it just be my imagination?

Was my sense of guilt making me feel pressure when none was really there?

Was the thing I ought to say simply, "Thanks for reining me in"? Was she just demanding my gratitude?

"Mm? What's wrong?" asked Shinobu.

"Uhh…"

I couldn't tell.

In contrast to Ononoki's expressionless face, Shinobu was wearing a truly gruesome smile… But it was still a smile, which tended to be difficult to read.

Hmm.

Maybe I'd try tricking her into telling me.

With a perfect question, I'd pin down the moment she woke up—but Shinobu wasn't going to fall for any regular trick.

I decided to be roundabout.

"Hey, Shinobu. You can adjust your hair to be however long you want, right?"

"If 'tis thy kiss scene with the shikigami girl thou art wondering about, I saw it."

"You're too good at piecing things together!"

I'd attempted a detour, but she'd taken a shortcut and grabbed me by the scruff of my neck.

I looked at Shinobu.

She was grinning.

Grinning with her fangs exposed.

"Um. Miss Shinobu?"

"What, an apology? He'll apologize? I cannot wait to see how this man will apologize. For leaving me, his life partner, to the side and doing this deed with the little shikigami girl from who knows where."

"…"

Now she was just annoying me.

She was openly enjoying it… She looked like an eight-year-old child at the moment, but she was five hundred, or as I recently found out, closer to six hundred, a vampire vamp as mature as they came.

I had heard before that they live to be about two hundred on average, so even by that standard she had a lot of life experience (not that she was exactly alive).

She might actually be understanding enough to laugh off me "cheating" on her and even turn it into a joke… Too bad she wasn't ready to overlook a dalliance with Hachikuji, too.

Well, if Shinobu was going to be an adult, I needed to act like one too.

Instead of grumbling that I was the victim or that there was no evidence and sour my relationship with Shinobu, I'd apologize straightaway. I'd make her see that she really was the only partner for me.

"Um, Shinobu. I'm sorry, it was my—"

"Not any of my concern," she nipped me in the bud.

Cut off at the best possible moment.

I had a pretty good line in mind, too!

"Thou art constantly flirting and pawing at the girls around thee, after all."

"You're going to regret this for the rest of your life, Shinobu... You just missed out on the most beautiful *dogeza* in the world."

"I've no interest in seeing my master on his hands and knees while he's in nothing but his underwear, regardless of how beautiful it may be... 'Tis taken me long enough, but to answer thy question as to when I first awoke, 'twas the moment ye shared a kiss with that tsukumogami girl. Aye, the exact moment. Thy heart was pounding and throbbing, beating as though ye'd just sprinted with all thy might, and I awoke, alarmed."

'Tis as if my heart had a vibration feature installed in it thanks to our shared senses, Shinobu laughed.

Wait, hold on a second.

Don't make it sound like I got so impossibly shaken and excited about kissing a tween girl that it was enough to wake you up.

She was making me sound so naive and inexperienced.

"And so I understand little of the situation," she continued. "What exactly is going on here? At first glance, the only explanation seems to be that ye've kidnapped a young girl and a tween girl, imprisoned them, but allowed the tween to escape when a kiss provided an opening."

"How can you interpret it like that, you've got a filthy mind."

"'Tis thy hands that are dirty here..."

"Anyway, listen."

Going any deeper into what just happened with Ononoki would be psychologically taxing, but the bigger issue was learning the true nature of the Darkness.

Even if Shinobu doesn't know, I'd said to Ononoki...but only as a possibility I couldn't quite rule out. I was pretty sure that she'd know.

In which case, I wanted to find out as soon as possible. I wanted her to tell me.

The Darkness.

Appearing out of nowhere and following us like it was giving chase—it suddenly got ahead and swallowed my cherished bicycle. That Darkness.

If Ononoki hadn't shoved us off that bicycle, the two of us might have been swallowed up as well, it wasn't difficult to imagine—no, I didn't dare imagine it, and to be frank, it defied my imagination.

To begin with, I wasn't certain that the Darkness swallowed up my granny bike and caused it to vanish—it's not as though I witnessed the moment.

I was just linking the phenomenon of its disappearance, simplistically, with the fact that the Darkness was ahead of where my bike was going.

I couldn't stop associating the Darkness with a black hole, so the bike seemed to have been sucked in... But even that was something I couldn't be sure of.

I understood so little of it.

During spring break, during Golden Week, with Senjogahara and Hachikuji and Kanbaru, and everything else since then, the phenomenon itself was quite clear—like a vampire on the verge of death or a cat monster on the prowl in town.

But this time, I wasn't even clear on the phenomenon itself.

Sure, you might remind me that aberrations are, fundamentally, symbols of what's less than clear... And I'd agree, but couldn't you also say that, through them, "what's less than clear" comes to exist in a "clear form"?

Then the Darkness, from the very outset—wasn't consistent with what an aberration should be.

It seemed to be a symbol, but of the most heterodox sort.

Nothing but blackness—

"It's not like it's a soot sprite," I muttered.

"Hrm? What's that?"

"Oh, nothing... I definitely wasn't talking about Ghibli movies."

"Liar. Ye just made a reference to *My Neighbor Totoro*. I ought to warn thee I'm quite fussy when it comes to *Totoro*."

"I'm begging you, please don't get us off topic..." I never thought the day would come when I would be the one making this request.

"Huh, I was hoping to do impressions of all the lines, of all the characters."

"That'd take an hour and a half."

"The real sight would be how the anime adaptation deals with it. The rights issue will be fairly complex."

"Don't worry, they're not going to adapt this far into the series… there's just no way. I assure you, unlike the novels, the anime will follow the original plan and end at *Nise*."

"Excuse me? What a rude thing to say to the leading actress of a feature film."

"…"

Miss Leading Actress of a Feature Film was clearly getting carried away.

You didn't get to speak a single line during the anime's first season, did you now.

"I can hardly wait," she said. "The scene where I stick my hand in my head to search my memories—I cannot wait to see how it unfolds on screen."

"Going out of your way to mention a scene that's sure to get cut… And why are you leading with this stuff? Just listen to what I'm trying to tell you."

"Hmph. I refuse, fool. For all of thy usual chattering on with girls, the conversation must move forward without idle talk now that thou hast a topic ye wish to discuss? Heaven may forgive such smarm, but not I. The next hundred and fifty pages or so shall promote the *Kizu* anime, and the rest of this tale will be summed up in bullet points, I hope thou art prepared to—mrrgh?!"

I shut her up with a kiss.

Wrapping my arm around her back and pulling her toward me.

I was clearly the instigator, and there was no fudging the picture.

"Wh-What art thou doing… A-Are ye Italian, my master?"

"Just listen. To me. Something bad happened—actually, I don't even know if it's bad, but please listen. I need your insight."

"W-Well, if thou dost insist..." she reacted bashfully, fidgeting and fiddling with her blond hair and blushing. It was this kind of thing that made her so cute.

She's so naive that you'd never think she's lived for six hundred years—where was her mature and understanding personality from a moment ago?

"I shan't refuse to listen. Now talk."

"Making it back with you from all of that time travel, I met Hachikuji right after we climbed down the mountain."

I felt like I moved the story forward at a fast pace, but the preamble still ended up being pretty long. I glanced at Hachikuji, still sound asleep (if anyone, maybe she was the one pretending to be asleep?), and started explaining everything to Shinobu.

Telling her about it would let me get the story straight in my own mind, too.

That is—if there was anything in this tale to get straight.

"Ah. 'Tis almost too convenient."

"Um, I think it's too early for that line... Anyway, Hachikuji left her backpack in my room yesterday, and she was looking for me in order to get it back... In order to return it, we headed to my house together, in a friendly, friendly, so very friendly manner."

"Why art thou emphasizing the friendliness?"

"..."

I wasn't going to tell her that Hachikuji's utterances today betrayed an odd antipathy toward me. I had nothing whatsoever to gain from showing my partner (any more than I already have) just how fragile my heart is.

"And, well," I said, "we didn't run into any trouble in particular up to that point. I was able to return her backpack normally... I handed over to Hachikuji, who waited outside my house, a backpack that hadn't been searched through at all."

"Every aspect of thy story exudes remorse. 'Tis as if I'm conversing with a sordid, petty criminal."

"Can you not compare your partner to a petty criminal? Wait, how far did I get into the story?"

"Up to where ye schemed to bring her into thy home somehow."

"Right, and just as I was about to break out every trick in the book...nope. I never said anything of the sort. As any older person would for a younger person, I kindly offered to take her out to lunch, to promote her physical development."

"Yet a ghost shan't ever develop. And 'twas only fast food."

How was she so sure it was fast food? How was she able to read me so well? Way too sharp of her.

"And that's when—*it* appeared out of nowhere," I said, lowering my voice.

Not even I could mix jokes into the story from here on—suddenly, the Darkness appeared near us.

Our immediate flight. The chase.

How we were saved by Ononoki, who just happened to be passing by, and finally, how we got away from the scene with the Disengagement Edition of her Unlimited Rulebook—I eloquently, if I do say so myself, rattled off everything that happened, speeding through to the end.

I'd hoped recounting the story would help me get it straight, and as you might expect, I was completely wrong. If anything, the more I talked, the more confused I became.

Now that I thought about it, even needing to run away screaming with Hachikuji seemed dubious... Instead of telling a jumbled story to Shinobu, who must still be only half-awake, shouldn't I go home and call Senjogahara and Hanekawa to apologize? That's how dubious it all started to seem.

"...There we have it, but what do you think? If it doesn't bring anything to mind, it doesn't bring anything to mind, of course," I naturally started sounding deferential by the end. You know, I think I even felt a little embarrassed.

"..."

Yet—despite my almost servile attitude, Shinobu met me with a serious look. There wasn't a hint of her trademark gruesome smile.

Actually, the more she heard my story, the more I spoke about the Darkness, the more her expression turned grim.

She looked like she was enjoying my story at first...but by the time I got to the end, she almost seemed mad at me.

Could she have been thinking, *What a tedious account ye've forced upon my ears, brat, 'tis a vulgar ghost story, no tale of an aberration...*?

I mean, I guess I'd get mad, too, if someone woke me up while I was sleeping to tell me about some weird hallucination that wasn't particularly harmful—

"What a tedious account ye've forced upon my ears, brat."

Then, as I was thinking so, she spoke the exact line I thought she might—but the nuance was a little different than expected.

Pretty different, in fact.

"—Ye've reminded me of something unpleasant."

"Hm?"

"No... I am merely venting. The responsibility lies not with thee... If anything, this is my fate. Or perhaps my karma... Then the one it was after was..."

Shinobu mumbled on, not making any sense. She looked lost in thought...or rather like she was trying to remember something.

If it were still available to her, she might have used that mnemonic technique of hers and stuck a hand in her head and rummaged around her brain.

"What, Shinobu... So you have some idea what it is?"

"Hm? Some idea... Aye, I do... Nay, I am uncertain as to whether I can say that I do..."

Indecisive words—rare for Shinobu, whose stock in trade was speaking directly to the point of having a declaration habit.

Then again, recently...during our time travel, she sometimes did show a similar indecisive attitude, but we're talking different cases here.

This time, all she'd done was sleep in my shadows.

"What's the matter, Shinobu? We promised not to keep secrets from each other, remember? If you know something, then tell me. It means you have an idea if you're acting that way, right? You must know what this thing that I'm calling the Darkness really is."

What kind of aberration it is.

You must know—

I ended up hounding her with my questions, but neither surprised nor intimidated by my vehemence, she said, "Well," maintaining her ambiguous demeanor. "If thy question is whether I know, then I suppose I do."

Some part of Shinobu's attitude, however, still felt like...anger? Wrath? At first, I'd thought she was mad at me, but that wasn't it, she seemed to be irritated by something more undefined.

"Tsk... What a bother. Thinking upon what is to come makes me naught but melancholic... Why must I encounter this trouble after, and I say this without exaggeration, saving the world? But this, too, must be my lot..."

"Um, like I was saying, Shinobu—"

"I know not."

Her expression clearing at a moment's notice, as if she'd taken all of the threads of emotion tangled around in her and snipped them loose at once, she turned toward me and spoke those words. Quite the opposite of what she'd said earlier.

"What? But... You just told me that if the question is whether you know, you do."

"I mean I've no clue what kind of aberration it is."

"Huh?"

"As ye've half-noticed thyself, this Darkness *is no aberration*—the Hawaiian-shirted boy would likely say the same. That 'tis no aberration—that 'tis not on the order of a mere aberration."

"...?"

Well, yeah, maybe Shinobu's answer wasn't that surprising. I, myself, had wondered if the Darkness really was an aberration... I thought it could be something else, a different kind of phenomenon.

So it wasn't anything to be surprised by.

It wasn't—but it certainly didn't mean I could go, *Ahhh, I see. What a relief, case closed!*

To begin with, the way Shinobu put it was weird—for her, the king of aberrations, to say that it wasn't on the order of "a mere" aberration?

"My goodness… What a hassle. Nay, I'm appalled. That absurd *phenomenon*—had *yet to end*?"

"Yet to end? What do you mean, had yet—"

"That phenomenon has no name."

No room for argument.

Whether she was finally reclaiming her mojo or just finally waking up, she said it with no room for argument.

A declaration.

"*It*, which ye term the Darkness, is something I have seen in the past—and that is what I've recalled."

"Recalled… You did say you were reminded of something unpleasant… But by past, how long ago do you mean?"

"Four hundred years, mayhap."

"Four hundred years? Isn't that when—"

"Indeed," confirmed Shinobu.

Soberly, solemnly—putting aside the assertive tone, such an expression was extremely rare on her.

"When I last visited this land."

"…"

"In other words—when I created my first thrall."

Back then.

I was caught up *in that Darkness*—Shinobu said.

"Nay—I suppose I should say swallowed up."

"Swallowed up—"

"Shamefully enough."

I was young then, she explained, despite looking like a little girl.

"Hm. I feel no nostalgia at all—nor the desire to speak of this, but under the circumstances I suppose that is not an option. Now that *it* has appeared, doing naught about it could, in the worst case—*bring ruin to the entire town.*"

"T-Town?"

And so they began.

Shinobu Oshino—scratch that.

The iron-blooded, hot-blooded, yet cold-blooded vampire.

Kissshot Acerolaorion Heartunderblade's recollections, from four hundred years ago, like it was better late than never.

007

"Now, then. 'Tis been quite some time since I've last thought of those days. Once one reaches my age, new memories are a rarity—to say that I live only in the moment would be a nice-sounding way to put it, but really, 'tis a transient, hedonistic existence.

"I remember only that which I enjoyed and forget that which was unpleasant.

"And so I cannot deny this unpleasant feeling—for I've suddenly been reminded of something forgotten from my past that I hardly wanted to remember.

"That said, I've no intention at all of blaming thee, so thou may rest easy in that sense—how should I put this. This time around, thou art, in a rare turn for thee, an entirely innocent bystander.

"'Twas not a case of ye sticking thine own head into a situation.

"Though I'm sure thou will make off for the jaws of death as always once ye hear my story—and I suppose I will be there with thee.

"This story will be a bit of a long one.

"It will require spending the great majority of the pages I'd planned to use advertising my theatrical film, at the very least—what's that, it doesn't bother thee in the slightest? What cold words. Just as my moment in the spotlight had come after all this time.

"But I suppose I do have memories of most of what happened that spring break. Of course, that memory came to a proper conclusion, thanks to that wretched Hawaiian-shirted boy, a bad ending though it may have been.

"Keheheh—but in those days I never would have been defeated by such a child, anyways.

"I was at my zenith in those times, after all.

"Not a child as I am now.

"Not looking like the kind of lolita preferred by thee.

"Not flat and smooth but big and buxom—Kissshot Acerolaorion Heartunderblade.

"The iron-blooded, hot-blooded, yet cold-blooded vampire.

"A legendary vampire, the king of aberrations.

"Bound by none, bound by no shadow, one who lived as she pleased.

"Suicidal?

"Oh, no, I became a suicidal vampire after that—I'm impressed that ye managed to remember such an early character trait of mine. This is why talking about the past always embarrasses me so.

"Still, strictly speaking, this will not be the first time I've spoken to thee about those days. I should have once told thee about the time I created my first thrall.

"Brief as the discussion was.

"Aye, during spring break, on the roof of this building.

"Though I never spoke of the circumstances around it—in other words, this was the same time I acquired the enchanted blade Kokorowatari, the one I've let thee borrow so many times.

"I will have to give a bit of a preface, or perhaps a few warnings before I begin… I'm about to tell thee the story of my first thrall, the story of when I created this first thrall…so take care not to grow jealous.

"No, 'twas not a joke.

"And 'tis no laughing matter—not to me.

"I suppose 'tis rare to find a vampire as chaste as I—but to create a thrall is, basically, to have one's breed flourish. One could say it is like creating family.

"While it may not have been a complicated, convoluted relationship such as ours, someone all but unrelated to thee having a master-and-servant relationship with myself, even temporarily, cannot but be an unpleasant story for thee.

"Or perhaps I merely wish ye would feel that way.

"'Tis something a bit different in nature from the way ye 'cheated' on me by kissing that little tsukumogami girl earlier—for I was, for what 'tis worth, serious about it... Aye, I felt about as serious then as I did when I made thee my thrall.

"Perhaps we could say I was more serious, as I made thee my thrall with the intention of turning thee back into a human.

"At the very least, 'twas not a frivolous act.

"So listen.

"Do feel properly jealous.

"To word it in plain terms, from thy perspective now, this thrall would be an ex-boyfriend of mine—sorry as I must be to disavow my virginity to thee.

"Well, no, that one was a joke.

"I know that the trust between us will not be shaken by my retelling, my rehashing of my past, not after all this time.

"So my true warning to thee is to listen closely—for this is no mere story of times past. 'Tis indeed a tale that still applies, that connects to this moment.

"Four hundred years.

"So the better part of my life, then... It all went by so fast.

"Like the blink of an eye.

"My memories are hazy. I'd forgotten them completely until just a moment ago, after all.

"Now, what should I start with.

"Rather, where should I begin.

"Aye, perhaps I'll begin with the circumstances—the circumstances that led to my visiting this land, Japan. Of course, it may not have been called by that name in those days.

"Oh, ye must know. The official name 'Japan' only came into existence a few dozen years ago, no? Prior to that, 'twas the Empire of Japan… What was it before that? Ye must know, thou art studying for thine exams.

"Ah, so Japan as a simple name existed prior to that? Hmm… I don't quite understand. 'The land of the rising sun'? Its derivation…

"But in any case, I didn't know any better at the time, even less than now. I didn't know, for better or for worse. I didn't know a thing about human culture or the like.

"Why, forget any name, I did not even know that these islands existed here. I dove expecting to take a dip in the ocean, only to find land there. What a surprise it was.

"Aye, a dip in the ocean.

"Vampires can't cross the sea? They can't pass over running water? Well, I wouldn't know what to say to such common sense.

"Having 'held' my power and 'fought' me, thou ought to know better than anyone that I am a special, rare species of vampire to which such rules do not apply.

"Not to mention that I was at my zenith then, in high bloom.

"In high bloom and in new bloom.

"Of course, vampires are still vampires—I do have those things ye would call vulnerabilities, such as being weak to the sun, or to garlic or crosses or what have ye, my properly 'established' rules and characteristics, but in those days I had regenerative abilities that far outstripped these weaknesses.

"From the moment the sun began turning my body to ash, nay, before it even could, my body regenerated—if my self of yore were to be biologically anatomized, I suppose I was an abnormally regenerative vampire.

"Even poison, which has troubled thee a number of times, would have done nothing to me in those days. My functions would have regenerated from the moment, or even before, the poison took effect.

"Prior to my visit, I was at the South Pole.

"Aye, the South Pole.

"I wanted to see the aurora… Like I said already, I was not suicidal then, merely a traveler.

"I was visiting the sights of the world.

"Even as vampire hunters around the globe sought to take my life—no, no, the hunters of those days were no mere Dramaturgys or Episodes or Guillotine Cutters.

"They would absolutely disgust you… Human rights and such weren't given consideration in those days.

"How the human world has changed in a mere four hundred years… Thy life would be hunted in those days simply for being immortal, even if thou were not a vampire.

"Not that I gave any mind to it—I enjoyed it, in fact. 'Twould not be until a little later that I began to tire of such battles, that I developed a distaste for them.

"That I became suicidal.

"I'm being serious when I say that I was simply, innocently, and purely enjoying my travels in those days—ah, the aurora was gorgeous.

"'Tis amazing, that aurora.

"Ye ought to see it once while thou art alive—well, I understand humanity is busy these days with global warming or whatever 'tis called, but I'm sure another ice age will come about eventually. It should be visible in Japan then, so don't ye forget to watch.

"If ye can live that long, that is. Ye seem to be bound for an early death despite thy immortality.

"But, to jump to the conclusion, 'twas a mistake.

"However much of an untrammeled traveler I wished to be, however much I wanted to see the aurora, the South Pole was the one place I should have never gone—indeed, the North Pole too.

"No, 'tis not as if I particularly dislike the cold. You could even say cold climes are my forte as a vampire.

"And being immortal also means having no body temperature… 'Twould get a bit complicated if I began down that path, as I'd need to explain the relation to zombies and ghosts and the like.

"Nay, the problem is that there are no humans at the South Pole. 'Tis what ye might call an uninhabited island. I have heard that technically speaking the North Pole is not land but floating ice…but thou must understand this well.

"Aberrations stand in conflict with humans.

"But they cannot come into existence without humans.

"Tales of aberrations cannot come to be without eyewitness testimony or first-hand experience—'tis not as if penguins and polar bears would speak of my immortality or my monstrosity, no matter how I exhibited them.

"Urban legends.

"The word on the street.

"Secondhand gossip.

"Without humans, none would exist.

"While I may not have frozen to death, I suppose I felt my existence weakening—*ah, 'tis no good, what a crisis I've found myself in*. 'Twas no time to be looking at the aurora, for I may soon become aurora myself.

"Nay, I meant nothing by that.

"There are no romantic legends that say a vampire turns to aurora when she dies—there do seem to be some that state the aurora consists of the souls of the dead, but even that legend had no speaker for it at the South Pole.

"There are now? Humans, at the South Pole? Antarctic Research Expeditions, ye say… Ah. So I was their herald. Not that I discovered, or researched, a thing. Regardless.

"I thought that unless I did something, the great being known as myself would vanish into thin air, what a loss for the world, I must not die until I have vanquished the sun, and so I escaped the South Pole in a tizzy.

"I escaped with a super jump instant air dash.

"Aye, even I had to bend my knees and crouch prior to taking off. Hm? The tsukumogami girl's jump? Ah, I suppose ye did speak of such things.

"The Disengagement Edition of her Unlimited Rulebook.

"Hmph, 'twouldn't even merit comparison. To be clear with thee here, the recoil from my jump threatened to destroy the Antarctic landmass.

"I took care not to, of course.

"While I may not have wanted to stay there, 'twas a pleasant land. My plan was to make it a vacation home, a place where I could sequester myself at times when I wished to avoid humans. Meanwhile, I had not given any thought at all to where I might land.

"It was a random, haphazard jump, and so I thought I would land in the ocean, anyway. My idea was to then take a little swim and refresh myself.

"Three quarters of the world is ocean, so probability would state that I was most likely to land in it, no? And while I said the jump was a haphazard one, I did have some kind of a target, I aimed for somewhere around the Pacific—but.

"But, much to my surprise, there was this country.

"Hm? What's that look on thy face?

"No, there's no need for worry. 'Tis not as if I crushed this nation underfoot. Perhaps I would have in the case of a solid landing, but that is where my good luck stepped in.

"I fell in a lake.

"Though it vanished when I did.

"The scale is needlessly grand, ye say? Again, this is a story of me at my zenith—but true, ye've barely seen me at the height of my powers. And that first impression was particularly bad. Ye see, the scale I fundamentally operate on is grand.

"But, the lake.

"When I landed in its waters—no, since I ended up with both feet on its bed, I suppose I ought to say that I landed on land after all—I made the lake disappear, and that is where the tale begins.

"This worthless tale of a demon."

008

"Well, I can't help the lack of excitement in my voice because I already know the ending to this tale, which is to say, 'tis already evident to me that it will come to an awful conclusion, but while I call it a worthless tale, 'tis by no means an entirely unpleasant memory, a flashback I wish to recall none of.

"As ye can see, I've a careless personality.

"Careless, or perhaps perfunctory, or perhaps improvisatory, but in any case, I've lived my life from moment to moment not thinking about matters too deeply.

"That must be why I've lived notably long for a vampire—because I've lived it as hedonistically as I could, never giving too much thought to anything.

"Which is why I do have my reasonably pleasant memories as well—of what happened in that village.

"I've forgotten its name, though.

"Nay, this isn't something I've forgotten, I never made the effort to remember it to begin with—as thou art well aware, I once had close to no interest in human society as a vampire—all of it looked identical to me, and I made no effort to distinguish any of it from the rest.

"I could barely distinguish one race from another.

"*What are the humans in this country, they're all so tiny in size*—that was about the only thought I had. A well-grown boy is no uncommon sight now, but four hundred years ago, every one of thee was about thy height.

"Hmph.

"But well, I am the tiny one now. One never knows what the world may bring—in any case, I apologize for making the story complicated, but the names of villages and humans and all those other kinds of proper nouns won't be accurate going forward.

"In fact, I shan't even try.

"As my senses direct me.

"They won't even be guesses—'twould not necessarily be incorrect to call them nonsense. For about the only distinctions I was making were 'village,' 'man,' 'woman,' and 'child.'

"I may have even mixed those.

"All in a messy tangle.

"I presume the lake whose disappearance I caused had some sort of name as well, but 'tis not one I remember…though 'twas a rather large pond.

"Now that I think of it, I recall that annoying Hawaiian-shirted boy speaking of legends stating that your Lake Biwa was made by the footprint of an inhuman existence, but the opposite would hold true in my case—for my footprints caused the lake to vanish.

"That said, 'tis not as though I did it without any tricks.

"Or perhaps not tricks, but there are always what thou might call advantageous conditions on my side whenever I perform any such large-scale acts—it seems the lake lacked much of its water in those days.

"Aye, from a drought.

"'Twas an age with no dams or the like, so the damage dealt by global warming…or rather, long droughts was quite serious.

"To the point where it truly was a matter of life and death.

"It may be hard for one such as thee who lives in a blessed age to understand…but this was a time when the very concept of infrastructure did not exist—but while it may nearly sound as though I feel sorry for the humans back then, I of course had no such conception at the time.

"While I say that aberrations cannot exist without humans, that aberrations only come into being as such when they are first witnessed by humans, all of that is but theory speaking—to go further, 'tis naught more than an empty idea.

"Why would I ever give my thanks or show my gratitude—in fact, I cackled and joked that if the sun's rays were causing them to grow weak and die, then why, 'twas nearly as though they were vampires.

"'Twas dark comedy, of course.

"But—by chance I had saved those helpless humans. How, ye ask? I thought I'd explained that already…

"I said I'd made the lake disappear, did I not?

"But 'tis not as if I'm an explosive.

"And I spoke of how I have no body temperature—I would not say I have none whatsoever, due to my remarkable regenerative abilities, but let us put that aside.

"This is to say that no matter the speed, Mach whatever, at which I landed, I may have made the lake run dry, but 'tis not as though its water would vanish.

"'Twould not evaporate, ye see.

"True, the high speeds may have heated me to some degree, but I regenerate from even such hot temperatures back to a regular one—when I land, whether on water or land, my body temperature must be quite pedestrian. Let us ignore the un-pedestrian notion of landing there from the South Pole in the first place.

"And with that ignored—what dost thou think would happen then? Think of it as a stone having dropped into a deep puddle from directly above—nay, there's no need to give it any special thought, just think about it normally.

"Aye, the water would splash up.

"Nearly all the water in the lake.

"While I may have been able to negate my heat, I could not go so far as to negate my kinetic energy—now, as for what happened to the water that flew into the air, that too was something utterly regular. After dancing in the sky for a moment, it followed the law of gravity and fell back down to the ground.

"As 'rain.'

"Nay, the word will suffice—if water comes down from the sky, 'tis rain. Dost thou expect me to be able to speak on the mechanisms of weather phenomena, anyway? 'Tis not as though I know everything merely because I've lived for a long time. Expect not the wisdom of the wizened from me, I told thee I've lived my life in the moment.

"In any case, I 'made it rain.'

"And here's the funny part—in those days, to do so was nearly the most virtuous act any being could perform.

"Thou must be thinking, what's so impressive about making it rain, or at least thou must not understand why doing so was such a virtuous act. So I shall be kind and rephrase what I did in a single word. Aye, 'twas a 'miracle.'

"The age was one where men staked their lives on praying for rain—they did not need me to split the land in two, for a long drought was damaging enough to do just that on its own.

"I do think that the sun has mellowed since those days—though it depends from place to place. In any case, I want thee to understand the era's historical background.

"And it was in this time and these conditions of this land—that I made it rain.

"'Twas only as a result—but I saved not just many lives but entire hamlets all around the lake, far and wide.

"I mean not to boast, I have no interest in bragging. 'Twas not my intention, after all. I do not consider saving a human life as any great deed, either—and one false step would have turned the miracle into a disaster.

"Had I landed in a place away from the lake, the center of a village, for example, I may have kicked up not the water of a lake but the drought-cracked land itself. While I would not go so far as to say that I'd have flipped these islands upside down, a number of towns would have met such a fate—a disaster.

"That is in part why I aimed for the sea when I leapt…while 'tis true that I generally have no interest whatsoever in human culture or life, 'tis not as if I'd take pleasure in massacring them on a large scale. Of course I'd want to avoid doing so if I could.

"But if I couldn't, I wouldn't.

"I am an aberration, after all. And a vampire.

"One of a degenerate tribe where suicide and the slaying of kin are chronic issues—humans had different ethics in those days compared to now, and I would say that perhaps mine are different as well. Maintaining the same character for four hundred years is an impossible task—especially in my case, I can now show some bit of understanding when it comes to humans by way of the strong influence ye've had on me, but in those days?

"I'm sure this is rather unpleasant for thee to hear, a modern man and one closer to the human side, but 'tis the truth. What I'm trying to say is that I did not upend the water in the lake to become any savior of the villages around it.

"Allow me to state that much.

"There would be no point at all in telling the legend of a savior rather than of a vampire. And anyway, while I said I'd prefer to avoid mass death if possible, I failed to do just that in reality.

"The lake only happened to be there.

"And, in a stroke of bad timing, I was witnessed when it happened to happen—nay, perhaps I ought to call it good timing?

"I mean, I'd executed that super jump instant air dash from the South Pole in search of 'witnesses' of the aberration that is myself.

"In fact, this prompt witnessing would be a resounding success. I ought to give a hip-hip-hooray for having been witnessed—and of all the times, in the instant I caused that 'miracle.'

"Nay, I suppose it really was poor timing when I think of what came after... The worst timing.

"By the by.

"Dost thou know what ye humans call one who performed a miracle?

"What one, whether aberration or human, is called upon performing a miracle—thou must have an idea.

"Aye.

"The performer of a miracle is called 'god.'

"To be more precise—the performer, whether aberration or human, is *made into* a god."

009

"*Made into* a god?"

I couldn't help but be puzzled by Shinobu's words—for one thing, what she was saying sounded so overblown, and for another thing, her story seemed pretty disconnected from the issue at hand, namely that Darkness.

"What, do I sound foolish to thee?"

"Oh, um... Well."

She rattled me by being exactly right.

I felt like I needed to learn how to hide my emotions a little better, though becoming as inexpressive as Ononoki would be too extreme.

It was way too easy for people to see them.

You didn't have to be Oshino to see through me.

"Well, yes," I admitted. "Oh, but didn't you tell me once about being invited to become a god in the past or something?"

I felt like she said it during spring break, right after I met her.

Right after she made me into a vampire.

Told that I wanted to turn back into a human, she said she understood how I felt.

Since she was once invited to become a god but declined—she understood how I felt.

And so she'd make me human again.

"Is this the time you were talking about?" I asked.

"Well, I suppose...but recalling it now, I wasn't invited to become one, in fact, as much as I was half-forced... There was no room for dialogue or anything of the like."

"No room for dialogue... I guess you did make it rain right in front of their eyes...as in, seeing is believing..."

Hm?

But wait, dialogue?

"Before we go any further, Shinobu, there's something I want to confirm. Were you able to speak Japanese back then? In other words, when you saved these villagers, were you able to have a proper conversation with the Japanese people who witnessed you? Or rather, were you able to communicate your thoughts to them at all?"

"Nay, I was not."

"Didn't think so."

So that was why.

There could never be a dialogue in the first place—Shinobu didn't even know about the existence of Japan, so of course she didn't know Japanese.

"So is that when you learned Japanese or something?"

"Aye, clumsily—of course, I was a bright girl in my glory days, and a multitude venerated me as a god. It didn't take a terribly long time to learn the language spoken by those humans."

"Is that really how it works?"

"And even now I'm learning modern language from thy kind. *Moé* and *tsundere* and *braided big-boobie class president*."

"You need to forget the last one you just said."

I didn't remember ever teaching her that phrase.

Don't say it to Hanekawa even by accident... She doesn't have braids anymore, anyway.

I love her no matter what her hairstyle is, though!

"But being half-forced into becoming a god doesn't seem like your style," I said. "Why not just escape from that with a super jump instant air dash?"

"Run? Me? I?"

Hah! Shinobu laughed in defiance.

I couldn't begin to figure out how she was able to look at her own partner with such an awful expression on her face.

"I turn my back to no one. I've never once fled since the day I was born as a vampire."

"..."

I dunno, it felt like she had a lot of times...

And wait, wasn't she originally born as a human before turning into a vampire? Or maybe she "didn't remember" that, either... What a convenient memory she had.

That's what happens when you live for so long.

"Well, 'tis not as if they had any need to court me by force, nor did I have any reason to reject them by force—I thought 'twould be a nice change of pace to be treated as a god...I suppose. To imagine my mental state at the time."

"Hmm... Still, treated as a god." Just like Shinobu said, I didn't really understand the historical background or circumstances, so I couldn't quite wrap my head around it. Was my point of view too peaceful? "I guess I can understand how making it rain was the most virtuous miracle possible in those days...but that seems like something other aberrations could do, too. Like, um...rain frogs?"

"Rain frogs aren't aberrations... But aye, when they saw rainfall so intense that it caused flooding, they must have treated that as an aberration. Everything is situational in the end."

"Situational, huh... Oh, but now that you mention it, I remember hearing that they can control the weather to some degree now. That they can force the sky to be clear or cloudy or rainy by moving rain-clouds around with planes or something... It's not quite genetic engineering, but it does feel like technology that's gone beyond the boundaries of humankind in some way. Maybe you could call that the other side of the 'miracle' coin?"

"Indeed. If someone appeared who could use genetic engineering to cure any illness in an instant, who would object to calling her a god? She would even be venerated. Though whether that's a good thing or not, I do not know."

"?"

"I mean to say that deicide is not out of the question in this day and age of weakened piety—those with outstanding skills are targeted. For their skills and their life. But no—deicide itself has existed in places around the world for millennia. Fortunately, that was not my experience."

"Oh, it wasn't?"

That was unexpected.

Since she said the story had a bad outcome, I assumed she was working up to that kind of ending—but then, in that case, there wouldn't be any place for the Darkness in her story.

So far, I didn't have any clue when or at what point the Darkness might get involved.

"What, are ye disappointed? That my plight in those days was not that I fell victim to deicide? This audience of mine has such cruel expectations."

"No, that's not what I meant..."

"Ye needn't worry, this story will be relevant. 'Tis not my plan at all to stealthily turn this into an advertisement for the film."

"Are you sure it isn't?"

"Why, I cannot believe it. I'd heard that it would be a theatrical feature but never expected it to be in 3D."

"Stop spreading false information..."

It's 2D, okay? 2D.

What was she doing trying to use lies to get viewers in seats?

"To think the class president's breasts would come bounding out so!"

"They won't, they won't."

"Well, putting aside whether they will, a film would be subject to fewer restrictions than television, so will we not be able to depict whatever we want, be it breasts or blood spray?"

"…"

I now knew this little girl talked about breasts and blood spray in the same breath. Very scary.

"Hold on, so stop sneaking in ads for the movie. Keep telling the story. About your past…or your first thrall."

And about the Darkness, of course, but if I'm being honest with you, I was interested in her first thrall, too.

Having it described as jealousy or envy, which made me feel like I'd been seen through, didn't sit well with me, but as Shinobu's—no, as Kissshot Acerolaorion Heartunderblade's "second thrall," I couldn't help but be curious.

I just had to be.

"You needn't tell me to continue," she said. "But I am recalling some of this as I tell it, so like anything from the past, my memories are a bit hazy, and I may not remember the precise details—"

"…"

How undependable.

Please, Shinobu. I'm depending on you.

"Allow me to continue by explaining a bit more about the background—though this would have more to do with the conditions of the land than it does the age."

"The conditions of the land?" I asked. "You mean how the whole area was suffering from a drought, right? I got that already—"

"Nay, not that but details of the lake I made disappear. It seemed that this lake, while perhaps not Lake Biwa, had been worshipped in one way or another. Those who lived around it revered it as 'a divine lake' and prayed to it as such. In other words, they prayed to it for rain.

'Twould seem easy to laugh at them for their foolishness—however many myriad gods they say this country has, seeing a lake of all things as a god and praying to it for rain? If thou art willing to go that far, why not scoop the water from the lake and carry it back with thee bucket by bucket."

"..."

Actually.

If she made a lake that people worshipped disappear, didn't that make her the god-killer?

I wasn't going to make the joke, though…

"Thus my witnesses," she continued, "were locals praying for rain—to that bunch, it must have seemed as though I'd come bursting out from inside the lake. As an incarnation of the lake's water."

"Um, it's a little awkward to say this, but if someone that blond, golden-eyed, and tall appeared out of nowhere in front of a Japanese person in those days, she'd seem pretty divine…"

Of course, she was doomful, not divine.

Then again, maybe there isn't that much of a difference in impression given off by the two words—even I was taken by her beauty when I "witnessed" her for the first time.

So much so that I was ready to throw my life away.

In that sense, maybe there isn't any difference between aberrations and gods—even the crab that had possessed Senjogahara was supposed to be a kind of god.

As for devils, which stood in contrast…um.

Would Kanbaru's monkey be one?

But even that devil—was a monkey that granted wishes, and you could say that it performed miracles.

Was there, or wasn't there, some theory that gods and devils are just two sides of the same coin?

"Hmph. Flattery will get thee nothing," Shinobu said, apparently taking my words as praise.

"Um, I wasn't trying to flatter you or suck up to you. Anyone from outside of Japan would have been a rare sight in those days."

"Did you not hear what I just said about flattery? Ye truly are a fool. The most it could possibly get thee is a pole dance."

"That'd be something."

She didn't simply not mind my words, she was jubilant.

A god who's vulnerable to praise...wasn't one I'd worship.

Still, she'd performed a miracle before their eyes, manifesting as a god to them, and she'd saved many of their lives as a result—if they were saved.

I could understand those people making Shinobu into a god—but. But...

"But that...couldn't have lasted for long."

"Hm? Why dost thou say so?"

"Well, given your personality—you're not the type to sit back and enjoy people just worshipping you..."

She was haughty and arrogant, domineering and condescending, discriminatory and egotistical, someone so hopeless that she really left you with no hope—but there was no way this vampire could enjoy being treated as a god for long—was my take on it.

Speaking of living only in the moment.

She might rise to that position on a lark—but I couldn't see her having any interest in ruling or reigning.

Given her personality.

It goes without saying, though, that the Shinobu that I knew, the one I was so close to, had a personality deeply influenced by none other than my own. So of course I'd think that, but I had no way of knowing her personality back then—and yet if she was the type to accept being treated as a god, she'd have made more than just two thralls over the course of six hundred years.

She'd have formed a hierarchical society of vampires.

In general, she preferred solitude over supremacy.

And I dare say that she placed herself somewhere above a god in her own mind—it was that incredible pride of hers that made me think she wouldn't decide to be a mere god for long.

Being a demon.

That's the one thing this vampire would never let go of.

"Hm? Aye, indeed, indeed. That is the kind of prideful creature I am. I seek no admiration from others at all, such vanity has no place in my life. Thou art wise, I see."

"..."

Considering how hopelessly weak she was to praise, maybe it'd be better to retract my previous statement.

"Well, true," she continued her story after savoring her delight for a moment. Fortunately. "As ye say, my time as a god did not last long—roughly a year, I reckon. Putting anything about my personality aside, it seems that I truly was not made to be a god—"

Shinobu looked out the window once she said this—the sky was still blue. No signs anywhere of aberrations or anything suspicious.

As for Mayoi Hachikuji.

She was still to our side, unconscious.

010

"I suppose ye could say that part of the reason I went along with those fools' attempts to exalt me as a god was to take a break.

"Living at the South Pole was demanding.

"Bitter, frozen blizzards—along with those many days when I was never once recognized as an aberration. While I may have been at my zenith, I was a little, just the littlest bit tired.

"The littlest bit, ye hear? Littlest.

"So now that I was in a place with plenty of humans that would recognize me, I thought I would take it easy and rest. Call it a whim if ye want. A whim quite befitting of me—being treated as a god meant free lodgings and food.

"'Twas a holiday of sorts.

"I was on an island nation, after all. Like being on Hawaii, were I to give a modern comparison. Aye, Hawaii—though that is one place I've never been despite having traveled the world.

"'Tis not easy to arrive on an island nation with a super jump. Hitting one's mark is difficult unless 'tis a large continent.

"Hm? Oh, no. When I said free food, I wasn't sucking the locals' blood. Don't look at me like that. Aye, I am a vampire and an aberration that uses human blood as energy, but I'd not consume any from humans showing me affection.

"Though it's hard to say what I'd do in an emergency.

"What about thee? Say there was a cow that showed thee affection and one that didn't. Thou would consume the latter's meat, would thou not? 'Tis the same thing.

"This country did still have a system of sacrifice in those days, so blood would have been easy to procure no matter how much I wanted—for thy reference, I've heard that ritual human sacrifice existed here until quite recently too.

"From who? That Hawaiian-shirted boy.

"Though I never told him this story—not once during the days I spent in these ruins with my arms around my legs did it feel appropriate to speak of my past.

"Of course, this is that boy we're talking about. He'd come to this town having researched everything he could about me, so perhaps he knew, without any disclosure on my part.

"Though I'm dubious of whether any records of those villages still exist—most of what makes me a legendary vampire are my acts in Europe, and not a person survived who could have related the event that happened here.

"Aye, that is what awaits us at the end of this story.

"Brace thyself. Every character that appears will die.

"While they avoided dying of drought, they all died anyway. Perhaps destiny isn't that easily twisted of a thing, in the end—though I'd prefer not to believe so.

"Well, I had no such values at the time—but ye'd better not misunderstand, I was not merely enjoying a vacation on an island nation in the Far East.

"I did my job as a god, too.

"Making it rain but once was not enough—I would wait a bit and then make it rain again.

"What's that? Didn't the lake disappear? Aye, which is why I gathered rain clouds from the area. 'Tis the method ye just described... I used no airplane or the like, of course. I collected them with my own hands. Hold on, don't tell me ye forgot I can sprout wings?

"True, 'twould only cause other regions to suffer through droughts—so I tried as best I could to gather them from above the sea, but I doubt my work was perfect.

"Gods are self-centered in that sense—believe and ye shall be saved, they say, and proceed to save only those who do.

"I did of course explain this to those humans, but they did not seem to particularly mind... In other words, they were faithful in appearance alone, and were in the end a regular bunch that thought only about themselves. While I don't dislike selfishness in humans, I wonder, dost thou find it a bit difficult to accept?

"Indeed, the karma of humans, or rather, of all living things—would be much easier to bear if ye simply became an aberration.

"Or a god.

"Of course, 'twas not a decision thou or I had the opportunity to make—ah, right, I'll skip over a bit.

"Shall we pick up the pace?

"Telling thee of how those humans came to venerate me could turn into naught more than boasting if I am not careful. About how I was extolled in this way and respected in that way. 'Twould be a dull story to hear, would it not? Not that this will be an entertaining story. Not a thing about this story is entertaining, unless 'tis the utter farce that was my youthful folly. Laugh if ye want to.

"Ye won't be able for long.

"So. While I spoke earlier of free lodgings, in fact I made them myself. In the bed of the lake that disappeared—the lake itself had been recognized as my land. As what ye might call my holy ground.

"It became home to my shrine.

"'Twas a gorgeous structure.

"'Tis not as if I could have settled in a village and lived among humans, after all—how would I have been able to maintain my divine majesty?

"What's that? I'm a horrible god for demanding a shrine from such a destitute village? Do not misunderstand, no one built anything for my sake.

"I built it myself.

"Have ye forgotten my ability to realize matter? And this was at my zenith. I was able to create a building and any sort of incidental gadgets in no time at all. In the blink of an eye, in the time it took them to gasp at such speed. It did not so much as tire me.

"I must say, though, ye truly are an awful sight there in your underwear and naught else. I'll make thee clothes, so just wear them. How long dost thou plan on providing fan service to that muscle-obsessed tsukumogami girl?

"Hmph. I like it. Aye, it suits thee.

"Wear that in the theatrical anime... What's that? 'Twould throw the timeline off? What do I care? Time is meaningless in my presence. Did thou not learn that for thyself just the other day?

"Ignoring the timeline is but a small price to pay if the alternative is putting thy unfortunate casual attire on the silver screen for all to see. Aye, ye disappoint.

"In any case, I built my pleasant home on the bed of the lake, but this too was considered a 'miracle,' only bolstering my godhood. It positively skyrocketed.

"I let them do as they pleased.

"A bunch that showed no interest in the logic of an occurrence and instead preferred to proclaim and hail a miracle was best left alone.

"There was no need to go out of my way to educate them.

"I commend thee in that sense for attempting to discover what the Darkness truly is in this way—I can see that the Hawaiian-shirted boy educated thee well. Or perhaps enhanced thee—but that said.

"The logic of the thing cannot always be understood.

"For even I, doing this explaining to thee, know not the identity of that Darkness—I am merely trying to explain how I do not understand what has not lent itself to understanding, 'tis forlorn to reflect upon.

"In that regard, this is no different from the idle chatter ye always engage in with all the girls. Shall we put this to an end? Skip straight to the conclusion and—I jest, I jest. Even I would feel uncomfortable saying this much and dropping it.

"I shall continue.

"With a perhaps meaningless story.

"While I said I let them do as they pleased, I did forbid that lot… or rather, my adherents, from doing one thing.

"*Naming* me.

"Calling me by a name.

"That is what I—forbade.

"As I already said, I do not remember any proper nouns, will not call people by their names, and do not so much as know the name of that village—since I saw no value in them.

"They, as a whole, were naught but humans.

"A single bunch of humans.

"But I did not allow them to call me by name for a different reason—after all, I was a 'god.' That lot wanted to know my name.

"Yet I did not allow them to—never did I allow them to call me by my given name, Kissshot, my alias, Acerolaorion, my heritage, Heartunderblade.

"I never gave them my name to begin with, of course.

"And I did not allow them to give me one, either.

"When that Hawaiian-shirted boy named me 'Shinobu Oshino,' 'twas to chain my existence by the name. Bound, hand and foot—and this was the one thing I had to avoid in those days.

"For if I were given a name, I would be chained to that land—while for me the title of god was but temporary, my time in that land but a vacation.

"Why should I allow myself to be chained?

"I may have acted like a god, but I had no intention at all of becoming one.

"Aye, I suppose I learned not the names of those people or the village for the same reason, if thou were to look at it that way. Because to call them by their names would breed affection.

"I may no longer be able to leave that land—but all of this is said in retrospect, and I had no such distinct awareness of the reason in those days.

"Now that I think upon it, I continue to remember few proper nouns—I feel the only full names I recall with clarity belong to thee and thy sisters.

"If thou were to ask me to write it in thy system of characters, I am dubious of even thy name. The difference of a few small lines here and there can alter pronunciations and meanings so drastically, changing *Koyomi*, 'calendar,' into *Reki*, 'record.'

"Stop it, don't act so mad—or rather, don't act so despondent.

"For I doubt ye can spell my former name correctly—but in any case, with the exception of calling me by a name, I permitted them everything.

"Not so much permitted, I simply let them be.

"I idly spent my time as I wished, slept, woke, and ate and made it rain as I wished, and blessed the occasional wedding.

"Aye, ye could call it pleasant.

"Looking back on it, I am dissatisfied in that Mister Donut had yet to come to this country, but that aside, 'twas a nice vacation for the most part.

"A way to kill time… Or rather, I savored all the time I had to spare. As much as I wanted, to my heart's content. I calmly and rather peacefully waited to recover from the small bit of fatigue I'd accumulated at the South Pole…but it ended up being for naught.

"My regenerative powers are, strictly speaking, different from powers of recovery—still, I'd assumed that the strength of my existence would recover if those people continued to witness me, but unfortunately, 'twas not how things work in the real world.

"How could it recover—when they were not witnessing me as an aberration known as a vampire?

"It took quite some time for me to notice this.

"My recovery seems to be progressing at a terribly slow pace, I thought as I lived my leisurely life. And at the time, in fact, I had no reason to be bothered by it.

"Say I'd continued to go witnessed by nobody—while I did take care to move so that I would be, say I had continued to live there at the South Pole. I think I would have survived for another century.

"In fact—looking back on it, that is what I should have done. I'd overreacted and in my haste made escaping the South Pole my only priority.

"Thanks to my doing so, I was able to live a pleasant life as a god… or so I thought, but 'twas not the case. I was utterly mistaken.

"'Twould've been quite alright not to be witnessed as a vampire—that was not the pressing issue.

"The issue was that I was continuing to be witnessed as 'a god'—in retrospect, simply refusing to be called by a name was not enough.

"Dance with a devil and ye too will become one—and so.

"Be called a god and ye too will become one.

"I was truly amiss not to notice—nay, not even know this.

"But let us put that aside.

"Judging by the history textbooks ye now study, the political structure in those days was known as the *bakuhan* system, but I am not terribly familiar with that sort of thing.

"They must have been ruled by something somewhere, as they went off to wherever they went to offer tribute each year—though serving something other than their god strikes me as unfaithful when I think upon it.

"Well, it seems that times have not changed much since then, who sits at the top of a country has only a limited bearing on those at the bottom.

"Perhaps it was a difficult time, but they did all seem to enjoy themselves. They seemed to live happy lives—humans are capable of finding joy in even the worst of conditions, and perhaps they can find misery in the best.

"That's how they differ from aberrations, who have more defined characters.

"Nay—my character had been wavering at the time…

"When I think upon it now, I ought to have refused their treating me as a god and left the moment I learned the land had no legends of vampires.

"One could put it in more simple terms, too. That I was punished for daring to act like a god for so long—at least, that's what he said.

"Him.

"Aye—my first thrall.

"In other words, he who possessed the enchanted blade Kokorowatari.

"I spoke the slightest bit about that man before—what did I say about him then? That he was a warrior…a samurai. Aye, that was it.

"But if we're to speak of the historical background, this land seems to have had the most peaceful political system in the world in those days—though this is something I learned not from thy textbook but from that Hawaiian-shirted boy.

"At any rate, 'twas an age when those who fought had the least to do. He and I were alike in that sense. Loafers.

"I heard something about how samurai was naught more than a title, an honorary post, something of the kind…but we can ignore those details.

"What is important is that despite those historical circumstances, the man was still a samurai.

"That he was still a warrior.

"The man fought—in that peaceful age, in some ways more peaceful than this one, he still fought.

"Against what? If not with humans, only so many options remain.
"Aye—against aberrations."

011

"He fought against aberrations… W-Wait, so you're saying he was an expert?"

Mèmè Oshino. Deishu Kaiki. Yozuru Kagenui.

Authorities on *yokai* and the like.

No, maybe not.

Somehow it didn't seem like they "fought against" aberrations—true, Kagenui felt pretty violent to me, but at the end of the day, they were experts.

They acted as mediators between two sides—as negotiators.

That was a better description of their station.

Something about the word "fighting" felt wrong.

In that case, wouldn't he be more like—

"A vampire hunter—"

Dramaturgy.

Episode. Guillotine Cutter.

That kind of person.

"Well, I suppose—while I'm sure negotiators similar to that

Hawaiian-shirted boy existed in those times as well, he was different from that type. The descendant of a storied line of those who made yokai extermination their calling—may be what he said, or maybe not..."

"What, your memory's fuzzy about something that important?"

"I cannot help it. Memories are worn away by time."

"Worn away..."

Um.

Listening to her speak, I was beginning to wonder. Didn't memories ever get idealized in her case?

My memories of the hell that was spring break and the nightmare that was Golden Week weren't pleasant, but when I actually tried to think back to those events, I found myself putting them in a fairly good light...

It didn't feel like she was altering her memories as much as simply forgetting them.

She was speaking like someone who was struggling to remember what she ate for dinner a week ago...like someone who was going back and recalling everything she ate to figure out what caused her food poisoning, for example...

But this was four hundred years ago, not a week. Maybe there wasn't anything left to see through any rose-tinted glasses... Still.

"This is an important episode about you and your first thrall, right? Even if your memories have gotten worn down, would they really get that vague? I mean, fill in whatever's missing with your imagination. Sentimentally. You told me to get jealous, but nothing about your words just now would make anyone jealous."

"Is that so. But now that ye mention it, he was a fairly different type of man from thee, and different too was the situation. Perhaps a direct comparison is misguided... Also, by now, if I may make something clear, and not out of any thoughtfulness for thee, the impression he left is not as strong as thine."

"Hm? Really? But wasn't he your first?"

"Being my first thrall does not mean he must be more memorable than my second... While ye may now be dating that tsundere girl and practically speak of her as thy first love, I'm sure that most strictly speaking, thou had a crush on thy dry nurse in kindergarten or the like. But ye've simply *forgotten* that—see?"

"..."

Well, I understood her logic.

But it did seem more suspect if you were to ask me if I thought my time in kindergarten matched up with Shinobu's experiences at two hundred.

No, wait, was this really about impressions and not memories?

In terms of romances, people always wanting to think that the love they're experiencing at the moment, first or not, is the best—the psychology of wanting to think so...

It seemed clear the story Shinobu was sharing with me wasn't a pleasant one for her—but even then, something still bothered me.

Did it matter so little?

Shinobu's first thrall?

"Didn't you call him something like a man you could entrust your back to?"

"I did, but then I came to know thee. He feels a bit lacking in that regard, looking back."

Hmmm.

She was being way too candid.

She still treasured his enchanted blade, carrying it with her in her belly, and yet—

"Also, doesn't your moniker 'aberration slayer' originally come from what people called your first thrall's sword?"

"Aye," confirmed Shinobu. "A sword passed down from generation to generation...among a clan of yokai exterminators. A sword that had slain aberrations since time past—that must have been worshipped like a god in its own right. I call it an enchanted blade, but 'divine blade' might accord better with reality."

"Divine blade…"

"And the human who wielded it would have been like a god—may have been a living god in his own right."

"I can't help but feel like you're putting a veil over everything you're talking about. You keep on calling this guy *he* and *him*…but don't you think it's about time you told me the name of your first thrall? I can't picture his face if you don't."

"Who knows."

"Huh, that's a weird name. Hunose? But maybe it wasn't that weird back in those days…wait, what?"

"Stop with thy surprise. Have I not told thee again and again? I recall the human world's proper nouns but vaguely, and call none by name. Listen when people speak to thee."

"…"

No…I was listening.

And yes, she did say that.

But I assumed there'd be exceptions…or rather, a limit?

How could she not even remember the name of someone that important, the name of the main character? Just how in the moment did she live her life?

"And I always called him Aberration Slayer—as I am called now," she said. "He was easier to distinguish from other humans as he held that blade, and he had the unique air of an expert about him as well."

"He was unique and special so it made him easy to distinguish… which was paradoxically why you didn't need to call him by his name?"

I could understand the logic there…

But it was too much of a stretch.

It sounded like an excuse, or simply too cold by anyone's standards—wasn't that just too cold-blooded?

Where did her iron blood and hot blood go?

"Look, ye've got it all wrong," Shinobu chided me. "Thou art an exception among exceptions for myself—as thou art the only one in my over five hundred years to whom I owe my life."

"..."

"Compared to that, my relationship with the man who was my first thrall was casual. When I think back to him now. That is also why I thought I may be able to arouse thy jealousy, but it appears as though I could not—perhaps jealousy for a man whose face thou cannot see, whose name thou dost not know, is a tall order."

"You've been living a lot more casually than I thought..."

In fact.

I was amazed she'd managed to survive for so long.

Maybe it just proved how powerful of an aberration she was...

"Then for convenience's sake," I proposed, "why don't we call him Aberration Slayer I? The First Aberration Slayer would be too long."

"'Tis the exact same length when ye say it out loud."

"Never mind."

She wasn't wrong to point that out, but "the first aberration slayer" sounded too impersonal.

Maybe it didn't reflect his personality if Aberration Slayer was originally the name of a blade (it might be like calling me "School Uniform"), but I wanted to do at least that much for my predecessor.

Forget jealousy, I was starting to sympathize with him...

You had to wonder.

"And then what? Did your slacker lifestyle change a bit when Aberration Slayer I came along?"

"Well, to some degree."

"If he was an expert in yokai extermination...that has to mean he showed up to exterminate you, right? He heard rumors about you from somewhere then appeared to attack you—"

"Nay. Not in the slightest—we did battle once, but he hadn't come to exterminate me. Think upon it, now. I was being venerated as a god in those rumors he heard. Not scorned as some target he needed to exterminate."

"Is that...how it works?"

Even if there weren't any legends of vampires in Japan at the time, there must have been aberrations that sucked human blood—so it felt like an expert would be able to detect that Shinobu was a vampire and not any kind of god.

"Oh, wait—I guess he found out in the end if you made him your thrall," I noted.

"Indeed—so why don't I focus in on that bit."

012

"So as I said, he came not to exterminate me but to check things for himself. An entire lake had disappeared and a god had manifested from it... 'Twas not a situation that one with his pedigree could ignore.

"Though I do feel it took him some time to arrive... True, information did not travel as swiftly then as it does in this age. His transportation methods were limited as well.

"Now that I mention it, he arrived transported in a palanquin.

"With a long retinue tailing behind—'twas a regular *daimyo* procession. Not that I've ever seen a genuine one.

"Still, all of those followers.

"He must have been as important as any feudal lord.

"I suppose thou could call them his thralls—he may have been connected in some way to those with effective control over the villages in the area.

"Perhaps he was even one of them himself.

"The villagers did kowtow terribly to him—but hierarchies within human communities are not something I am familiar with.

"What I am sure of, or rather, what was important was that he had come to my temporary abode—he posed no threat to me no matter how many humans came along with him, but something was different this one time.

"I did not feel threatened by him.

"Ye may think that odd, as he was an expert…or a hunter, but I had been dealing with those types year-round.

"I could not even distinguish them from regular humans.

"Call me too casual, but what am I to do when that is who I am? There's no need for me to distinguish between hunters and regular humans, anyway—the two are alike.

"Of course, the Hawaiian-shirted boy I met when I was weakened did leave a strong impression on me, as did Kaiki and Kagenui after I became a little girl.

"'Tis simply how it goes. Don't ye think poorly of me.

"That said, it woke me up. I was awakened by their arrival—which is not to say I had been sleeping in the shrine until then.

"He aroused my awareness of things for the first time in a while.

"In others words, as I was living my lukewarm existence as a god, I found a fine stimulus. But again, 'tis not to say that he—or that gathering—was what excited me.

"Those blades.

"The ones he had—hanging off of his hips. The ones he *wore*, would thou say? I'm unsure of the distinction there…

"In any case.

"The two blades the man had as he left his palanquin, one large and one small—those are what drew me in.

"Though it may sound a bit vulgar that my attention was drawn to a man's hips. Thou and I would then share a love of hips belonging to the opposite sex, so perhaps in that sense our connection is age-old.

"I jest.

"Hm? Aye.

"Two of them, two blades—the longer being the enchanted blade

Kokorowatari.

"The one whose replica ye've wielded—the true one is rather more dangerous.

"The replica has been de-tuned some.

"'Twas too dangerous.

"Of course, 'twas not that effective of a weapon on me...but it did at least open my eyes.

"'Twas enough of a stimulus.

"Hm? What about the smaller blade? The short sword?

"The second—of the two blades?

"Ah, have I never spoken of it? I thought I already had... Mayhap 'twas my imagination.

"Thou could say it was a backup...like something to keep the first, too dangerous Kokorowatari in check.

"Perhaps we could call it a sheath... Well, both the original Kokorowatari and this short sword had their own, separate sheaths, so the metaphor would only serve to complicate the story.

"A weapon that was too dangerous needed a follow-up, an accompaniment—my replica is but a replica, of course, so I've no need for the short sword.

"The second enchanted blade—the short sword was known as *Yumewatari*.

"Dost thou find it odd that I recall the name of the short sword, in addition to the one that I still use? Well, 'tis no special exception.

"That is simply how much of a set the short sword was with its leading blade Kokorowatari. The two, the heart and the dream, *kokoro* and *yume*, were one, and no sword could cut them apart, so to speak.

"If Kokorowatari is the aberration slayer.

"Then Yumewatari was—the *aberration savior*.

"A divine blade that has been passed down through the generations becomes something like an aberration itself, so my own radar was pinging like mad.

"I left the shrine the moment I felt its presence—well, to be precise,

I blew the shrine to dust. Moving was such a bother that I chose to have the shrine disappear.

"I compared it to a *daimyo* procession…but I would say he had, oh, fifty men with him? I believe he, its leader, was not the only expert, and that the other forty-nine were not mere underlings.

"Well, doing away with a shrine might not be enough of a miracle—but 'twas a sufficient display of power. Though if I truly made use of my power, it would be the earth I could make disappear, not a simple shrine.

"I suppose the sun is the only thing I cannot disappear. Aye, my one and only goal, which I continue to hold to this day.

"Oh, don't say thou would never allow me to. 'Tis my one and only goal… But in any case, I succeeded in surprising them, even if 'twas not the point of making the shrine disappear. 'Twas just too much of a bother to walk outside… To me, it was naught more than a structure I could rebuild.

"Yet that, and no more, managed to suppress them.

"For while they may have been experts in the field of yokai extermination, I was so far removed from any they'd known—the lot of them were gripped with terror.

"They collapsed on the spot. How disgraceful. I found myself losing my own will to fight, in fact.

"Only a few were able to continue standing in the face of my glaring countenance… Ah, I want to say about five of them.

"Aberration Slayer I, if ye want me to use that name as well… Only he, as well as the men directly under him, his four knights as it were, managed to stay on their feet and look in my direction.

"That probably is not to say they were unflustered.

"And 'twas not as though they recognized that I was not a god but a vampire—if anything, they believed me to be a true god.

"At least, one with enough power to be called such and venerated—and, as thou said, the color of my hair and skin were novel to the people of the land, so I must have appeared divine in the sun's reflection.

"Now. What do ye think I did next?

"What did I do in the face of this continued misunderstanding? To be honest, I wavered for a moment. For as I said earlier, I sensed that they were hunters due to those swords.

"I could see a battle unfolding were I to reveal my true identity.

"Vacations are nice, but so is the occasional stimulus—so perhaps I should ratchet things up a bit.

"I would be lying if I claimed not to have felt that way.

"Hm? Nay, to jump ahead, I did not reveal my identity, nor was there any battle. I am a pacifist, as thou art aware. Aye, a pacifist—one who hates to fight, a humanist who believes in love above all.

"I make myself want to laugh, taking on the title of humanist when I am not even human... 'Tis a white lie so audacious, I turn pale. My apologies, that was overdoing it, even as far as jokes go.

"The reason we did not find ourselves in a battle next was simply that they did not seek one.

"As a bunch of men who made yokai extermination their job, I would be the exact type of creature they needed to kill. But in those days, as I just said, I was not yokai nor vampire, but a god. I was evidently on the level of a god, at least in terms of sheer power, so that was all for them.

"Though they did ask, as a formality.

"'Are ye truly a god?'

"I still hesitated to call myself a god, though, so I answered, 'Think of me as ye wish...but do not call me by any name'... I was able to give that much of a response by then, as I understood some bit of Japanese... and apparently my answer was persuasive.

"Of course, they did not attend to me like the vicinity's inhabitants—their response was a realistic one in that sense. 'Twas not as though their attitude toward me suddenly changed, either.

"If anything, they were quite businesslike.

"A god, is that so, then please sign these documents here and we will call thee later—that sort of thing.

"Figuratively, of course.

"I presume they had already dealt with many gods other than myself—'twas as if they felt at home once they knew me to be one. Even those who collapsed upon first impressions stood right back up.

"Though I was not an actual god…

"Well, familiarity can be a frightening thing.

"I suppose ye could say familiarity was the main reason none of them feared a god, or that they even made light of gods, but I think the fact they were of the ruling class played a role as well. In other words, droughts did not particularly affect them.

"They would not have been saved by me.

"And not just I, they would not have been saved by any 'god'—they had conceived of, created, and implemented systems that allowed them not to have to rely on gods.

"Such men do not venerate gods. If anything, they see gods as their equals.

"*Believe and ye shall be saved,* as we said, but it may in fact be closer to the truth to describe it as a manner of hindsight bias, whereby having been saved, one believes.

"But let us return to the subject.

"The rest of our conversation turned awkward, in part due to my unreliable Japanese, but we agreed to some promises I would adhere to as I played out my role as a god.

"Every land has its own rules.

"While we did not put them into writing—paper was quite valuable in those days—to summarize they told me to 'not go too far.'

"Having no reason to agree to such conditions, I considered routing them after all, but stopped myself.

"That enchanted blade was about the only thing I was interested in, and at the end of the day, even it was merely a blade. If it was being wielded by a human, I had nothing to fear.

"I assumed that if the time came to fight, we would fight—I decided to leave it up to fate.

"I did not have any clue then.

"Of just how wrong that decision was—I never imagined what would come from leaving everything in the hands of fate.

"None of it would have happened had I used their visit as my chance to leave—my goodness.

"My goodness, what a wretched story."

013

"So, this short sword—" I interrupted Shinobu, suddenly curious, "what was it like?"

It was probably a digression that took us away from what I wanted to learn then, but I still felt like I needed to ask.

I needed to hear it.

I felt like I'd come to really regret it if I didn't ask her—which isn't to say that some serious development involving it promised to come up soon. It was a more basic feeling that she'd forget its story unless I put the question to her right there.

While I'd discussed Kokorowatari with Shinobu a number of times, I hadn't even heard of the existence of this short sword—I'd never gotten even a whiff of it in the past.

Actually, I was certain she'd forgotten about it until just now.

"Had I never spoken of it?" my ass.

Get off your high horse.

"So if Kokorowatari slayed aberrations, did the short sword slay humans? Wait, that would just be a regular katana…"

"Indeed. As I said, 'tis the Aberration Savior—the short sword known as Yumewatari is a blade that brings aberrations back to life. Though it does sound odd to describe aberrations as being brought back to life, as they were never alive to begin with…but in essence, 'tis a blade that can resurrect aberrations."

"I don't get it."

"A slice from that blade could bring an aberration slain by Kokorowatari back to life—in other words, 'tis an item with a healing property. Of course, the only wounds it heals, the only aberrations it revives, are those who suffered harm from Kokorowatari, giving it a rather limited capacity—"

Another reason my dull replica does not require that short sword at all, added Shinobu.

"And 'twould be heavy carrying around two blades."

"Light or heavy shouldn't be an issue for you…"

"True, 'tis just how I feel. Also, I only slay."

"…"

She was right.

If Yumewatari's role was to place a limit on the sharpness of Kokorowatari, Shinobu didn't need it.

She'd never try to return a slain aberration to life.

All aberrations were nothing more than food to her—

"In that case," I remarked, "it almost feels like you'd be able to eat the sword itself."

"I wonder. I doubt even I could have digested those two blades…"

The way she replied to a joke with a serious-sounding response made me think she really did try and fail to eat them four hundred years ago.

She'd definitely qualify as a glutton if she had.

"Well, forgetting about whether you could eat them, could you beat them?"

"Hm?"

"You said you did fight one battle with this Aberration Slayer I. So who won and who lost then? My assumption was that you won, since you're still here and alive, but having heard about Yumewatari's mysterious ability—"

"Ye dunce," she said before kicking me.

I got kicked by a little girl.

She was the type to bark and bite at the same time.

I of course had no objections to being kicked by a little girl's bare foot (don't take that the wrong way, I only mean that I'm not that petty of a person), so instead of taking her to task for the attack, I simply said, "What's the matter? Can't I imagine a situation where you were killed with one slice and brought back to life with another?"

"Nay, ye can't. How could I have forgotten Aberration Slayer I's name had he been so gifted that he could slay me? Have I not properly recalled the names of those three vampire hunters who stole my limbs from me in a true battle?"

"Oh, right..."

She remembered the names of strong people, in other words.

What a combat geek.

In that case, it was hard to tell if she remembered Oshino's name... While he did outwit her once, it wasn't as if they fought for real.

Then again, he could have left a strong impression as an expert with a love of harassment and a terrible personality.

And practically speaking, it felt like she only remembered the names of those three hunters because everything with them had taken place just half a year ago...

"I shall say this for the sake of my honor in any case. By no means was I slain by Aberration Slayer I—even what I call our battle was but a diversion."

"A diversion?"

"A little entertainment over drinks. I merely toyed with him for a bit—I did want to test those blades."

Aye, 'twas an item that could easily make history, Shinobu said, as if she was moved—and if she carried around a replica, her high opinion of it wasn't surprising.

"But, well, the real one *vanished*… It disappeared, tales and all, so unfortunately 'tis no longer part of anyone's memories, let alone history."

"Hearing you say all of this makes it sound like it was only the blades that were amazing, like this Aberration Slayer I guy wasn't impressive at all."

"Now, I would not go that far. If that was how my words sounded, it must have been the result of my consideration for thee. Were I to say it in a way that might wound, as an expert—as an expert in aberrations, he had twelve up on thee."

"Twelve up…"

How high up was he?

He might as well have infinite lives.

But no, of course he did. I was an amateur, not any kind of expert… So yes, she had put it in a way that hurt.

What a tough situation.

I felt sympathetic when Shinobu was being too rude about her former partner, or rather, I started to get strangely indignant, but it's not like that stopped me from feeling bad when she spoke highly of him.

It was tough.

Shinobu said he was an ex-boyfriend of sorts, but now it felt like he was exactly that, not as an analogy.

"Though he was limited in what he could do alone, strictly speaking. He was naught more than a talented leader—he directed that group of fifty or so experts to slice any aberration in two with a single stroke. That was how he fought."

So of course he was unable to defeat me mano a mano, Shinobu said.

"Perhaps if all fifty of them came after me—"

"You might have lost?"

"Indeed, I may have suffered a wound or two from their blades."

"…"

Just a wound or two, huh?

As an aberration-slaying sword, a wound from Kokorowatari, or even a scratch, should have dealt significant, in fact fatal damage. But that didn't seem to matter much. In Shinobu's case, and I guess mine as well, the moment the blade cut us, which is to say the moment it killed us, we would come right back to life.

That was another way in which Shinobu had no use for Yumewatari.

Even though it might have only been a replica, that thing made me suffer through the nightmare that was dying, then being brought back to life, then dying again, then being brought back to life again.

You could call it the drawback of my healing abilities.

"In any case, I was able to handle those visiting experts, that lot of hunters, well enough."

"Hmph…"

It seemed hard to imagine, given the haphazard, or even self-indulgent, slacker-like life she led…but then she was "handling" the locals well enough now too.

Though I wouldn't say she got along with them.

Though their relationship wasn't what you'd call friendly.

"They would come by regularly after that to speak with me, then leave. They did this again and again. As for their frequency, I suppose 'twas about once a month—perhaps a little more often. I helped them with their yokai exterminations a few times as well. That was when I entrusted my back to him. While 'twas difficult work dealing with yokai that were unique to Japan, aberrations are naught more than energy to me at the end of the day. They were little more than novelties to me. …Of course, I was not able to consume any of that energy, as I could not possibly eat while they were watching."

I had no choice but to watch in silence as my delicious-looking prey was tossed out, Shinobu lamented with true regret in her voice.

She looked so regretful.

Despite her worn-away memories, the aberrations she couldn't eat still seemed fresh in her mind... I couldn't believe it.

She lived according to hunger alone.

...That said.

"Hey, Shinobu? In that case, why didn't you just become a god? I thought you might not be cut out for it at first, but now that I've heard more, the job actually sounds like a good fit...or like you were perfect for it, really. You didn't oppress the people, and if there were any issues at all, I guess it would just be your vampiric impulses."

"Ye fool. Those vampiric impulses that ye call an 'issue' are problem enough—though I could simply have traveled afar if I was unable to suck the blood of those humans who took kindly to me, I was but a traveler. My vacation was naught more than that, a vacation."

"..."

Talk about obstinate.

Of course, that might have been how I looked while I was trying to turn from a vampire back into a human—not that I'd been able to at all.

When I thought about it, my immortality had saved me more than a few times, too...

Even if everything could be solved and I could suddenly return to being a regular human, I doubt I'd be able to say yes and go back on the spot—I've relied too much on my vampiric nature for too long. Didn't Shinobu feel the same kind of hesitation back then?

Not that it mattered either way now...

"Well, in fact—" Shinobu said.

Her expression suddenly serious.

"That was not the only problem."

"Hm?"

"That was not the only problem—it was not my vampiric impulses alone. For that could be solved without issue if it truly mattered—violent a solution as it may have been."

"Yeah... Okay, fair enough. This was four hundred years ago, anyway—you could have always taken a trip out of town, or if you really had to, you could have demanded a sacrifice. Actually, you could have eaten some aberrations when Aberration Slayer I and his guys weren't looking."

One year.

She said she lived as a god for about a year—which would mean she pretty much fasted for a whole year.

She might have enjoyed the food given to her as offerings, but they wouldn't have been nourishing—they'd be like the Mister Donuts she ate now.

I was impressed by her self-control, but maybe that just showed how utterly powerful she was at the time. Or maybe she'd been feeling that starved for witness testimonies.

I could only guess, given how vague Shinobu's story was…

"In any case—your vampiric impulses wouldn't have posed a direct threat. So, was there something else? Another, well…issue?"

"Aye. And 'tis one that you ought to know—and know quite well."

014

"Well, if I hold out like that, thou might feel disappointed again, so I shall go ahead and dispense a spoiler here—the issue was not my vampiric impulses or the like, but my very presence as an aberration, as a vampire.

"Thou must remember.

"The shrine we traveled to for that forelocked girl—that we used yesterday to travel through time. The shrine that has been the scene of multiple cases.

"Kita-Shirahebi Shrine.

"Why negative energy gathered in that place—thou must remember the cause quite well, eh?

"After all, ye were the one to accept the Hawaiian-shirted boy's mission to seal away that negative energy. Thou completed that all-important task.

"Indeed.

"The aberration that I am—I, the king of aberrations, or rather, my past self, the presence known as Kissshot Acerolaorion Heartunderblade—*gathers aberrations.*

"Like a bug zapper of sorts.

"There could be no more convenient a trait, when ye think of it. It left me free to eat as many gathered aberrations as I wished. My prey came to me to be eaten—though strictly speaking, I simply destroyed the balance, the ecosystem of aberrations. They knew not that they were coming to be devoured.

"And what gathered was not so much the aberrations themselves as the negative energy that precedes them. Aye, those 'bad things.'

"Indeed, that Hawaiian-shirted boy described them as such. 'Bad things'—does that ring a bell?

"Well, think of how ye described this Darkness as being incomprehensible—does that not feel similar somehow?

"'Tis ironic, in fact.

"I'd been careless.

"I'd forgotten the very reason I roamed, traveling from one place to the next—no, that was one thing I'd not forgotten. I'd been careless, and I'd been thoughtless, but I was not such a fool that I'd forgotten the reason I traveled.

"I ought not stay for long in one place—I utterly destroy the balance of its aberrational ecosystem.

"'Tis a troubling trait, it makes one question being too strong—but a bit of an upset balance does not allow that negative energy to form into true aberrations. The only harm that would come to a place is a darkening of its general mood.

"But it could certainly lead to a Great Yokai War—what that Hawaiian-shirted boy told thee was no exaggeration.

"Even then—that would not be a problem on its own. In reality, I would have been able to handle the situation had it arisen. Were I at my zenith, I could have dealt with this town's hangout with ease, no matter how it grew.

"It only became a problem because I lost my powers after attracting it here—and because that Hawaiian-shirted boy had me under observation.

"As a bug zapper, I was at least able to handle whatever I attracted—that said, I'd be no match for them if I allowed so many to gather that they were out of control, and so I moved as appropriate.

"Dost thou understand now?

"Why I could not stay forever as a god—'twould become a crucible of aberrations had I continued to be there. Heaven to me, 'twould be hell to anyone else.

"Hedonist though I may be, I am no decadent.

"'Tis not my desire.

"And so I thought—perhaps I should cease this vacationer's life at an appropriate time.

"But I had been careless here because I'd previously been at the South Pole, a land where neither humans nor aberrations exist.

"It had caused my senses to go awry—I had not noticed one bit that despite my presence in that village, those 'bad things' *were not gathering at all.*

"'Twas hard to notice, as local yokai appeared from time to time. Even I would have surely felt that something was off had not a one appeared.

"They're taking awfully long to gather this time.

"So perhaps I could stay here for a little longer.

"I suppose I can let them treat me as a god.

"The food is good, and I can sleep as much as I wish.

"Ah, what joy... That is how I felt.

"Oh, do not call it self-indulgence. 'Twas not as if I traveled because I wanted to, so of course I'd want to sit down and rest from time to time—their treatment of me as a god aside.

"So I made an exception and put off leaving again and again, staying there for one long year.

"'Tis still okay, 'tis still okay, 'tis still okay—I thought.

"But each seemingly peaceful day that passed was another lost opportunity to avert a tragedy.

"It all happened—nay, 'twas *noticed to be happening* not by me or that group of experts, not by Aberration Slayer I, but by the residents of the area.

"Aye, that bunch living around me.

"You see, aberrations spread by word of mouth—by the time they imbue the common populace and make it to the 'top,' 'tis already too late. There is not a thing that can be done then—though this was not an aberration, of course.

"This was their story.

"People are disappearing, they said.

"People are going away, they said.

"People are vanishing, they said.

"They leave and never come back, they said.

"That on its own sounds like a case of humans being 'spirited away.' But 'twas hard to explain it all as such, for I was there, a god living in a readily found location, which was an ironclad alibi after a fashion.

"If they thought it a case of me 'spiriting away' men and women, they would only have to come to my shrine and search it from corner to corner to find them—though none did so in reality.

"I suppose my daily good behavior was enough to convince them— laugh not, I truly did act in a benevolent way then.

"Though 'tis awfully ironic that 'twas my acting like a god that cleared any suspicions that I had spirited anyone away like some god.

"But it seemed this truly was occurring when I looked into it a bit myself—at the very least, it was no simple case of runaways, kidnappings, or murders—

"'Twas a linked series of aberrational phenomena.

"Nay—as I said, 'twould be hard to call it such.

"I did think, *Ah, so 'tis here at last*—that staying in a place for so long had caused a chain reaction of negative energy, but something still felt off.

"Namely, there was a lack of eyewitness testimonies.

"'Twas as if I was only learning of the results of a phenomenon, not about the phenomenon itself—not one who either witnessed or experienced this 'spiriting away' came forth.

"Humans were simply disappearing.

"That was all.

"These kinds of phenomena, which is to say these kinds of ghost stories, normally involve someone alongside the human who disappeared who sees it all happen—such people should have existed, or if not, someone who had disappeared needed to return, even if their memories were not intact.

"There were none.

"They disappear, they go away, they vanish.

"And they don't come back.

"If they had someone accompanying them, that person did not return either.

"That was all—'twas self-contained.

"So much so that there was nothing we could do about it—I tried speaking to Aberration Slayer I, and we investigated it together, but ultimately we never found any evidence. Our conclusion was that perhaps these were crimes committed by a human.

"For while there may be no such thing as a perfect crime for aberrations, perfect crimes by humans do exist.

"This was not our job—that was the conclusion we came to, that 'twas not a job for either a god or an expert. 'Twas a job for the police.

"Well, in those days, the job of the temple schools…nay, what was it again? The *doshin,* or something like their kind?

"In any case, it fell upon another type of expert—while I would make it rain as a god, I was not getting involved in any opaque strife amongst humans.

"Though this was a dreadful shirking of responsibility in hindsight. I ought to have wondered why that aura of negative energy had yet to arrive this one time alone—aye, I ought to have wondered.

"About how just in the way the humans disappeared.

"So had the negative aura.

"I ought to have wondered about that.

"But in reality, I nearly failed to notice the mere fact they had never come. Why would I be bothered by them not arriving? Meanwhile, I would have no choice but to notice, had a mass of them come creeping and crawling, and I surely would have considered their cause. But humans, and vampires for that matter, cannot take seriously those dangers that are not pressing.

"I regret it, but I doubt my lesson will ever be of use.

"In brief, I did nothing.

"I lived as I had.

"And as I did they disappeared—the residents of the lands around me continued to go missing.

"Until no one was left.

"It kept continuing."

015

My first thought was that I misheard her. Or that she misspoke—
Until no one was left?
Not one?
"What's that supposed to mean? Until no one was left... So, until all fifty of Aberration Slayer I's group of experts was gone?"
"Why would that be the case? I suggested nothing of the sort. Ye need to learn to piece together the logical progression of a story."
"Your stories don't have a logical progression to them... Your memories are so worn away that the details are completely fuzzy... I don't know if I should say this, but you're even worse at telling stories than me."
She wasn't a poor talker, she was a poor storyteller.
I was truly relieved that, per Hachikuji, there was a rule saying that aberrations couldn't be the narrator.
"Hmph. Ye've got some nerve. But apparently, that monkey girl is being called the best storyteller up until now, which is unexpected. Looks like ye've been overshadowed."

"No, I think people only said good things about Kanbaru because her narration wasn't nearly the mess they thought it'd be... In other words, couldn't you say she let them down?"

And hold on, can you stop talking about future events like it's nothing?

We needed to hurry up and get rid of the rule saying that aberrations are allowed to give meta-commentary... Of course, you could also say it's beyond too late for that.

There's only one book left, after all.

"By the way, I understand the last book will be narrated by that tsundere girl."

"What, really? Not me?"

That was kind of a shock.

Did that mean I was done after this?

That easily? That unceremoniously?

They wouldn't really do that, would they?

"I simply can't wait to hear how that tsundere girl truly feels," Shinobu said. "I wonder what kind of verbal abuse we'll get from her."

"Verbal abuse? Like, about me? No, she doesn't badmouth me. She's reformed now. She's become a clean-hearted Hitagi Senjogahara."

"No, no, oh no. We have no idea how a woman truly feels. In my estimation, that woman is surely thinking about how to break up with thee."

"Why are you acting like you're so knowledgeable about human psychology? You were just talking about how you got into a huge mess because you didn't understand it."

"She's holding back out of sympathy, as 'twould surely affect thy entrance exams if she discussed breaking up with thee right now."

"You do hear that one a lot!"

Umm...

Yikes, hearing that really makes me think...

She might be reformed and a lot more expressive now, but I still can't quite tell what she's thinking.

Even at that moment, I couldn't begin to imagine what she might be doing... Though the most likely option did seem to be that she was thinking about how to criticize me for skipping the start-of-school ceremony.

"Enough about next volume," I said. "We don't even know if there's going to be a next volume at this rate, and it almost seems like this flashback of yours could take up the entire story this time."

She needed to realize that everyone's getting worried.

Worried about this surprisingly long story about her past.

"What's the matter," she retorted, "flashbacks are the cornerstone of any popular manga."

"As a reader, I'd be more inclined to call them a bad practice than a cornerstone..."

"Flashbacks are a part of this, but wouldn't thou say that the more popular a manga, the slower the progression of its story?"

"Do we really have to talk about this now?"

Weren't we at an important part of your own story?

Even the most important part.

"A deliberate pace might be vexing to readers, but it must be vexing to the creator as well," she forged ahead. "'Tis not blood flow restriction training. Writing that slowly must make even the creator lose the thread."

"Well, if I stepped back from looking at it as a reader and looked at it as a fan, what's really going on is that the title's getting dragged out at the publisher's request."

"Hm. But I don't think a publisher would ask a creator to go slowly..."

"Sure, they probably don't want them to go slowly. They'd want them to speed ahead if possible, but one person only has so much talent. The only way you can stretch a title out is by watering it down to some degree."

"Ah, I see. While I understand thy logic, would an author so popular that the publisher asks for his work to be stretched out need to listen to what the publisher says? Could he not simply put an end to a story he wishes to finish?"

"Part of a publisher's job is to control its authors, so they probably get talked into stretching the title out without even realizing they're being controlled."

"So at the end of the day, even creators are in the palm of capital's hands!"

"On whose behalf are you getting mad here..."

It wasn't the position of a reader or fan.

And given Shinobu's lifespan, it shouldn't matter how long any popular manga gets stretched out... Not that I know Shinobu's exact lifespan as she is now.

I had to admit, though. Those are a rare sight these days.

Final chapters of popular manga series.

"So, Shinobu. Now that we've reached a conclusion on that topic, can we get back to our main plot?"

"Hmph. I've yet to be convinced, but very well."

"I'm going to send you flying if this story ends up having nothing to do with the Darkness, you know. I'm gonna grope your breasts until they double in size."

"To me, a chest groping is nothing more than proof of loyalty from a slave."

"Oh, right."

I guess some such thing was established at some point.

Her initial character traits had grown pretty vague, but it seemed like that one was still alive and well.

"Okay, then. If your story ends up having nothing to do with the Darkness, I'm gonna grope Hachikuji's breasts until they double in size."

"Very well. I've already told thee this much, so I'm willing to take that risk."

We'd just made an unthinkable deal that ignored the human rights of a girl who was still passed out right beside us.

"So, no one was left—what do you mean by that? You can tell me to attend to the logical progression as much as you want…but the way you talk and your delivery makes it sound like every person who lived around you disappeared."

"That's correct," Shinobu blithely confirmed. "So thou dost understand. I see that my abilities as a storyteller are superb after all. In fact, I think we may change plans for the next volume and, in a twist, make its narrator none other than me."

"That's too much of a twist, and disrespectful to Senjogahara. And wait—everyone disappeared? And then there were none? This isn't an Agatha Christie novel we're talking about here."

"Hmph. But that told the events on an uninhabited island. This was far worse, as an entire village turned uninhabited."

"…"

The scale was so big—too big.

It was hard to comprehend when she put it in roundabout ways, like the village disappearing or the town vanishing, but…

How many people disappeared, exactly?

Fifty—was just the start of it.

I shouldn't be sure since I didn't know the population at that time, or the area's population density, but it felt like it'd have to be more than a couple hundred people…

They'd been "spirited away" on that big of a scale?

"Hold on a sec… So unlike the time you made the lake disappear, these people disappeared not all at once but gradually, right? Little by little, they vanished—so you should have been able to notice before it got that bad. What in the world were you doing before you realized, 'Then there were none'? Sleeping?"

"If ye wish to put it that way, then aye, I was sleeping," Shinobu responded to my line of questioning, tinged with criticism, without a shred of discomfort—but while she didn't seem uncomfortable, there was a bit of awkwardness in her words. "I lazed around the entire time—but really, isn't it all the same?"

"Hm?"

"Had they all disappeared at once, there would have been nothing I could do about it—in any case, the community was doomed from the moment I made no active effort to prevent that from happening."

"Well, true…"

Logically speaking, there was no difference between them disappearing all at once or disappearing gradually if they all disappeared by the end—but I didn't want to speak logically here.

"Thou must have had the experience of feeling as though ye had a great deal of money, then using it gradually, until suddenly thy wallet is empty. 'Tis the same."

"I don't know about that comparison, either. At the same time, I guess it was actually harder to realize what was happening if they got thinned out over time instead of disappearing all at once… It might have been hard to recognize the gravity of the case. You did fail to notice what was happening during your initial investigation, after all…"

Had hundreds of villagers suddenly gone missing, even Shinobu—and Aberration Slayer I would have done something.

But it might take longer to respond if it was at a pace of one person each night, or five people every three days. And to notice, too.

The gravity of the matter…

"So how did you end up noticing in the end? You know, that this… abnormal situation was going on."

"Which one dost thou mean? That no negativity came flowing in despite my sojourn there—or the steady disappearance of villagers until no one was left in the end?"

"Both—but I guess I meant the latter."

"I suppose I noticed the latter, then noticed the former moments later… I would have had to notice the latter sooner or later, regardless of how thickheaded I was. Those believers who venerated me stopped coming to pay their respects entirely."

"Ah, right…"

"Though I thought at first that they had at last exhausted whatever patience they had for my cold demeanor. I had dismissed them saying that their being spirited away was none of my concern, and that neither I nor any yokai creature had anything to do with it. I'd left them to figure it out and take care of it on their own, so I thought they had gotten fed up and discarded their belief in such an unreliable god—resulting in a drop in visitors paying their respects, but it was undeniably odd for their number to reach zero. No matter how rampantly they were being spirited away, those humans still had to eat to survive. In that case, they wouldn't have stopped praying to me for rain—drought was naturally a far more immediate problem for those who hadn't been spirited away. They wouldn't have forsaken me and brought another famine upon themselves…and so I noticed."

'Twas the logical conclusion, she said.

For some reason, I got annoyed just hearing the word "logic" come out of her mouth…

"Something—was strange."

"…"

"And so I left my shrine and descended to the village—though strictly speaking, I was on the floor of what was once a lake so it was more like ascending—and what I found was a scene resembling the Mary Celeste."

"Of course, that comparison wouldn't make chronological sense."

A deserted village.

A community with no one in it.

The villages Shinobu ruled over as a god—had turned into ghost towns.

Every man, woman, and child who followed her had disappeared.

They disappeared gradually—while she hadn't noticed.

"How did that make you feel?"

"Hm?"

"Okay, it might be cruel to ask for your impressions of the sight…

but I'm interested to know what you felt back then, when you were at your zenith and uninfluenced by me."

The humans who venerated her had disappeared, unseen by her—but within reach.

When something she couldn't undo happened, how did she—how did Kissshot Acerolaorion Heartunderblade take it in?

I wanted to know.

"Nothing special. I was surprised, like whoa, they're not there."

"..."

She hadn't taken anything in.

She just passed on the ball.

Or just passed on it.

"Could they have all left, I thought, perhaps to find work? Then from there, I may have been outraged that they'd leave me and sneak off on their own and vowed to kill them all."

"You're the worst..."

She was just short-tempered.

But maybe that's how it was... There was probably no point in blaming her, it was a different era then. I was the fool for asking the question in the first place since Shinobu simply wasn't what she is now.

I asked, "It would be different now, right? You wouldn't react that way if it happened today."

"Indeed. Now, my reaction would most likely be, *AAAAAAGH! THEY'RE GONNNNNE!!*"

"So it would just be louder..."

She was posing, too, if you're curious.

Give me a break. Was the only thing she learned during her time with me how to react in a stupid way?

She needed to learn some emotions.

What it means to have a human heart.

"I'd find it hard to learn such things from thee... But after that, I traveled around all the neighboring villages."

"Uh huh."

"I emotionally traveled around, with heart."

"You don't need to add any pointless descriptors. Just tell me the facts."

"Then what I understood from this investigation was that no one remained in any of the nearby communities—though all the villages beyond a certain point were fine, as though a boundary had been drawn."

"A boundary—so in other words, the line separating the people who believed in you from the ones who didn't? Geographically speaking—"

"Indeed. To be more precise, I would say 'twas whether they knew of me or not. Faith had nothing to do with it—for there were those in the neighboring villages who had none in me despite knowing of my existence. They were a minority—I thought that perhaps they may have still remained, but such hopes turned out to be false."

"Hmm... In that case."

In that case, I said, but didn't know what came next—it was like I felt bewildered, or that I was grasping at straws... Despite all I'd heard from her, I couldn't grasp the essence of what she was saying. Regardless of her abilities as a storyteller, though, Shinobu was the narrator, the protagonist here, so for me, a thread still ran through it—otherwise it would have been too meandering as a tale about aberrations.

Not a tale about aberrations—but a ghost story.

Of bad things—of the unclear—and the incomprehensible—

Just like the Darkness.

"Aye, in that case," Shinobu continued where I left off, though I doubted it was because she'd read how confused I felt—no, perhaps she had.

Our hearts and minds were connected, after all.

"Even I understood that something was going on."

"That's where you were at, despite all that happened already... Just how happy-go-lucky are you?"

"I wish thou would describe that as my being a big shot—but it did seem that something was happening, and I also realized that I seemed to be the cause."

"Hm? Wait, the cause? I don't know if that's exactly right. Even if you realized that you had something to do with the phenomenon, that should have been as much as you could've said at that point—"

"Nay, it was my experience speaking. When something happens, in most cases 'tis because of me."

"..."

Yeah.

It was, I guessed.

Not that I could complain when I'd been getting Shinobu to help me solve these things that did happen and to take care of the aftermath.

"And aye, I noticed at last—now that I thought about it, I had stayed there for a rather long time and yet no negative energy had accumulated at all. I noticed that none had come. So if anything had caused the situation, it was that I had lived there for too long, causing that energy to do something somewhere—or so I thought, but that didn't seem to be the case when I looked around."

"..."

"And the fact that it didn't—was odd."

'Twas abnormal. An abnormal situation, Shinobu muttered, closing her eyes.

"'Twas odd that nothing supernatural had occurred—and odd that an abnormal situation obtained despite this. I suppose thou could say—it didn't line up. I could not ignore how uneven it felt. To be honest, the fact that all of the neighboring villagers had disappeared was not as strange as the comparable fact that *nothing was gathering nearby*—that's what made me feel unwell."

"..."

"Since I felt unwell, I returned home and slept."

"Hey."

"Hm? Is it not best to retire and rest when ye feel unwell?"

"It is, but still!"

So when there was something that she didn't understand, going home and sleeping made her feel better? What a handy constitution she had.

"Now that everyone was gone, I thought of going off somewhere. Not with a super jump this time, but by spreading my wings and gliding right off, as if I'd Doraemon's bamboo copter on my head."

"Again, those didn't exist back then."

Not that they existed now.

I wonder when they'll be invented.

"I need not worry about the battery running out, though. Didst thou know that bamboo copters require a break every four hours if they're to be used over an extended period?"

"I know facts that you can find in a manga in my little sisters' room, okay? Wait, what? Don't tell me you really flew off to another country after that. That you really went to sleep, woke up, and forgot it all—"

"But of course not—ye shouldn't underestimate me so."

"I don't know, I feel like you do everything at such a big scale that it always deserves respect... That's why I wanted to be sure."

"Though thou art correct to say that I went to sleep, woke up, and forgot it all."

"Big!"

Downright unfathomable, seriously!

"I jest. Even I am not so simple that I can forget everything after sleeping and waking. I awoke and still remembered. Like oops, no good, it's turned from a short-term memory into a long-term one."

"Well, yeah... I find the carefree attitude ever so annoying, but I suppose humans—or I guess brains—aren't built so simply..."

"And so I plunged my hand into my head, scrambled and destroyed my brain cells, and forced myself to forget. About everything that happened in recent times."

"You can mess with your brain like that not just to remember things but to forget them too?!"

Now that was scary!

No matter how much her body might be able to recover, the idea of picking and choosing her memories like that was almost unthinkable. Even Hanekawa, who knew everything, would be surprised to hear that. She wouldn't be able to accept it.

"So I forgot it all and tried to go back to sleep—but then someone appeared to prevent me from doing so."

"I'm glad they did, the way your story is going. I'd want someone to if it were me. I was wondering what to do if nobody did."

Of course, that would have meant getting free rein over Hachikuji's chest, and in that sense I didn't mind, and in fact nearly wanted to recommend it, but nope, not gonna happen.

"Someone appeared… It was the enemy?"

"Nay, the one who appeared—"

Was Aberration Slayer I, Shinobu said.

016

"*Awaken, god*—he said, waking me up, but thou art well aware of how much difficulty I have getting up.

"'Twas not as bad since I'd merely gone back to sleep, but he seemed to lose his temper when I did not respond and stomped right into my shrine.

"The inside of a shrine is the most sacred part of any sacred ground.

"Or so I'd said, stating that none shall enter outside of an emergency—a decision made, of course, to maintain my pleasant lifestyle.

"Though 'twas by happenstance, they treated me as a god.

"'Twould not be seemly for them to see me lazing around…but now he saw me at last.

"*What insolence,* I yelled, trying at least to act appropriately divine, but it must not have had much of an effect after he'd seen my nearly naked body lying face-down on the floor—he didn't seem very surprised, either.

"'Twas as though this was not the time for such things.

"In fact—if anyone was surprised, 'twas I.

"Because he was alone—a man who always used to bring a massive retinue with him as if he were showing off his favorite medals and decorations.

"I was surprised to see such a man acting on his own. I was sincerely surprised—to the point that I snapped wide-awake. Ye may think I was too surprised, but listen, that's truly how unusual it was.

"Well, 'twas not as though that entire throng would enter my shrine, so perhaps he entered alone after making them wait outside—perhaps I could have speculated so, but the chances of that, too, seemed slim. If that is what he required, he would have sent in one of his underlings.

"Thou might say he was a man who hated being alone—did he always need attention, ye say? Hm. He was quite a different type of man than thee in the sense that he enjoyed mixing with people. Then again, 'tis not as though thou art alone by choice…

"But that kind of man was acting alone.

"Surprised, I asked, 'What happened?'—by this point, I had fumbled about in my brain and erased my memories, so I realized not at all what had happened to the neighboring villages.

"In fact, I was astounded to hear of the calamity he then spoke of—but then even I began to recall it as he spoke. His words caused my brain cells to regenerate in that shape.

"How I criticized myself, saying, *Ah, how could I forget such an important thing?* I did a great deal of reflecting.

"'Tis a lie, of course… My only feelings were, *Oh dear, what an unpleasant memory. Perhaps I'll forget it by the time I wake up if I go to sleep*—I suppose my thoughts were repeating all over again in a cycle.

"I certainly wasn't going back to sleep yet again with Aberration Slayer I there—not to mention that he'd brought me new information.

"It concerned his underlings—the reason why he hadn't dragged them along behind him as he always did.

"Well, 'tis exactly as ye predict.

"In fact, 'tis exactly as I just said.

"They too—were gone.

"Gone—disappeared.

"Off to somewhere.

"He said they'd disappeared just as the villagers had—to start from the beginning, it seems that the group of experts noticed the communities being empty quite some time before me.

"And they properly investigated it, unlike me—what an admirable bunch, not going home and sleeping. Nay, I jest not. I admire those who work, even I respect that.

"Thou, too, must feel a sense of admiration looking at worker ants and worker bees, 'tis no different from that—though that is as far as my praise can go, as it ended with them vanishing without exception.

"It sounded as though they too disappeared gradually, not all fifty-or-so at once—and Aberration Slayer I noticed at some point that he was alone.

"Unlike me, he must have felt quite menaced—or perhaps more frightened than menaced. That lover of crowds must have come to me alone not out of any sense of duty but out of a feeling of fear. He had grown desperate.

"But whatever his reasoning, it did not really matter. He was ultimately moved to action, making him admirable all the same.

"Far more praiseworthy than I.

"And for my part—I, with my divine affection, naturally decided to hear him out before solemnly offering to investigate the matter. Not that there was any point in trying to act like a god in front of a single person... And 'twas not as if Aberration Slayer I was a follower of mine.

"'Twas habit.

"While I'd already traveled 'round the neighboring villages and understood the situation, the premise was that I'd forgotten—explaining it to him would reveal that I'd fiddled with my brain—so I traveled the villages again, this time with Aberration Slayer I—over the course of two full days.

"'Twas like locking a door I'd already latched—there were no changes, of course. The populace who'd been 'spirited away' had not all reappeared out of the blue.

"And so—no one was there.

"Well, unlike me, a monster who only ate, Aberration Slayer I was, at the end of the day, an expert. Rather than haphazardly search here and there, he verified the situation from this angle and that—but he came up empty.

"I castigated him, saying that he truly craved company. But he was more than a man who merely acted important, dragging his flunkies around with him everywhere—not a man who was useless on his own.

"I, more than anyone else, had seen him in such a light.

"I saw him in a bit of a new one, and admired him.

"To describe it as I once did with thee—perhaps I grew fond of him. For the way he searched for the disappeared villagers, his disappeared men—aye.

"Though his efforts were for naught.

"He neither gained nor found any results at all—'twas almost strange how little there was. In retrospect, that in itself was abnormal—'twas a time when aberrations…when the dark had a deeper, closer relationship to humans than today.

"'Twas unthinkable for there 'to be nothing.'

"Though guilt beyond a reasonable doubt may be a suggested standard, there was not even anything about which to be doubtful. 'Twas as if…oh, how should I put it… Aye, there we go.

"'Twas like a perfect crime.

"While there may be no such thing as a perfect crime with aberrations, humans are capable of perfect crimes, so this was a perfect crime committed by a human, I decided in what now strikes me as a bit of a shallow syllogism, and washed my hands of a 'spiriting away' that I deemed to be the work of men—Aberration Slayer I did as well—but there was a flaw in this logic.

"The possibility that there may be perfect crimes committed by aberrations? Nay, we're not trying to examine such a claim, there's another possibility to consider before we start splitting hairs.

"Aye—*the possibility that 'twas not the work of an aberration, nor the work of a human.*

"A third possibility.

"It had taken us long enough, but we arrived at it—Aberration Slayer I and I. But rather than arrive, perhaps we'd been cornered into a position where we had no choice but to think it.

"Even so, given my devil-may-care, happy-go-lucky personality, I was not depressed—the way Aberration Slayer I was.

"Had it been caused by an aberration, 'twould have been one thing—or had a human been the culprit, but both he and I had not a clue how to deal with a case that was neither.

"'Twas beyond our expertise.

"While I eat aberrations and suck the blood of humans—I am a vampire who does that and nothing more, if I did also act as though I was a god then. As for Aberration Slayer I, though he had his knowledge, he had already lost the forty-nine underlings who acted as his arms and legs. His trusty enchanted blades, Kokorowatari and Yumewatari, were indeed valuable and divine items, but as one can tell from their names, Aberration Slayer and Aberration Savior, they could only be used on such.

"Aberration Slayer I was also a man in a position of power—but that power could only be demonstrated on humans.

"Our performance would have been impeccable had it been an aberration or a human—but we could do nothing in our situation. Rather, there was naught to do.

"What we could—had vanished.

"But as I've already said time and again, I was not diligent, and was not particularly saddened or depressed to find I had naught to do—but Aberration Slayer I was…and he wasn't recovering.

"How weak the elite are in the face of setbacks.

"'Twas no time to be so depressed, in all honesty—myself aside, 'twas no time for Aberration Slayer I to be enjoying the full range of his states of mind so.

"After all—how could one see human after human disappearing, vanishing like smoke, and think that ye are the one exception? Then again.

"'Tis human to be able to do just that."

017

"Able to do just that..."

"In other words, though Aberration Slayer I felt scared that all of his underlings had disappeared by the time he noticed, he felt no unease whatsoever about the possibility that he may be the next to vanish."

"Huh... Your tone makes it sound like you're criticizing him, but weren't you the same? Despite your presence, no negative aura, none of the stuff that aberrations are made of, was gathering there—if you were to think of that as aberrations vanishing, wasn't it just as likely for you to vanish too?"

"..."

I'd only voiced my straightforward impression, and honestly, I was expecting a logical counterargument from Shinobu, but she was giving me a stunned look.

Her expression eloquently stated—
Wow.
That's true, isn't it?

She really did live without a care... We'd been referring to concepts like "danger" and "fear" and "anxiety," but maybe you didn't have to deal with those kinds of things if you were as absurd (in more ways than one) as Shinobu at the height of her powers.

We sometimes talk about animal instincts, but maybe it's only weak animals that have them...

Shinobu was too extreme to be an example, but maybe the strongest animals just lie around sleeping all day.

Just as humans lost their feral nature—

"W-Well. Well, well, well," she openly fibbed, but she was just as bad at it as she was at narrating, and all she said was *well*—she wasn't actually going to bother. "An existence on my level is able to handle any situation. Of course I remained cool, as I didn't feel any pressure."

"And didn't Aberration Slayer I feel the same way? But you sounded like you were criticizing him for it..."

"I did not mean it as criticism—and by the way," Shinobu changed the subject by brute force, "what would thou have done?"

"Huh?"

"If thou had been in that situation—in the same position, what would thou have done?"

"What could I have done? I'm not an expert like Aberration Slayer I, and I'm not a monster like you. In that position I'd be trembling like a normal person... I'd probably try to run away for real. To the other side of that boundary."

"A wise decision. But the boundary I spoke of is but a convenient expression that arose as a result. The actual distinction was made not according to geography but knowledge. In other words, thy fate was sealed if ye knew me as a god—coming into that notion, what would thou have done?"

"Do my best to forget about you, I guess... Fiddle with my brain or whatever?"

While I said this half as a joke, Shinobu replied, "Indeed. Ye ought to," and showed me a deep nod as if I'd read her mind. "*That was most likely—the only method.*"

"...?"

"Or so I say, as if I am giving it consideration, but in truth there was no time at all to make any sort of decision. I suppose ye could say the timing was the worst—it happened so suddenly."

Suddenly—out of nowhere.

It appeared.

"Once we visited the last home of the last village and discovered that 'twas uninhabited—at the very site where Aberration Slayer I acted so depressed and delicately wounded. It appeared there. To quote thee, the Darkness—for no good reason whatsoever, despite it being the middle of the day."

"___"

And so it finally appeared.

We'd reached the main subject.

I wasn't getting free rein over Hachikuji's chest.

018

"There it was.

"Or there it existed?

"Were it an aberration, the former would be fine—but embarrassingly enough, I had nary a guess as to *it*'s existence.

"I thought 'twas a weather phenomenon at first, to be honest—while I may be able to go out into the sun, 'tis my natural-born enemy all the same, and I was not intimately familiar with it. Perhaps 'twas a phenomenon that occurred when sunlight was reflected, I thought—when.

"When I witnessed that Darkness.

"That black mass—feels like the best way to express it, but it did not seem solid enough to call a mass. In fact, it seemed to spread vaguely about—its size about the same, human height as thou saw.

"But even that was uncertain.

"I could not gauge our distance, so how could I know its size?

"Its identity was entirely unknown to me. I lacked any idea—in fact, 'twas as if I was missing a part of my vision. As if I simply could not see a portion of the sight before me...

"Like 'twas empty.

"Thou said thou intuited something dangerous about *it* the moment thou saw it and darted away... But unfortunately, I had no such intuition.

"What in the world is this, I thought as I looked at it like a fool.

"Ye could say I was as curious as one could be seeing this new sight—'tis rare for me to experience something novel. In fact, I nearly felt joy.

"I'd lost my feral nature? That may indeed be appropriate—lacking any sense of danger sounds like mockery, but perhaps thou art right.

"And Aberration Slayer I was the same—and no, not because of his dampened spirits. Emaciated, enfeebled, down, or depressed, an expert hunter from a fine pedigree he was all the same—his body would have reacted on its own had an aberrational phenomenon occurred.

"Yet he did not react.

"As though he were dumbfounded—while in my case 'twas an excess of experience, 'twas the excess of knowledge in Aberration Slayer I's mind that left him unable to move, dazed and vacant.

"He knew not what it was—and.

"He erred in trying to understand this thing he knew not.

"Thou art an amateur who does not even attempt to flaunt his smatterings of knowledge, and it must be this amateurism that allows thee to up and leave without a second thought when faced with the unknown.

"That may sound as though I am calling thee a fool, but nay, this is praise—in fact, thy decision was the correct one.

"I was the mistaken one—we were.

"And before we could even recognize our error—it engulfed.

"Thy bicycle was too, was it not? Likewise, it engulfed. Not sucked up into blackness or absorbed into shadows—I can only describe it as being engulfed by the darkness.

"Who was? Well, the both of us.

"Both of us were engulfed.

"The legendary vampire Kissshot Acerolaorion Heartunderblade and Aberration Slayer I, wielder of the two enchanted blades—together.

"*Ah, now I see.*

"*So this was the truth behind the spiriting away*—I realized, however late. Aye, however late. For half of my body had already been engulfed by the Darkness. Nay, not merely half. About three quarters—come to think of it, I'd met a worse fate than having all four of my limbs taken from me.

"But of course, I still had a quarter remaining, and that was more than enough—to flee, that is.

"Wait, no, not flee, I did no such thing. I've never once fled in my life—um, so as I was saying, a quarter of my body was more than enough to disengage from the scene.

"Ye spoke of the Unlimited Rulebook's Disengagement Edition—but I disengaged, allow me to repeat, with a disengagement far exceeding that poor excuse for one. I would never pale in comparison to that tsukumogami girl, no matter the activity. I surpass her in everything.

"In that sense, I was not entirely joking when I spoke to thee about circling the earth seven and a half times in a single leap.

"In any case, I left the scene behind. Or not the scene so much as—that Darkness.

"Hm? The tsukumogami girl's withdrawals could only reach a few dozen miles at best, no? 'Tis cute to call it disengagement—for I flew to the South Pole.

"Yes, to the same South Pole I'd saved as a vacation home.

"Those three quarters engulfed included a leg of mine—so I flew a hundred thousand miles with what thou may call a one-legged jump. On a different level, am I not?

"…'Tis not a hundred thousand miles to the South Pole? 'Tis only ten thousand at most? Hmph. How boorish of thee to make such minute corrections for the sake of comedy when I clearly speak of my perceptions.

"In any case, I disengaged. With all my might.

"Even after I reached the South Pole, I was convinced 'twould come after me. I was not able to feel as though I'd truly gotten away—I simply wanted some time, even a moment, to renew the parts of my body that had been swallowed up.

"And that is why I escaped—my plan was to jump elsewhere next, perhaps even Mars. I'd know I was in a safe place if I could withdraw to space...though going beyond the stratosphere offered no guarantee.

"Even I had never experienced having my body shaved away *thus*, so my first instinct was to get some distance from the thing.

"But moving on, there was no need to go so far—once I'd arrived in the Antarctic, once I'd reached the South Pole and instantaneously regenerated my body, and lay in wait—the Darkness never came after me.

"No matter how long I waited.

"Aye, I did wait for it. For I craved a powerful enemy—I was starved for an opportunity to display my full powers, or rather, I barely had any chances to do so in the first place.

"So in a sense, I did enjoy this game of tag—yet never received another visit.

"It seems to have followed thee quite a bit, but I had no clues as to its logic then—I determined that perhaps it may not be the kind of thing that follows, moves, or the like, and so I allowed my guard to fall for the time being.

"It does seem to move, according to thy story, and apparently it can even teleport. Our stories do not match up there...but perhaps 'tis able to follow someone moving at the velocity of a mere bicycle.

"I only mean to say 'twas no match for my all-out speed—and it seems the tsukumogami girl's Unlimited Rulebook was able to elude it, after all.

"Perhaps there are individual differences—if we're to permit any individuality to it.

"I feel as though 'twas not even a solid body.

"It seemed to be liquid, or perhaps gaseous.

"But whether it gave chase or not, its identity was unknown to me all the same—that said, 'tis difficult to constantly be prepared for war.

"I would have to stop concentrating sooner or later.

"And so I stopped sooner.

"Again, stop castigating me as being too nonchalant, 'twas my personality at the time. I could not help it—I thought that if I were going to have to stop sooner or later, 'twould make no difference if I did so sooner.

"And whether or not I was focused, I'd not act differently—in any case, this is how I left Japan.

"From there, I did not return.

"The next time I visited—was half a year ago. Which would be when I met thee."

019

"...Hm? Hold on a second."

I couldn't help but be captivated by Shinobu's story once the Darkness finally appeared, but now I had to disrupt the melancholic mood.

I mean, there was some important information missing here.

"What happened to Aberration Slayer I?"

"Hm? I told thee. Swallowed up into the Darkness together with me—he had no time to draw either the Aberration Slayer or the Aberration Savior. While only three quarters of my body fell victim to it, his situation as the first to be engulfed was worse—it went and got just about his entire body."

"Went and got... So you just sat there and watched it happen?"

"I was not watching, to be exact—the Darkness, which had appeared by the time I realized it, had engulfed us before I realized it."

"..."

Paying more attention to Aberration Slayer I in their situation was a tall order—and there wasn't any reason for Shinobu to protect my

157

predecessor, anyway.

The man wasn't even Shinobu's thrall at that moment in time, which is to say he was just plain human, not my predecessor—hm?

Hold on, no, wait, that can't be it.

"That doesn't make sense, Shinobu. If he was swallowed up by the Darkness, wouldn't that be the conclusion? Don't tell me you were pretending to suck at storytelling but setting up a clever narrative trick? As in, making me assume that the head of the group of experts was my predecessor, when in fact..."

I'd have to look at her in a new light if that was the case.

Not many mystery novels these days employ decent narrative tricks—maybe the spring of such tricks, once thought to be endless, is in fact starting to run dry.

But now!

Was my partner Shinobu Oshino about to make a big stir?!

"Ne'er-active tricks? I can't say I've ever heard of those. Sounds terribly like an oxymoron to me."

"..."

Of course not...

"In any case, that woman, in fact man, attacked, in fact was attacked, four years, in fact four hundred years ago by the Darkness—"

"Forget about narrative tricks," I cut in, "this had better not be about you simply having misspoken at some point."

"Oh, no, 'tis not so at all. Worry not, I've neither tricks nor mistakes in my story—the Aberration Slayer I of whom I've spoken thus far is the predecessor, for thee and for me, no mistake about it—listen more carefully. I believe I said the Darkness swallowed *just about* his entire body."

"You did. And that's why I'm asking. If that's the case—"

"Just about. In other words, a part of him remained," Shinobu said before appearing to roll up her right sleeve—not that she had one since she was wearing a sleeveless dress.

"His right hand remained."

"Hm?"

His hand?

"I did tell thee he was engulfed first—and when he was, he grabbed onto my wrist as if to seek my help. He snatched onto it, like so," she said, grabbing my arm with her right. It was a tight grip, like she was placing a lock around it. "As if to seek my help—or so I put it, but I believe that in reality, 'twas a reflex. Had it been a vine of ivy or a twig of straw there, that is what he would have grabbed—'twas an action guided by instinct."

"So you think—he would have literally grasped at straws?"

"Aye, and so 'twould be harsh to criticize him in any way. 'Should he not have grasped the sword at his waist instead?'—would be too cruel a charge. I doubt it'd have meant anything even if he had—the Aberration Slayer could not have cut through a plain darkness that was no aberration."

"..."

"That said, grasping onto my wrist as if to seek some bond is questionable. He could have botched my escape in doing so."

"Well, you say that, but when you've got boosters on you big enough to fly to the South Pole, a human's grip wouldn't do anything—hm? In that case, don't tell me—"

"Precisely." Shinobu gripped my wrist tighter. "I flew to the South Pole together with his hand."

020

"I am unsure.

"Did the strength of my jump tear his wrist from his body, or had the Darkness already engulfed him up to that point, leaving me no need to tear it at all—I feel it was the latter, given the clean cross-section.

"He'd grabbed on so tight that his nails dug into my skin, so I may have taken all of him with me to the South Pole instead were it the former...

"No, he'd have been dead on arrival in that case, given the ultra-high speeds, the drop in oxygen content, and the changes in gravity and air pressure... However much expert knowledge he may have had, his body was but a human's.

"That's all the backstory there is here.

"In the end, I remained alone at the South Pole with his hand— 'remained alone' may be a poor choice of words after having traveled at such an incredible velocity, but none better describe my sentiment at the time.

"That Darkness was not pursuing me in the least.

"And every one of those people I'd come to know in those days, though I may not have known their names—Aberration Slayer I included—had gone away.

"In all likelihood.

"Because that Darkness—had swallowed them all.

"There I remained, alone.

"I'd been left to myself.

"*For the first time in a hundred years*—I thought. Nay, I had likely erased that memory—yet it had been revived.

"A woeful sense of isolation gripped me.

"Aye, isolation. That thing ye always feel. As I've transcended that dimension, I've never once felt lonesome, but everyone ought to, everyone can afford to have that kind of an experience a couple of times in one's life.

"Having just encountered the unknown phenomenon known as the Darkness no doubt affected me. While feelings of fear or anxiety may be a stretch—I did sense its menace.

"While you said I'd lost my feral nature by being too strong—that precise nature revived within me for the first time in ages.

"And so—I revived him.

"I created my first thrall—just like that, as with thee. When I create thralls, 'tis only for quite selfish and egotistical reasons.

"There's something known as the suspension-bridge effect—aye, the one in manga and the like. One confuses the heart-pounding fear from standing atop said bridge with the heart-pounding of romantic excitation. Explained in that manner, 'tis an easily understood phenomenon, but I believe the effect may be interpreted differently.

"That is, when a living creature feels 'tis in a situation where its life is threatened, it thinks of creating progeny and more easily falls in love.

"In my situation, my life had never before been in any sort of danger, and so I never felt like creating any thralls—and in fact, I cannot deny that I was on the verge of death during that time with thee, too.

"Perhaps I was far closer to death then than when I met thee—and so I felt that way.

"Romance, love, family, thralls—'twas not that emotional of a thing, but an impulsive, contemptible reason. My heart was simply weak. Aye, I permit thee to feel disappointed here.

"Though 'twould be nothing short of misguided to expect human emotions out of me—as a man who abandoned his humanity out of such misguided feelings, thou dost have the right to feel disappointed.

"I think. 'Twould allow me to rest easier as well—hm?

"What was that?

"How did I revive him when there was not so much as a corpse? Aberration Slayer I's body had been engulfed by the Darkness?

"Come, now, how many times have I told thee to listen—stop making me repeat myself so often.

"Not all of Aberration Slayer I's body was swallowed up by the Darkness—I said his right hand came with me to the South Pole.

"Aye, from the wrist onward.

"'Twasn't even his head—but a hand is more than enough.

"Who dost thou think I am? So long as I have any part of a body with me, a fist or whatever else, I can use it as a sample from which the whole is revived.

"True, if the cells of the part in question, the right hand in this case, were to die off completely, then 'twould be beyond me.

"Strictly speaking, I am not reviving any corpse. I take that which is alive, make it immortal, and ensure that it does not die.

"So while I need only a part of a body, using a broken nail, a strand of hair, or a flake of skin would indeed be impossible—and of course, there must be blood within that part.

"As I am a vampire.

"While I understood the theory behind this as my character profile, 'twas my first time putting it into practice. I had no idea what would happen until I tried.

"And so, chomp.
"I bit into that right hand—and sucked its blood.
"Not as sustenance.
"But to create a thrall—I sucked its blood.
"Unable to stand being alone—
"I quit being a god and returned to being a vampire."

021

"That's so intense I have no words. Or room to be jealous or sympathetic," I simply spoke my mind, giving her my unvarnished opinion.

Or rather, what I felt all over again listening to her story was: *I see just how much of a different level you operate on.*

Forget levels. Just everything.

It was too different.

Resurrecting a human being from his hand alone? Ridiculous—I knew it wasn't exactly fair to criticize her for it, but frankly, it seemed like she was playing around with life itself.

She said "returning to being a vampire," but that, to me, felt the most like a divine act—it's a little late in the game to be saying this, but in terms of power, she really was nothing short of godly.

I keenly understood how those people felt when they recognized her as a deity for making that lake disappear—keenly and anew.

"...And you did it?"

"Hm? Uh, no, no, hold on a second. I do admit to speaking of the suspension-bridge effect and the desire to propagate in the face of a mortal crisis, but that was merely a figure of speech, and I know not how to respond to such a direct question—"

"…?"

Shinobu was blushing and staring daggers at me for some reason—hm? Wait, so did she fail? Figure of speech? Was the vampirism stuff a figure of speech? Mmf…

"Wait, no! I wasn't asking if you *did it*!"

"What? Ye weren't? Thou art not interested in hearing of what Aberration Slayer I and I did under the cover of darkness?"

"I don't even want to imagine if the two of you had love scenes! No, I'm asking if you managed to do it when you tried to regenerate the rest of him from his hand!"

"Hah," Shinobu instantly laughed, a note of superiority in her voice.

This little girl, she was the best in the world when it came to looking down on someone.

"I know not how to fail. When I said 'I had no idea what would happen,' I meant 'twas unclear what manner of success I would achieve, what else? In fact, I wish someone would teach me how to fail. Otherwise I would be flummoxed when I do somehow manage to fail one day. Ah, indeed, 'twould be nice to know. I wish someone would write a self-help book or such on the topic, *How to Fail Better!*"

"…"

Well.

The scary thing is that there really are books like that.

"So then, what was thy question again? If I did it? Is that what you want me to answer? Very well, I shall."

"Yeah… No, you're virtually telling me that you did it. Right?"

"I failed," she answered—

Successfully faking me out.

Her gleeful, self-satisfied expression quickly vanished—transforming to one of gloom.

She looked at the floor instead of at me.

"Y-You failed?"

"To be more precise, I succeeded for a time—but the end result was failure. I've told thee already, have I not—about the fate met by Kissshot Acerolaorion Heartunderblade's first thrall—"

"…"

Right.

I'd already heard—during spring break.

On the roof of this abandoned cram school—I'd heard about the fate of my predecessor.

About his end.

I'd heard it, and been shocked.

I'd already been—spoiled.

"Aberration Slayer I returned to life just as I'd planned—his entire body was regenerated from his right hand. A full and complete transformation into a vampire—there were no missteps in my execution unlike when I turned thee into a vampire over spring break. Nor did I turn into a little girl. I would say the first thrall I created went better than my second, were we simply discussing the degree of my craft."

"And I have to just sit and listen to this…"

"But—perhaps he was not as strong mentally as thou. While I suggested earlier that the elite are weak in the face of setbacks, that man must have been fragile in some more fundamental way."

In retrospect.

I may have been lacking in consideration.

So she said—but I didn't think you could expect Shinobu to be considerate to humans back in those days.

That's why she couldn't avoid it.

It was unavoidable.

Aberration Slayer I's—suicide.

"Didn't he throw himself into the sun, turn into ashes, and disappear?"

"Aye. Suicide—that oh-so-common cause of vampire death, about nine out of every ten. If there was anything uncommon, anything divergent about it, then—'twas that he ended his life after but a few years of being a vampire."

"As a thrall, he might not have had your level of endurance, but I presume he didn't die swiftly just because he went out into the sun."

Burning, regenerating.

Burning, regenerating.

Burning, regenerating—until he burned away.

It would have required quite a lot of time.

It would have required—quite a lot of suffering.

I'd experienced something similar—so I knew.

That it really was a living hell—but a vampire probably can't die unless he does that. Especially if you're Shinobu's thrall—

"…You didn't save him? The way you did when I accidentally went into the sun over spring break?"

I was asking her if she didn't, but perhaps the better question was: if she *couldn't* save him.

And in fact, "'Twas impossible," she replied. "Nor did I really understand the meaning of his actions at the time—well, we'd spoken at length prior to his decision to end himself, but my relationship with him was essentially bankrupt at that point. I had no way to stop him."

"Bankrupt?"

"To put it simply, Aberration Slayer I was angry—angry that I had made him into a vampire."

"…"

"'Tis no complicated matter. For my part, I felt that I had bestowed upon him something for which he could never thank me enough. Not only had I brought him back to life, I had made him the thrall of my mighty self. 'Tis an absurd attitude to take after having done so out of loneliness, but that is something I am able to regret only now, after four hundred years. I truly felt that way then. If anything, I meant to be modest about it, telling myself, *No, I shan't be so childish as to demand his gratitude. I merely did what was proper.*"

But I was off the mark.

Quite off the mark, regretted Shinobu.

After returning him to life from just one hand—after Aberration Slayer I had been given new life as a vampire, the very first words he spoke were:

"'You monster—how dare you deceive us!'"

"..."

A demon, and not a god.

She'd been found out—to be a vampire.

That must have been what "deceive" meant.

At least in part.

But he probably also meant something else by it—

"—'So it was all your fault!' he shouted. Perhaps it was more rebuke than shout. That's when he spoke his bit about 'divine punishment.' By continuing to pretend to be a god, I brought down divine punishment—he claimed."

"So in other words, he made everything your fault, from the people being spirited away to all the rest? He was saying the Darkness was part of your plan or something... Well, I mean—I can kind of understand why he'd think that, but—"

His sense of scale was off.

Even if he was the leader of a band of experts, even if he knew real gods, he surely hadn't ever dealt with an aberration of Shinobu's—Kissshot Acerolaorion Heartunderblade's caliber. And being forcefully brought back to life via his remaining right hand after being engulfed by this mysterious Darkness and disappearing—it would have been strange if he did stay on an even keel.

The fact that he'd been regrown from his hand, especially, concerned his very identity as a human—they say that planarians can regenerate forever, and an earthworm that's split in two turns into two earthworms... But where do you find your sense of self when that happens to you?

An impossible question to answer—

Had been put directly to him.

"So—what did you do? No matter what your reason for saving

him, you did it all the same. You couldn't have stayed calm when he said that to you."

"No, 'twas not that bad. Correcting his misconception was a bother, so I let him say whatever he wished. He may be confused and deluded now, I thought, but he would calm down eventually."

'Twas similar to the way I'd pouted here in these ruins, she remarked.

"…"

I wasn't naive enough to buy that it mustn't have been that bad just because she was making it sound like it really wasn't.

How Shinobu thought then.

And what she thought—I couldn't begin to imagine.

Since I'd never met him face-to-face, there was no way for me to know exactly how delicate Aberration Slayer I was, but at the end of the day, Shinobu was just as sensitive as him.

Being that way, she was only acting like a villain sometimes… She consistently cast herself in a bad light and said that turning him into a thrall was just a self-centered impulse, and she wasn't lying, but she also seemed to be presenting it in far too one-sided a way.

She'd reigned over a region as a god, even if she called it a whim—and he was its last survivor. Did she really, truly, unequivocally not want to stop him from dying? I wasn't going to believe that.

If she was that kind of woman—

I wouldn't be alive like this.

I wouldn't be alive—halfway vampire.

"But he did not calm down. He was confused and deluded, he antagonized me at every turn, before flinging himself to his own death. Cursing me again and again, slathering me in words of remorse and resentment, he threw his body into the sun as I watched—and then he died."

I could not stop him.

Nor could I save him.

Indifferently, apathetically, in a flat tone, Shinobu described the outcome.

"I even told him my true name after we reached the South Pole—and yet the only time he ever called me Kissshot was immediately before he cast himself away."

"..."

Still—he'd called her Kissshot.

Not Heartunderblade, not Acerolaorion—but Kissshot.

Just like me.

In that case...

"And then he died—though 'twould be more accurate to say he met his demise, as his was an immortal body, but in any case, he died. Leaving behind as a memento a replica of the enchanted blade Kokorowatari that he worked himself to the bone to make. I am sure he made it with the intention of slaying me... I only happened not to have made a thrall before him, 'twas not as if I had remained resolutely single—but when I watched his corpse burn blue and fade away, I decided that I would never again create any—I swore that I would never drink human blood for any purpose other than nourishment."

To God, at that, she added.

How ironic the words sounded—when she'd played at the role.

I certainly wasn't laughing.

Nor did I find her words clever—because ultimately, both as a god and as a vampire, she hadn't been able to "handle" humans.

The demon's monologue.

Her tale of what was now past, four hundred years old.

So did its curtain fall, on an unhappy ending.

022

"Or so I say, but four hundred years later I created a new thrall without so much as a second thought. It seems my principles aren't much to speak of. In fact, I failed even worse than I did my first time around, causing even myself to lose power. I managed to get myself locked not in a god's shrine but a man's shadow. Hahaha, oh how splendid!"

"..."

Well, she was right.

If you wanted to say that she hadn't learned, you really could... Or rather, Shinobu must have seen what happened four hundred years earlier as something in her history, something from long ago, at most a lesson she should work to live by.

Memories, mementos, they all get worn away.

The follies of her youth—it had to have been a story from her past that she felt just a little embarrassed telling, a flashback scene. She wasn't going to get emotional over it or let it burden her as if she still dragged it along to the present day—aside from one part.

Right. In Shinobu's story—not her, but her story—there was

one issue that had yet to be resolved.

One affair that hadn't come to an end.

That was—the Darkness.

"In other words—you never discovered the identity of the Darkness, that thing that murdered your followers and your first thrall."

"Aye—I never did," Shinobu humbly nodded. "After it all—in other words, after Aberration Slayer I disappeared from this world, *it* never again tried to come after me, nor did it ever follow me. Once the dust settled, I traveled to Europe—I'd been a bit traumatized by super jumps, so I swam there—but I never saw the Darkness even after I arrived. Quite the contrary, as negative energy began to gather around me once again...so I thought 'twas all over. But I'm no fool. I was constantly worrying about the Darkness for another five years, but it never once showed any signs of appearing."

And so I eventually forgot.

That's what Shinobu said—I wasn't going to question her about whether she forgot by messing with her brain or if she did so naturally, but regardless, I was amazed all over again by the thoroughly happy-go-lucky way she lived her life.

She really was incredible.

She was able to forget—something like that.

"And so I've remembered it for the first time in four hundred years—ahh. What a truly awful thing to recall. And 'tis all thy fault."

"My fault... Well, all I can do is apologize if you're going to blame me like that."

"I jest, 'tis not thy fault. In fact, it must be my own—that Darkness has to have come chasing after me at last. Our game of tag that I'd arbitrarily decided was over had in fact continued on—and as one who's been linked with me, thou art now its target."

How embarrassing to know that even Hachikuji has gotten caught up in this, Shinobu rued, this time sounding genuinely sorry.

While I was one thing, as the two of us were nearly one in body and mind, it seemed she found it inexcusable that Hachikuji had gotten involved in this mess.

It was odd. Hachikuji was a ghost, which is to say she was an aberration. Shinobu should have seen her as nothing but energy…but maybe she felt some sympathy for her.

Who knows, maybe they were both members of a Koyomi Araragi Survivors Group.

"I know not its cause, I know not its identity, I know not a thing about it—to be frank, I was powerless even at my peak against this Darkness, a mysterious phenomenon whose mysteries beget mysteries—but 'tis no excuse. So, now what?"

"But—it didn't come after you four hundred years ago, right? So it's possible that we ended it again this time by getting away from it…"

"Perhaps, but perhaps not—for as unlike last time, I cannot jump to the South Pole. We do need to put together a plan, and I'd even propose to attack it ourselves if we can—for 'twill be too late if we meet it only after the residents of this area are spirited away."

"…"

Of course it would be.

This issue went beyond Shinobu and me—we needed to act with the understanding that everyone living here in this town where I was born and raised could go missing.

Hitagi Senjogahara, Tsubasa Hanekawa.

Suruga Kanbaru, Nadeko Sengoku.

And when I added Karen Araragi and Tsukihi Araragi, my two little sisters, to that list—I knew it was no time for me to be hiding out in a safe location feeling like everything was over.

Even if it wasn't an aberration.

That phenomenon—wasn't something I could ever let myself ignore.

"Well, that thing is just as mysterious as it was before you began your story, but I at least have some ground to stand on now. Because four hundred years ago—the same thing happened, and you fell victim to it then as well."

"Indeed, thou art correct."

"In that case, we should start by gathering information, like Oshino would. We'll start with data about the lake you eliminated and those villages that got emptied out, and then—oh, but—"

Even if we were starting by going to the library to do research, I needed to leave Hachikuji somewhere first. She had run away with us due to the way everything had transpired, but if what Shinobu said was true, I couldn't let her get any more deeply involved.

In fact, now that Hachikuji had started showing a face that was weak to adversity, it felt like she'd be something like dead weight during any adventures we might go on in the future… She'd basically be a backpack.

"Aye. I'd like to take care of this issue before thou goest to school tomorrow—so for now, let us explain the situation to Hachikuji once she awakens, then part ways with her to begin acting in earnest—"

And just then.

Right as Shinobu was beginning to put together our plan, a voice to my side interrupted her.

"I think you should probably not do that," it wedged itself in—like a bookmark. "Kind monster sir."

I looked over to find—though I didn't need to look—a tsukumogami.

Expressionless, in a cute outfit.

It was—Yotsugi Ononoki.

Standing at the entrance to the classroom, she gazed at us soberly.

"Ononoki—"

"You're in for a nasty surprise if you buy into everything that geriatric is telling you. I do owe you for that time you bought me ice cream, kind monster sir—so I can't turn a blind eye when you might find yourself in a fix after letting this foolish aberration incite you, which is why I'm warning you now."

"…"

Wait, forget about that for the moment.

How long had she been there?

She interrupted our conversation like it was normal—and given the know-it-all tone she spoke in, did she actually finish her job and come back here because she was worried about us?

Ononoki wouldn't call something that only takes a few moments to settle a "job"—it would have taken at least one or two hours.

Which would stand to reason that, um, how would you put it...

"Yeah," Ononoki said. "I heard everything. By coincidence."

"Coincidence..."

"It was coincidence that I was standing in the hallway outside of the classroom with my face against the door and struggling to hear your every word. The world is just so full of coincidences, isn't it."

"Not ones like that."

I felt like I'd been had...

So she pretended to leave but had actually been in the hallway the entire time?

But why would she...

"Hmph," Shinobu snorted—actually, she seemed downright grouchy.

All of the wind had been taken out of her sails.

Or no, maybe this would actually be wind to Shinobu's sails.

"I'm surprised ye still have the guts to call me geriatric to my face, tsukumogami girl—despite how much thou must be shaking inside. In consideration of that courage, I shall make a special exemption this one time and not eat thee alive."

"I don't know. I think that might be hard for you in your current state..." Ononoki riposted confidently.

She was right—Ononoki had been trounced by Shinobu in the past, but that was when Shinobu had some degree of her power back.

Now that she was a little girl—she probably wouldn't be able to kill Ononoki, Kagenui's top shikigami, at least not without a fight.

If anything, Shinobu would find the tables turned on her.

"If ye insist, I wouldn't mind taking thee on—of course."

"Hmph. A rematch—"

"H-Hey. Cut it out, you two," I reflexively jumped in to stop them.

My body moved on its own to get in the middle of this volatile situation.

"You know this is no time to be doing this—and anyway, Ononoki."

"Yes?"

"Um, why did you feel like you needed to sit in the hallway and wait? You could have just stayed in the room if you wanted to listen, so why go to the trouble of lying about work and—"

"It was a coincidence," Ononoki stuck to her story, but she seemed to know quite well that her excuse was a stretch. And so, "I didn't lie," she corrected herself somewhat. "It wasn't a lie that I had a job to do. I just delayed my plans—and anyway, that geriatric over there has a petty personality. I thought she might hold back if I were here."

"Hold on, do not misjudge me so. Do I really seem that small-minded to thee?"

"..."

"..."

She did.

My thoughts lined up perfectly with Ononoki's.

Shinobu must know the identity of this aberration— that was my prediction, and Ononoki must have decided to step out into the hallway in order to hear what Shinobu had to say.

Which would mean that her little goodbye kiss was specifically meant to wake Shinobu up... Ononoki did know that our senses were linked.

Oh. Just as I thought she'd fallen for me, it looked like I was wrong.

That was depressing.

It was going to take me three or so days to recover from this.

"But it was worth delaying my work, since I got to hear a surprisingly interesting story—I had a feeling I might."

Ononoki was expressionless.

But I could see in that lack of expression her clear feeling of having gotten one up on Shinobu—as if to say this was part of her payback.

"Urgh!"

Shinobu had noticed the same vibe, and not so good-natured that she was going to sit back and accept it—she crawled under my legs to get past me and dashed toward her target.

Oops. I'd let my guard down.

Crap, a fight was about to break out—I braced myself, but instead Shinobu went around Ononoki and locked down both of her arms from the back.

"Now! Do it!"

"You're assuming that I'm going to be your accomplice."

"Ye can grab her chest to thy heart's content!"

"Um, it needs to be one-on-one for me..."

With that, I actually took a step back to put some distance between me and Ononoki. Since Shinobu was linked to my shadow, I was essentially dragging her away.

From there, I just kept walking away.

Until we were at a good distance.

"Still," I said, "this is like a dream situation when I think about it. I'm here in a classroom where around me are a little girl, a young girl, and a tween girl. Hold on, is this Shangri-La?"

"Dost thou know thou art uttering all of thy thoughts?"

"Whoa, I need to be more careful. That was borderline dangerous."

"Well, thy words were indeed borderline."

Putting aside the issue of age with these little, young, and tween girls—you couldn't deny that I was in an awfully lavish situation.

Shinobu Oshino.

Yotsugi Ononoki.

And, though she still hadn't woken up, Mayoi Hachikuji.

Who could have ever imagined that these three would end up congregating under one roof?

So there were benefits to dragging out a series.

What an amazing bonus level.

It was like every monster had turned into a coin.

"What are you grinning about, kind monster sir?"

"'Tis the kind of man he is. Thou ought to be careful, he's the type who'll follow thee around for life after a single kiss."

Look at that.

I thought the two were irreconcilable, but was I starting to see signs of them making up thanks to a common enemy, better known as me?

Heh.

Looks like playing the villain was worth it after all.

Actually, forget bonus levels. Being in a cramped room together with three girls was practically being in a dating sim.

Not bad at all.

"By the way, I'd hate to let this opportunity go to waste. Why don't ye settle it once and for all. Which of the three among us dost thou like the most?"

"What?!"

Agh!

Sure, it might have been a dating sim, but it was still about to turn into a bloodbath!

Why would she ask me a question like that out of nowhere?!

"You're right. He really does need to make that clear." I couldn't believe it, but Ononoki agreed.

She was letting herself get carried away.

"Ah, um, out of the three of you? Well, of course that would be you, Shinobu, the partner I share a body and mind with—"

"I'd like to hear thine answer were we not partners or of one body and mind," Shinobu backed me into a corner.

Why even back me into a corner, at this juncture?

She was so clearly taking her anger out on me. What was this if not harassment…

"Nay, rather than this situation, which is to say the three of us here, I think I'd like to hear ye choose among me, the tsundere girl, and the cat class president."

"~~~~~~~~~~," I shook my head back and forth.

You can't ask that! Didn't she know it would be all over for us?!

We'd end up in a quagmire!

She'd taken the triangle I'd successfully created through clever shifts in how I liked each of the three and put them all together in the same sentence... I was in big trouble now.

"Forget about that, Ononoki, what did you think about what Shinobu had to say? I know you told me you have no clue what the Darkness might be, but maybe you made some connections when you heard her story?"

"Forget about that? Is the person you like most a topic you can forget that easily, kind monster sir?"

Ononoki wasn't playing along.

Shinobu was one thing, but I couldn't recall ever earning Ononoki's ire, any reason she'd want to vent her anger at me...

She was doing it entirely to amuse herself.

"Mnnn—"

And then.

While I wasn't exactly surrounded on all sides, I was hemmed in on two sides, front and back, but a voice from a different side spoke up to rescue me.

Well, it was more like someone talking in her sleep.

"—nnn. Where..."

...*am I*—she said.

Mayoi Hachikuji did.

At long last—she'd woken up.

023

"Hachikujiiiiiiiiiiiiiiiiiiiiiiiiiiiiiiiiiiiiiiiiiiiiiiiiiiiiiiiiiiiiiiiiiiiiiiii iiiiiiiiiiiiiiiiiiiiiiiiiiiiiiiiiiiiiiiiiiiiiiiiiiiiiiiiiiiiiiiiiiiiiiiiiiiii!"

I charged into Hachikuji after giving myself an Unlimited Rulebook Disengagement Edition-level rocket start.

I ended up tackling her, or rather, I aimed a little too low and hit her bed made out of desks—even so, that only sent her flying off of her bed and ultimately onto my sliding body, and it all worked out in the end.

"AAAAAAAAAAAAAAAAAAAAAAAAAAAAAAAAAAA AAAAAAAAAAAAAAAAAAAAAAAAAAAAGH!" she shrieked.

It had been so, so long.

It was almost as if I was listening to a relaxing piece of classical music.

"Great, you're awake! I was so worried that you might've taken a nasty hit or that something you could never recover from had happened because you weren't getting up at all! I was doing so much soul-searching, thinking about how we never should have ridden two to a bicycle even if we were trying to get away! I was planning on watching every next-episode preview from *Carrangers*, the fighting traffic-safety squad! Oh, but I'm so glad that you're awake now!"

"AAAGH!"

"C'mon, lemme touch you more, lemme lick you more, lemme slurp you up more!"

"AAAGH! AAAGH! AAAGH!"

Grah!

Then, for the first time in a while, Hachikuji bit me.

Not just Hachikuji, actually. A vampire and a tsukumogami bit me too.

I was being bitten from three directions, by a young girl, a little girl, and a tween girl.

What utter bliss.

"Grah! Grah! Grah!"

"What art thou doing, fool, acting in such a brazen manner before my very eyes!"

"I just, um, felt like it."

It was a beatdown. Punches and kicks rained down on me.

You could call it a mild case of mob violence. Or a severe one, even.

"W-Wait, you three! I understand how you feel, but calm down! Is right now really the time for this?!"

Of all the people they could have heard the words from.

I was probably the one person they didn't want to hear saying them.

"Phew..." I took a deep breath. "It had been so long since I got to act that way that I lost control of myself. I was on a total rampage, almost like I was a member of the Blastasaurus Rampage Rangers."

"How dare ye speak the name now," Shinobu scolded me.

Did we have another fan of ranger shows?

"Yeah, don't you utter that name. That's righty-tighty," Ononoki scolded me too. For some reason, it involved using a weird phrase.

It really made me feel like I was speaking to children.

"Anyway, Hachikuji. Are you really okay? It didn't feel like it when

I was palpating you just now…"

"What are you, a doctor?" Hachikuji asked as she straightened herself out.

It didn't take any time at all for her to return her clothes to the state they were in before I made them come loose, but it looked like she didn't have any spare bands, and her hair, which had come partly undone as we escaped on my bicycle, remained disheveled.

If anything, she should have just undone her other pigtail to balance things out… Was she picky about her antennae's design?

"I'm okay. No problem at all. All clear, all lights green, perfecto," Hachikuji said—taking her backpack from where it was on the floor (you weren't expecting her to wear it while she slept, right?) and popping it up onto her shoulders. "I never thought that unknown thing was a problem to begin with, Mister Araragi."

"…"

Given just how agitated she was while we were being chased, she was acting awfully composed—her attitude felt like it took its own kind of courage.

"Still, Mister Araragi, allow me to thank you."

"C'mon, I know that friends ought to respect each other more than anyone else, but there's no need to be so formal with me," I said, giving her a thumbs up. "Holding you in my arms right after you wake up is something like my calling."

"No, I'm not talking about that hug. I wanted to thank you for taking me with you and not abandoning me… I'd been convinced that you'd try to shake me off and escape all on your own in a situation like that."

"Sheesh, she's got zero trust in me!"

What a shock, seriously…

That's how little Hachikuji believed in me? But when I thought about it, she really hadn't gotten the chance to see me do much of anything cool.

In fact, it seemed like all she ever saw was me acting like a loser…

I felt as though she was the biggest victim of my loserdom out of anyone, like just now, for example.

"Plus," Hachikuji added, "I'm happy that you didn't ignore that traffic light—it was out of consideration for me, wasn't it?"

"Hachikuji..."

"I really wouldn't have minded, though. I'm not that neurotic."

"I'm so disappointed in you!"

Why did she always have to have a punch line ready?

Of course, it was thanks to the ridiculous turn I tried to make that we slid right toward Ononoki as she wandered around town. When I thought about how we were brought together by fate, it seemed like maybe I'd made the right decision to obey that traffic light after all—wait, no.

I'd ignored that light, as it turned out.

Then came the divine punishment.

"All right, everyone. Now that I've woken up, why don't we change gears. Miss Shinobu, Miss Ononoki? Though I treasure your individuality, we're going to need to work in lockstep this time. Our ability to operate as a team is going to be tested today."

"O-Okay..."

"Yeah..."

Hachikuji was taking the lead for some reason, and for some reason the other two were following.

What was going on with them?

They say just taking leadership first is the best move in any chaotic situation, and in that light, Hachikuji had done well for herself.

She'd been characterized at the outset as shy, or rather, poor at communicating in general, but maybe that didn't apply when she was talking to other aberrations.

"Then, Codename: Gold," she said. "I'd like you to give me a status report."

"Aye, ma'am—hey. Know when to quit," Shinobu came back to her senses.

Hachikuji's brief reign ended.

"Don't make me eat thee."

"Hah. You think you would be able to eat me?" Despite her reign being over, Hachikuji remained confident. It totally came across like she was hiding her true power. "You know that I'm extremely toxic. I might even give you food poisoning."

"…?"

Shinobu looked dubious.

Like she wasn't able to respond.

Maybe she was wary that Hachikuji might have a leucochloridium inside her.

I didn't know why Hachikuji was able to still act so confident, but her over-arrogant attitude was, in a way, the ultimate protection.

Maybe that was how she defended herself.

"Kind monster sir. About what we were saying earlier."

And then.

Ononoki walked away from the little skit to tug on my sleeve. What a shy little thing, she oughta just get my attention with a kiss the way she did before.

"Hm? Earlier?" I asked.

"About any clues I might have—you were thinking that I might have remembered something new after hearing that geriatric's story."

"Ononoki… I'm sorry, but really, could you please put a rest to calling Shinobu that?" I insisted, unable to just let it pass. Once or twice was one thing, but hearing it over and over was rough. "People are starting to move away from using that term, to begin with."

"Then what should I call her?"

"Kind monster ma'am, or something?"

I tried to come up with a title that lined up with mine, but in terms of appearance, Ononoki looked older than Shinobu.

Shinobu = eight years old.

Hachikuji = ten years old.

Ononoki = twelve years old.

Or thereabouts… So "kind monster missy"? No, while I didn't like Shinobu being treated as elderly, her being treated like a kid felt a little weird, too.

If we ignored appearances, Shinobu was nearly 600 years old, and Ononoki was a newborn—

"Then just go with Aberration Slayer," I concluded.

"The former Kissshot Acerolaorion Heartunderblade" was also an option and would have been easier to get, but it was a little too long… It might double our page count.

"Phew," Ononoki sighed audibly. So clearly on purpose. "Fine, then. I guess I'll do it to keep you from losing face."

"…"

Again, why did she make every little thing sound like a big favor?

Was this about the tsukumogami attitude of not letting anything go to waste?

"So," she began, "if you'll allow me to state the conclusion I came to after coincidentally hearing that Aberration Slayer's story—"

"Oh, so you thought of something?" I said, but wasn't particularly hopeful—Shinobu's story helped us to establish a standpoint, but it didn't change the fact that we had no idea what the Darkness was.

If anything, mysteries only begat mysteries—you could say that things were twice as mysterious now.

Yet more hopelessly, even Shinobu at the height of her power had had no choice but to run (though I'm sure she wouldn't admit it)—only.

Only our despair grew, it was that sort of predicament.

While the danger hadn't quite sunk in for me yet because of the gorgeous situation I found myself in, surrounded by three young ladies, I found myself facing the biggest crisis so far in my life—

"You're not going to present us with a convenient development like having figured out what that Darkness is, are you?"

"I am. I've figured it out for the most part," Ononoki rattled off the words. She went and said them.

"Huh? Sorry, what was that, Ononoki?"

"Do you mean Miss Ononoki?"

"..."

This is why I could never get a read on her personality...

How exactly did she want to position herself when it came to me?

"I think there's a certain attitude you ought to take when you're begging someone to teach you something, kind monster sir."

"My attitude... What, are you saying you want me to bow my head and beg?"

"I'm saying you need to be rubbing your head against the floor."

"Kick."

I kicked a tween girl.

I kicked a tween girl in the stomach.

While she was a sturdy little aberration, it seemed to do a decent amount of damage, possibly because it caught her by surprise. Ononoki fell and curled into a ball.

"Urgh... Grrghh..."

She even started to let out an awful groan. The girl's nerve.

You'd better not think I was going to feel guilty.

We're talking about someone who's terrorized Mayoi Hachikuji numerous times.

"If you've realized something, then hurry up and spit it out. I can't afford a single moment's delay."

"Okay, I get it already. Okay, okay," Ononoki said, standing back up. She held the palm of her hand out toward me and sued for a cease-fire. "I get it, so please, no more violence."

"..."

It was a normal, honest request.

Her low resistance in the face of violence said something about how Kagenui usually treated her.

"To cut to the chase, kind monster sir, this is pretty bad."

"Yeah, I was well aware of the fact that things are bad... In fact, I know that all too well. That's why we're in a fix to begin with..."

"That's not an aberration. It's something else," Ononoki told me.

"That's why the Aberration Slayer—and Aberration Slayer I or whatever he was called—couldn't handle it. Of course they couldn't, it was acting under a different set of rules."

And of course you can't handle it either, kind monster sir.

Something about Ononoki's words made it sound like she didn't care.

No, that was always a facet of who she was. Maybe I was being a little too sensitive in considering that a change.

Still—not an aberration?

That was a possibility we had considered from fairly early on—and one that was somewhat supported by Shinobu's story—but I didn't understand what it meant for us when she stated it so definitively.

Just like the Darkness itself.

I didn't get it.

"If it's not an aberration—then what is it?" I asked. "Isn't that the real question? What exactly *is*—that Darkness?"

"I don't know its exact name—but I do know someone who does. I only have secondhand information about it, which is why I didn't have any clue at first—but when I heard the Aberration Slayer's story, I made the tiniest little connection."

"The tiniest little—connection."

If Ononoki had heard this information second-hand, that must mean directly from Kagenui—but who had Kagenui heard it from?

If we could talk to whoever that was.

We might not be able to resolve our situation, but we'd at least be able to move forward—wouldn't we?

"Who is it? Who knows what that Darkness is? This tiny little connection you're talking about—who does it connect to?"

"Izuko Gaen," the name came out of Ononoki's mouth. "She knows—everything."

024

Gaen.

But before I could search my mind for any memories related to that name, *it* appeared. Right there.

It "was" right there.

That—Darkness was right there.

In the very center of the abandoned classroom, which we were using as our sanctuary.

The desks I'd tied together to make a bed for Hachikuji had been there just a moment earlier—I was sure of it.

But they were gone.

Gone without a trace—there was only darkness there now.

Deep and black, it was impossible to gauge its distance—present but unclear as to where, seen, without being seen.

The Darkness.

"—gh!"

"…gh!"

"~~~gh!"

"Guh…"

Mayoi Hachikuji, Shinobu Oshino, Yotsugi Ononoki.

And I—shuddered.

We'd been left speechless by *it*, the way it had appeared so suddenly, without warning, seemingly illogically.

I just kind of had my guard down.

I really mean it when I say "just kind of."

For some odd reason, I'd convinced myself that this former cram school was safe—I do make the worst assumptions, don't I?

"Guh, uuugh—"

"It's time to run, everybody!"

It wasn't me, in my clear confusion, or Shinobu, who was seeing *it* in person for the first time in four hundred years, or Ononoki, who stood closest to the Darkness—

But Hachikuji who was the quickest to act.

Her judgment was the swiftest among us all.

"Y-Yeah!"

Run?

But how?

We could have Ononoki activate the Disengagement Edition of her Unlimited Rule book like before—that'd be a good idea.

But as I mentioned, she stood closest to the Darkness—we couldn't approach her position. Getting any closer to her might make the Darkness engulf her—along with us.

Ononoki was going to need to run toward us, but she didn't seem to comprehend this sudden development quite yet.

She was probably trying to comprehend it, though.

Which was exactly why—she couldn't move.

Still, she was the only one with a way to escape at that moment—Shinobu couldn't run off to the South Pole since she'd mostly lost her vampiric skills.

I was pretty much in normal mode, too.

As for Hachikuji, that went without saying—what were we

supposed to do now?

What could we do to get away?

Faced with a "phenomenon" that we weren't certain was our foe, which seemed to lack a will of its own to say the least, what in the world might we do—to get away from it?

Or maybe not?

Should we be fighting here instead of fleeing?

But we didn't even have the first clue as to how to fight it.

True, the Darkness had devoured my beloved bicycle. I should have hated it, in other words, but I didn't know what to think of it.

I didn't even know if it was our enemy.

How was I supposed to feel any enmity toward it?

"Guh—"

Our stare-down only continued.

This situation, where we were all frozen in place, dragged on and on—it may have been just a few seconds in reality but felt so much longer.

Ononoki was the only one with a way to escape from this place—but with her in a stupor, no one could move.

No.

I was wrong to think that no one could—there was an exception, though it might not have been "someone."

The Darkness could.

That's right—it did move—but not toward Ononoki. It could have swallowed her whole just by moving forward a few feet, but *that* isn't what *it* did.

No—instead it moved toward Hachikuji, who stood farthest from it.

Slowly—none of us noticed that it had started to move.

"Hachikuji!—" I yelled, hoping to get to her before the Darkness—but only hoping. I didn't know if I should really move yet.

We didn't know what might stimulate the Darkness—*it* might react to my movement and start to move faster like Ononoki said.

That'd be one thing, but it could also start teleporting around again, engulfing Hachikuji in one go, or possibly even everyone present—

So all I could do was holler.

"—Come this way!"

In any case, the Darkness seemed to be gliding toward Hachikuji—which meant that no matter what, she and she alone had to act. And in that case, I wanted her to come toward me at least.

Shinobu and I were connected by my shadow, so there was no need to do anything about her—once Hachikuji joined me, we could grab right onto Ononoki and have her activate that thing—activate the Disengagement Edition of her Unlimited Rulebook.

If it was too hard to make it out through a window, she could just crash through the ceiling—it didn't matter where we went, she just needed to put some distance between us and it at an incredible speed, and we should be safe.

Temporarily, at least.

"O-Okay!"

Hachikuji's fragility in the face of adversity actually seemed to work in her favor... She was usually such a rebellious girl when it came to me, but not only did she not question my words, she obeyed them immediately.

While I might leap onto Hachikuji, it was extremely rare for her to leap onto me. Come to think of it, this made two times in one day, which was even more rare.

The strangest things can happen over the course of a life, I thought, which is precisely why I can't die here—as I caught Hachikuji in my arms.

The Darkness didn't stop moving—it passed where Hachikuji had been, engulfing a few more of the desks that had stood behind her.

It really was like a black hole.

Then again, I thought of black holes as something with suction—and while this thing could swallow you up, it didn't seem to suck you closer. In that case, we could get away. Even if it got to our destination before us, we could get away as long as we were fast enough.

I held Hachikuji tight (a split second)...

I leapt toward Ononoki (a split second)...

I grabbed onto her body (a split second)...

"Ononoki," I yelled (a split second), "now!"

"Huh? H-Hey, kind monster sir, that's going too far. Stop it, already. Don't touch me there. What are you thinking? Consider the situation we're in."

"What are YOU thinking?!" I screamed as loud as I could and head-butted her.

I couldn't put my hands on her because they were holding onto Hachikuji—and Shinobu had already sunk into my shadow. Our feelings weren't linked for nothing—having secretly worried that she might needle me later saying, *Ye abandoned me*, I was seriously relieved that she understood me without any verbal exchange.

"We're escaping, Ononoki! Like before!"

"Oh, so that's why—"

I even felt anger at how she seemed to have forgotten about the option entirely, but naturally didn't have the time to pursue the matter.

The Darkness changed direction.

Now it came toward us.

Or at least—looked to be, though it was probably an illusion.

"Unlimited Rulebook: The Disengagement Edition."

025

We were transported in an instant—I heard later that Ononoki was able to go through the window normally and didn't have to crash through the ceiling.

Not that I should call flying out of a window "normal"…but Ononoki just maybe hesitated to destroy the abandoned cram school that was home to so many of my memories.

I'm using phrases like "just maybe" and "I heard later"—the reason I don't sound sure is that I couldn't read Ononoki's expression at the time or our trajectory.

We were simply going too fast.

Ononoki was no match for Shinobu's peak-state super jump instant air dash, according to Shinobu—judging from our velocity, though, Ononoki's leg strength might have been comparable in this case at least.

Actually, I was knocked out by the kinetic impact—it wasn't even close to the kind of speed that my consciousness could withstand.

"That's because I didn't go easy unlike when I first did it—it was an all-out escape this time. You should consider yourself lucky that your body wasn't torn to pieces from the sonic boom, kind monster sir," Ononoki explained.

Actually, it was more like an excuse.

This girl never apologized...

Then again, she probably figured we couldn't get away unless she went at that speed, and we did in fact manage to get away. I should have had no complaints...but still didn't feel like thanking her.

Humans are emotional animals.

"So... Where are we now?"

When I regained consciousness, I was somewhere I'd never seen before—it seemed like we were in the mountains, but I didn't know which.

All mountains tend to look the same when you're in them...but at least it didn't seem to be the ones I knew so well...or rather, was deeply tied to, that featured Kita-Shirahebi Shrine. I felt no familiarity with this place.

Hmm...

Actually, forget where. What about the time?

It was a...night sky...approaching daybreak, actually.

"I don't know where we are, kind monster sir. I didn't have the luxury to pick a target—though I'm sure I went roughly north from that abandoned cram school."

"North... Um, but why are we in the mountains?"

"Three quarters of Japan's land is mountains. A haphazard jump is probably going to land you in them."

"..."

Shinobu had said that three quarters of our planet is covered by water so that's probably where a jump would land you. Ononoki was making a similar point at a reduced scale.

"Well, I don't think we're that far away..." she told me. "I jumped almost straight up the first time, which is why we only had to travel a few miles as the crow flies."

"Is it not...following us? I mean, the Darkness?"

"It seems that way. I guess it's true that it's bad at dealing with vertical motion... That is how the Aberration Slayer got away four hundred years ago, too. I should have jumped more upward this time, too—we ended up flying like a cannonball because I aimed for the window and traveled at a shallow angle."

We probably went a few dozen miles, maybe even more than a hundred, Ononoki estimated with a nonchalant look.

It seemed like we'd escaped without thinking of what might happen next.

Well, she'd gone fast enough to make me black out, so maybe we'd broken the hundred-mile barrier...

And it wasn't even per hour, so I was really lucky that I hadn't gotten thrown off.

"Wait, where's Hachikuji? Don't tell me she got thrown—"

"She's fine. Thanks to the tight grip you had on her chest, kind monster sir—quite the seatbelt, I must say. She's sleeping in the shade over there."

"Sleeping... Did she pass out again?"

"No, she was awake when we landed. She said she was sleepy because it was night, and went to bed."

"..."

Such audacity when she didn't have to face adversity head-on.

Nerves of steel.

"Oh, because it was night... Right, the time... When is it? I mean...how long was I out?"

"How long? Just long enough for Miss Hachikuji and I to have our fun with you."

"What did you do to me while I was passed out?!"

And hold on, "Miss Hachikuji"?

Sheesh, were they getting along?

"To be specific, one night—ever since early evening," Ononoki enlightened me, "so I guess that would be about twelve hours."

"Twelve hours..."

What a good night's rest.

I was mentally exhausted too, so my body probably used the opportunity it had when I blacked out to go into sleep mode—not that I felt at all refreshed.

"Though I said Miss Hachikuji and I had our fun with you, actually we tended to you, kind monster sir."

"O-Oh... Sorry for the trouble."

"Are you really? Saying so doesn't cost you a thing... If you're being sincere, why don't you swear you won't get angry even after you see everything we drew under your clothes?"

"How about I get angry now?"

Kick.

No, I wanted to but stopped myself.

Whether or not they'd really tended to me, a guy passing out during an escapade was nothing but a burden—I was grateful that they hadn't abandoned me there and simply run off.

"At any rate, if we're being cautious, our rule that it won't follow us if we travel vertically is just based on past experience. It's only worked so far. There's no telling how it'll go next time."

"Yeah... Past experience aside, I can't figure out the first rule about how this Darkness works. What *is* that thing?"

I might have been less anxious if it actually kept on chasing us.

Even at that moment, the Darkness might pop up right next to me—I'd breathed a sigh of relief, but that wasn't our situation at all.

"So, Hachikuji..."

I stood to go check up on her as she slept, just to be sure. There was a chance that she'd been injured and that Ononoki was trying to be thoughtful.

Then again, I wasn't too sure whether Hachikuji, a ghost, could sustain an actual injury...

Either way, I was worrying too much. She looked the very picture of health as she slept there under the trees.

I even touched her and made sure.

Yup, she was in good health.

"Okay, then... Now what? If we don't even know where we are..."

Muttering, I pulled out my cell phone.

Hmm.

I should have expected as much, but it was out of service—which meant we were deep in the mountains, far from any towns...

It seemed unthinkable, but could Ononoki have put in so much effort that she took us to another country? What if we were in the Grand Canyon?

...I guess the Grand Canyon isn't a mountain.

"I'd love to launch a counterattack, but can that thing be counterattacked?" I wondered out loud. "And it's hard to tell if it's really coming after us in the first place... We can't even be sure if it's following Shinobu, since that's just based on experience too..."

"The first step of our counterattack will be listening," Ononoki said.

"Listening?"

"Gathering info—did you forget what I was saying right before that thing appeared? I told you there was someone who knows about this thing that isn't an aberration but a phenomenon. Remember?"

"..."

Um.

Now that she mentioned it—it felt like she'd said something like that.

My memories were vague since I'd passed out right afterwards... but I believed the name was...

"Gaen..."

Gaen—Izuko Gaen.

So we needed to hear what she had to say? She knew Kagenui... right? Were we going to have to approach Kagenui first to get to her?

"Ononoki... What about your job? Is everything going to be okay?"

"Of course it's not going to be okay. But I can't just go back to my work now—I'm not that cruel."

"Do you have any way of contacting Kagenui? You couldn't yesterday, but some time has passed since then. She must be close to done with whatever she was doing, right?"

"Contact my sister... Hm. Considering our predicament, we might have to try, even if it's no good, even if she's still working. In that case, I do have a few tricks up my sleeve to gain access...but I can't use any of them this deep in the mountains."

"Can't you telepathically communicate with her or something?"

"Unfortunately, our bond isn't that strong. To approach her, we'd have to climb down this mountain, then call her or text her—not that I'd expect an immediate reply. I have a negligent sister."

"Negligent... Well, I guess I don't see her as the type to reply to text messages within the minute."

Whatever her personality, though, Kagenui was our only hope—she appeared to be our only route for contacting Izuko Gaen.

"Telepathy is too much to ask for, but it'd be nice if my sister could at least use her sixth sense—that said, I'm sure she'd readily abandon someone as inconsequential as me if she had to."

"..."

"In fact, kind monster sir—don't you think it's about time you pulled that Aberration Slayer out of your shadow?" asked Ononoki. "Either she doesn't want to talk to me or she's sound asleep, because she hasn't come out at all ever since we landed—I doubt the acceleration knocked her out too."

"Wait, Shinobu?"

What?

Now that Ononoki mentioned it, my partner wasn't around—no, I'd noticed from the start that she wasn't. That's why I naturally assumed that she was in my shadow—unlike Ononoki and Hachikuji, Shinobu and I couldn't be separated.

Our shadows.

Our hearts—our very being connected us.

We couldn't part ways—in other words, if we didn't see Shinobu, the natural, logical conclusion was that she was hiding in my shadow—but.

But when I thought about it, that didn't make sense.

Because right now—it was night.

Not exactly the middle of the night, since it was close to dawn, but unmistakably an hour you'd classify as night—there wasn't a hint of the sun's rays.

So then why?

"*Why isn't Shinobu—awake?*"

"Why? Don't ask me, kind monster sir," answered Ononoki, sounding confused despite her emotionless expression. She had to have wondered, too, for her part—and now that I'd asked, her suspicion that something was off was deepening. "I mean, what am I supposed to say? It's probably because she hates me—"

"I realize that you and Shinobu don't get along, and she certainly doesn't like you, but that's not enough of a reason for her to literally hide in my shadow at such a critical time… That's not the kind of person she is."

"So you trust her," Ononoki noted with a sarcastic overtone.

That was her only rebuttal, though.

It seemed like even she had no choice but to recognize how, well, magnanimous Shinobu was. Hence the sarcasm, I suppose.

"In that case… What could it be?" she asked. "I thought it was impossible, but could she really have fainted inside your shadow? Or maybe she got seriously injured somehow…"

Right now she can't regenerate the way she did when we fought, yes? Ononoki checked with me—and she was right, but still.

"Can you even get seriously injured while you're in someone's shadow? It's like she's in a dimension of her own in there. She shouldn't be affected by those kinds of physical shocks…" I mused, touching my shadow.

It was a dim, moonlit shadow, but there was no mistaking it for anyone's but my own—that was where Shinobu should be. It'd be strange if she wasn't—

"You can't enter your shadow, kind monster sir?"

"Unfortunately, no... But."

I patted it all around and got no reaction in return—the anxiety and impatience I felt should've been communicated to Shinobu through my shadow, too, but she wasn't reacting to that either.

Despite her reacts being incomparably better than they'd been four hundred years ago.

Which meant... What did it mean?

"Ononoki? You know what this means. I'm just going to have to kiss you."

"How did it come to mean that?"

"Our only choice is to reach her by making my heart pound, like yesterday. We're gonna have to kiss—a big sloppy French one!"

"If you say so...though I'd rather not."

Not really, Ononoki demurred.

She didn't wanna—how sad.

But there was no other way.

No matter how much she didn't wanna, my only option was to steal a kiss from Ononoki!

"Um."

Just as I tried to grab onto Ononoki's small frame, Hachikuji popped out from under the trees to show her face.

"Mister Araragi."

Oh.

She seemed to be asleep just a moment ago, but it looked like she was awake—had Ononoki and I been too loud?

I'd been trying my best to keep my voice low...

"What is it, Hachikuji? Jealous?" I said, looking in her direction. "In that case, I'd be fine kissing you instead. You might've spoken up sooner."

"Please die, Mister Araragi. Sorry, I meant to say please wait, Mister Araragi."

"Wait for what? Are you taking responsibility for the character I am and committing suicide?"

Out of confusion, I was saying and doing things that didn't make any sense, but I'd have you know, at least I was aware of that.

I was concerned if I could take back any of it.

"Um, er—I'm sorry I went to sleep during such a crisis," Hachikuji said, as if she really regretted it, and felt guilty about it.

But what was she supposed to do?

It's not like I could criticize her after being unconscious for all that time.

"It's fine. You slept, that's all. Anyway, Hachikuji, why do I need to wait to kiss Ononoki?"

"No—Mister Araragi. There are a countless number of reasons why, but before that, or more importantly, regarding Miss Shinobu..."

Hachikuji approached me as she spoke. She must have called out to me right after waking up because she didn't have her backpack on.

"She's not in your shadow at the moment, correct?"

"Well, I wouldn't say that she isn't..."

Whether Shinobu was asleep or unconscious...

She was bound to my shadow, after all—but maybe there were exceptions? In fact, she did temporarily leave my shadow when she fought Ononoki.

But she'd regained most of her power as a vampire then, so—

"Kind monster sir. Allow me," Ononoki followed up on Hachikuji's words—and touched my shadow the way I had moments earlier.

Closing her eyes—she seemed to be feeling for something.

"Ononoki—"

"Be quiet. I'm checking right now—searching," she shut me down, focusing on her palms as they touched my shadow, with her eyes still closed—but even I wasn't optimistic enough to believe that she was waiting for a kiss.

I simply waited.

For Ononoki to come to a conclusion.

Her conclusion—an answer I felt I could foresee.

"She's not there..." Ononoki uttered at last.

In her affectless voice.

"She's not there."

026

"I saw it happen as I was being carried by you, Mister Araragi—the Darkness appeared where your shadow should have been," Hachikuji said.

She had joined me and Ononoki in crouching around my shadow.

"Could it be possible that Miss Shinobu was swallowed up by this Darkness? It probably didn't, but is it at least possible?"

"…"

The Darkness had touched my shadow?

I never noticed that—or maybe I had forgotten thanks to the impact that followed… But could that really happen?

It wasn't like it touched her directly, right?

It was absurd to think that the Darkness could engulf the *contents* of my shadow by simply touching it—but I needed to think carefully about this, to really think. Weren't we up against an absurdity?

A mysterious phenomenon that we couldn't even place—that's what we were up against.

So in that case.

"Shinobu got swallowed up...by that Darkness? No way..."

"I don't think that's it," Ononoki said, just as I gulped, confronting the cruel possibility thrust in front of me—there wasn't any particular emotion in her words. To put it another way, they didn't contain any note of consolation or consideration—which is what made them convincing. "If *it* really engulfed the Aberration Slayer—then you would have lost your vampiric nature entirely, kind monster sir. You should have returned to being a regular human—but you haven't."

"I haven't... Wait, but can we really say for sure that I haven't lost my vampiric nature? Oh, I guess—you can, Ononoki."

She'd figured out I was a vampire the first time we met—and had called me "kind monster sir."

As a shikigami—as an aberration.

She had the ability to figure that out—just as she figured out that Shinobu wasn't in my shadow.

"Well, there's a way even you can be sure, kind monster sir—you can *see* Miss Hachikuji right now, can't you?"

"Oh..."

"Miss Hachikuji is an aberration, and if you can clearly make her out, that means you haven't lost your aberrational nature—it means you haven't lost your vampiric nature."

Hearing this, I looked at Hachikuji again.

I could see her.

I saw her—she was definitely there.

Which meant—I was still a vampire—I guess? Which in turn meant that the Darkness hadn't engulfed Shinobu—

"But seeing her isn't enough for me to be sure. I'll have to touch her to be certain."

"Stop messing around and die, Mister Araragi. Sorry, stop messing around, Mister Araragi."

"You've been asking me to die a lot today, you know that?"

"In fact, you put your hands all over me while I was sleeping over there under the shade, didn't you?"

"She knows!"

This wasn't good!

Crap, I couldn't think of an excuse!

"I just thought of it as a bug clinging to my body. It was too much trouble to bother doing anything about it…"

"That's all I am to you?"

She wasn't even treating me as a pervert.

I'd lost to her drowsiness.

Being on the same level as a bug—was pretty thrilling.

"In other words, the Aberration Slayer is fine—no, I'm not sure if she's fine, but at least, she hasn't 'disappeared'…or as she put it, been 'spirited away.'"

"I see…"

A wave of relief hit me.

My mental state turned around entirely within the blink of an eye—but what was so cruel was that it did nothing to confirm whether or not Shinobu was okay, just like Ononoki said.

Because the fact was still that she wasn't in my shadow now.

"The Aberration Slayer hasn't disappeared…but, kind monster sir, I think it would be best for you to consider the link between you and her severed."

"Our link's been severed?"

"It might be more precise to say that your link has disappeared—because it overlapped with the Darkness."

You might say it stepped on your shadow as a child at play might, Ononoki put it poetically by her standards.

So it cast its shadow over mine?

"If my link to Shinobu was cut because it overlapped with my shadow…then what? So she isn't bound to my shadow anymore? In which case…"

"In which case we probably left the Aberration Slayer behind—you were clinging to my body and Miss Hachikuji's, but you were relying on your link to do the work with her."

"This isn't funny. So you're saying I abandoned Shinobu there under a Darkness we don't know anything about?"

I held my head in my hands—what had I done? Had I really left her behind in that dangerous of a situation?

I was overwhelmed with regret.

"Please calm down, Mister Araragi—don't blame yourself. It's just as Miss Ononoki said. You can still see me, which means that Miss Shinobu is still alive—the worst hasn't happened."

"You're right... Yeah, that's true."

Hachikuji was right—while I'd left Shinobu there under the Darkness, she hadn't been engulfed by it yet.

Even in the most pessimistic scenario, at least it was more likely that she hadn't been swallowed up—so this was no time to be feeling discouraged.

I needed to hurry back to town and reunite with her.

I wanted to hurry and apologize to her.

I wanted to apologize to her for leaving her behind.

I wasn't sure if I could get her back on my side with some Mister Donut—but I still wanted to apologize.

Most of all, I wanted to see her.

Shinobu and I had been together for so long, but now she wasn't in my shadow—and I never imagined the fact would make me feel such a profound sense of loss.

Which was also why—I felt angry.

The Darkness was so unknown to me that I didn't know what to think of it or how to deal with it—but real, tangible anger toward it was starting to bubble up in me.

Enmity was starting to rise up in me.

I was able to recognize it now. As an enemy.

I couldn't forgive it.

I could not forgive it.

Because—Shinobu must be feeling the same way.

Without me—she must be suffering her own sense of loss.

The same feeling she had at the South Pole four hundred years ago—

Of solitude.

I knew she had to be feeling it again—how dare it.

How dare it make Shinobu feel like—

"Let's climb down this mountain," I said to the two. "I don't know where this is, but if we're in Japan then it shouldn't take more than a day to get back to my town... We need to hurry and meet up with Shinobu."

"I understand how you feel, kind monster sir—but don't get impatient. I'm for climbing down this mountain, but we ought to contact my sister before trying to reunite with the Aberration Slayer."

"Oh, right—I guess that's right. We need to learn more about this Darkness at the same time..."

Agh. My anger was keeping my brain from working properly.

It was good for me to establish how I felt about the Darkness, but I couldn't lose myself in that and get sloppy.

An order.

I needed to figure out—the best order to do this.

"Well, we'll be using the Disengagement Edition of your Unlimited Rulebook to get out of here either way. Three quarters of Japan might be mountains, but the remaining quarter is towns. We'd eventually land somewhere with roads or train tracks if we used it a few times."

"No...that's not true, kind monster sir. Unfortunately, I can't use the Disengagement Edition of my Unlimited Rulebook anymore."

"Huh?"

I was bewildered by Ononoki's response.

The fact that I was counting on her to get us down the mountain made her words feel that much more unexpected.

"Why... Are you out of juice or something? Can you only use it so many times a day?"

"That isn't it. The skill consumes a reasonable amount of energy, but that's not the problem since I was able to rest for a night."

"Then why can't you—"

"The problem is you, kind monster sir," Ononoki said. "If your link with the Aberration Slayer has been severed, your vampiric nature should be that much weaker, even if it persists."

At the very least.

You're not immortal right now.

"That's why you weren't able to withstand our disengagement earlier. It was fairly strange to me at first, but now it makes sense. You certainly wouldn't have blacked out had you still been linked to her, and you wouldn't have been unconscious for twelve hours, either."

"…"

"You're weaker now, kind monster sir—this isn't just about the Disengagement Edition. You'll have to refrain from the kind of nonsense you've been pulling for the past couple of months."

027

I was weaker now.

That's how Ononoki put it, but she wasn't exactly right—she should have said that I was returning to normal, not that I was weaker.

I hadn't lost my vampiric nature, but it was waning—and while my immortality wasn't gone either, it too waned.

What an effect the removal of our link was having—well, it made perfect sense when you thought about it, but this "perfect sense" wasn't good news in any sense of the phrase.

What was going on here?

The situation was only getting worse and worse.

"But maybe it means the opposite happened to Shinobu, and she's more vampiric now? Now that our link is cut, she'd be relatively more—"

"No, she's probably less vampiric herself, just like you. That's the way your relationship works—though if you'd lost your life instead of your powers, kind monster sir, she'd probably be back to her peak state."

Right.

That's how it worked.

In other words, it wasn't only my situation that was worse. She was in just as much trouble—all we could say now was that she still existed, and there was no telling when she might disappear.

But stay calm.

It wasn't like this was over yet.

The tale—was still on.

"I do think it's the correct decision to hurry to the vampire, considering the emergency that is your link being severed. It's also the correct decision to climb down the mountain. It's not like there are any places that are safe from the Darkness, anyway," Ononoki concluded. "However, you're going to have to rely on your own two legs."

And so—that's what we did.

We weren't at all equipped for climbing down a mountain, and doing so was no easy task—though saying "it was no walk in the park" might be a little too affected.

We indeed were traveling in a downward direction, but in the dead center of a mountain range, if that's where we were, up or down didn't always matter.

As an aberration, Ononoki wouldn't get tired from climbing up and down, but I couldn't say the same for myself—nor could Hachikuji. Although she was an aberration, she wasn't a combat model like Ononoki. While her vitality was a different story, her stamina wasn't much different from a regular ten year old's.

Well, it did feel kind of inconsistent that she could survive high-speed mid-air travel but not a hike... Maybe she was one of those characters whose stats doubled when her health was flashing red?

"Hey, Hachikuji. You walk in front."

"Huh?" My words were utterly unexpected to judge from her expression, or maybe more like utterly unpleasant. "What are you talking about, you worthless piece of garbage?"

"'Worthless piece of garbage,' huh. You know, you don't actually get to hear that phrase too often in real life."

"Shouldn't the man walk in front on a mountain path as dangerous as this? I read that in *Rurouni Kenshin*."

"Why is a manga your source?"

"Well, I'm something of a wanderer myself," Hachikuji said with an air of self-satisfaction.

True, she was a lost tribe.

"My reverse-edge sword thirsts for blood tonight!"

"There was no such line, I'm pretty sure…"

What kind of reverse-edge sword was that?

Then again, its strike would probably still draw blood.

"Why that expression, Mister Araragi? Are you the kind of boor who reads a manga and thinks yourself clever for complaining, *That guy claims to have vowed never to kill again, but if you hit someone in the head with a metal rod, they're going to die, reverse-edge or not!*"

"Come on, my mind hadn't gone that far," I shrugged. "I just thought that as the smallest of us, it'd be better if you walked in front. I have a big stride so we might even get separated if I took the lead…"

My thinking was that if I walked behind Hachikuji, I could step in if something happened. Unfortunately, though, she didn't seem to be a fan of the idea.

In fact, she might have felt like a canary in a coal mine.

"When you walk with a woman on a sidewalk, you stand closer to the street," Ononoki commented quietly. "You open doors for her, then you wait until she passes through to close them. Naturally, you don't let her hold anything, and you don't sit before her, either. When you climb stairs, you stand behind her, and when you go down them, you stand in front… So maybe you should be the one standing in the very front when we go down a mountain, kind monster sir."

"…"

I'd been schooled by a familiar on how to be a gentleman.

It had come from someone who normally let her master, Kagenui, ride on top of her shoulders as they roamed around…

Hm?

Hold on, what did she just say?

"It's recommended for men to stick behind a woman when you're climbing upstairs? Even if she's wearing a skirt?"

"..."

"..."

Hachikuji and Ononoki held down their skirts at the same time—how upsetting. I'd asked a simple question.

"Kind monster sir. It's so that the gentleman can use his broad embrace to catch the lady if she is to slip that he stands behind her on the stairs."

"Yeah, I know. In fact, I caught a girl falling down the stairs just half a year ago."

"Hearing that makes me think that you must have had some kind of ulterior motive from the start..."

"Hmph, I wonder if I ought to tell on you about this to Miss Senjogahara..."

Both the tween girl and the young girl were piling baseless accusations on me.

Hmph.

It looked like this would require further explanation.

It wasn't manly to offer excuses, but it would be a great loss to these girls if they continued to misunderstand just how much of a gentleman I was. I needed to tell them, out of kindness.

Sheesh. What a softie.

But it's just who I am.

"Listen up, you two. Yes, my heart does start pounding just looking at a woman wearing a skirt, but I don't necessarily want to see what's under it. In fact, just getting to see the way her skirt swings and flutters in the air is more than enough. Compared to the skirt itself, what's under it is just icing on the cake. In fact, I might even look away if I saw under a girl's skirt."

"Please walk in front."

"Please walk in front and get bitten by a snake."

The tween girl and the young girl disappeared from my sight.

I couldn't believe it...

I'd told them the truth to clear up a misunderstanding, only to do more damage to our relationship. Perhaps I ought to have let them have their wrong idea.

Well, they at least understood just how much of a man I was, in a way...

Though you do also hear that mountain snakes don't bite the lead hiker, they go for the second person in line...

Or that bringing up the rear is the riskiest.

Maybe it just means that no position is safe when you're marching through the mountains.

Or that if you want to be a chivalrous gentleman, you shouldn't be bringing ladies deep into the mountains to begin with...

"Mister Araragi, I'd wondered if turning into a vampire had made you more of a pervert, but it seems that had nothing to do with it, now that I see you acting this way even after your link has been cut," Hachikuji said—out of my sight as she stood behind me. "It seems that you were just a plain old pervert."

"Stop throwing the word around like that. Don't be so quick to call someone a pervert. It's almost like you're making me out to be a pervert."

"True, using 'pervert' too easily could rob it of its gravity, and it might even stop sounding like a big deal... But if someone like you really existed, Mister Araragi, wouldn't it be a social issue?"

"I'm not fictional."

"Speaking of perversion," Ononoki said.

Was she really going to use that word as her jumping-off point? She was actually going to go from one perversion to the next?

She meant something else by the word, though.

"When a caterpillar turns into a butterfly, is that a kind of perversion? What kind of phenomenon is it?"

"Huh?"

"Well, it's as if one creature is evolving into a different creature... I'm really just talking off the top of my head, though. It's not like I know anything about biology..."

"Hm," Hachikuji began in a solemn tone, "in terms of metamorphoses, I know that both complete and incomplete metamorphoses exist—so bringing it back to you, Mister Araragi, which would you be? Labeling you a complete pervert might be going a little too far."

"If you want to talk about going too far, Miss Hachikuji, there's also something called hypermetamorphosis, where one creature becomes something that's more or less completely different... But I wonder, what happens to your identity as an organism in a case like that?"

"A hyper-pervert, you say. Yes, that seems to be just about the right term for Mister Araragi."

It was hard to say if the young girl and the tween girl were talking past each other or not.

Actually, Hachikuji was just badmouthing me the whole time.

"What about a human becoming a vampire," I interrupted them, finding no reason not to elbow my way into a conversation between a young girl and a tween girl. "Does that count?"

"Well, that's more than a creature turning into another creature," replied Ononoki. "It's a creature turning into an aberration... Hmm, I wonder."

"There's no chrysalis stage, so it'd be an incomplete metamorphosis. I see, Mister Araragi, so you're incomplete! Incomplete perversion, those words describe you so well!"

"..."

Could you shut up for a second, Hachikuji?

Rare as it was for me to feel that way about her.

"But it's not just vampires. In general, all aberrations are born through a transformation. So maybe you could call it a kind of perversion," Ononoki went on.

She wasn't responding at all to Hachikuji.

Actually, it kind of felt like Ononoki was consistently failing to do so.

"When something transforms..."

"Yes," Ononoki nodded. "When it turns aberrant. That's why they're aberrations, right?"

"..."

"We're aberrations because we 'aberrated'—it's an aberration when a human becomes a ghost, I'm an aberrant corpse—and thoughts, foxes, and raccoons can all turn aberrant and end up as aberrations," Ononoki said, seeming to cite every example she could think of. "Which is why you can say that a human turning into a vampire is an aberration—a deviation from its original form, a perversion. Again, a metomorphasis."

"You mean me-*ta*-mor-*pho*-sis."

"That's what I said."

I pronounced it right, Ononoki insisted.

She wasn't even going to try to own up to her mistake.

"In that case," I said.

It did seem a little silly to be discussing the topic in those steep mountains, a treasure trove of metamorphosing insects where shape-shifting foxes and raccoons seemed ready to pop out at any moment.

"Could you call it a perversion when Shinobu, a vampire, became a god?"

"Hm?"

"Well, like we were saying." I decided to go into further detail because Ononoki didn't seem to take my point. "Would one aberration turning into another count, is what I want to ask... I guess it's all semantics, though."

"Well, that does happen. They say yokai shift forms all the time—but,"

But, Ononoki said.

"I wonder. Would it count as a perversion in the Aberration Slayer's case?"

"Huh?"

"Well, it's not as if she had *become* a god four hundred years ago—she was worshipped as a god, but at the end of the day, she continued to be a demon."

"…"

"Yes, she lived as a demon—and continued to be a demon."

The tale of a demon that the Aberration Slayer told remained a demon's—it wasn't of a god.

That's what Ononoki said.

"Hm."

Well, sure.

You could put it that way, of course you could… For whatever reason, it felt like her obvious statement was in fact pretty important.

But I didn't know why…

"By the way, Hachikuji, what about snails? Are snails perverts?"

"Could you not treat me like I'm some sort of expert on snails?"

"…"

I tilted my head in confusion at Hachikuji's reply.

Our conversations were strangely awkward today.

Asking her if snails were perverts was such an obvious attempt to make her seem like a pervert too and should have been a decent setup, but she didn't bite.

I'd been hoping to advance our banter about perversion with Hachikuji.

Maybe this mountain really was proving to be quite a hike for her.

She was a ghost that haunted streets, and maybe mountain paths were unanticipated…not that this area even had paths.

"Snails have shells from the time they hatch from their eggs… I don't think you could say that they change in form," Ononoki replied to my question in the end, and in the most straight-laced manner possible.

"What? Snails are born from eggs? Oh, but I guess so. They're shellfish, after all."

"How did you think they multiplied?"

"I just thought they must divide or something… I mean, they're molluscs."

"You know that molluscs lay eggs, too… Have you never eaten octopus eggs, kind monster sir?"

"Octopus eggs aren't exactly a common dish…"

Still. Ah.

Yeah, that made sense.

It was simpler creatures that multiplied through division, like hydras.

Not to allude to the story of her first thrall or anything…

"They apparently discovered fossils of a pregnant dinosaur, and it just means that organisms multiply in a lot of different ways," Ononoki said.

"How about this."

"Hm?"

"Well, even with my link to Shinobu severed, we know for sure that I'm showing the aftereffects of becoming a vampire… In other words, you could still describe my state as 'not human.' What if, one day, I start a family in this state and become a father? What of the kid?"

"…"

Ononoki stayed quiet for a long moment after my question. "Really?" she asked. "Our situation couldn't be any more serious, and you're worried about what's going to happen if you engaged in intercourse with a woman? You've got a filthy mind."

"No! I just skipped over all of that stuff! I'm going straight to the cute part, or rather the totally serious part, aren't I?! Like what to name the child."

"It was a serious query about a series of events sans sleaze?" asked Hachikuji.

She'd rejoined the conversation now that we were off the topic of snails.

I was impressed. Her enunciation was so clear that I didn't have to think twice about the sentence.

"As I said earlier, humans and vampires are organism and aberration. Their entire biology is different…so I wonder. That might be close to asking if it's possible to have a half-dog, half-human. No, given that vampires aren't even organisms, it might be closer to a half-television, half-human."

Ononoki was kind enough to tilt her head and ponder my question.

"Then it's impossible" was her answer, however. "If you simply need to reproduce and leave behind offspring, kind monster sir, you may have to turn the woman into a vampire… No, hold on, vampires reproduce in the first place through vampirism… So maybe you can't even if you're both vampires? But I'm sure there are legends about vampire parents and children, vampire siblings—"

"Actually, at the risk of answering my own question, I did meet a half-vampire man, now that I think about it." It came back to me; while not quite Shinobu's story of her past, it was a memory I didn't care to recall. "Doesn't that mean he's half-vampire, half-human?"

"I see. Then maybe it depends on which side is the vampire, the male or the female… If you simply have to know, then I think you should just ask Miss Gaen that as well."

"Er, I'm in no particular rush about it…"

It was just a thought that had popped into my head.

I wasn't more interested in it than I was in the Darkness, at least… Even if that were an issue for me, it wouldn't come up for a while.

"Anyway, I don't think it's something we can figure out based on past cases, kind monster sir… After all, you're a mockery of a vampire, not a real vampire. My personal view is that since you're practically human, you shouldn't have any trouble begetting a child."

"Begetting…"

That word.

It sounded both indirect and very to the point.

"If it was with a human, I'm sure the child that's born would be more human than you, at least… Oh, kind monster sir, I'm sorry."

"Huh?" I tilted my head when Ononoki apologized to me out of the blue. Did she make some kind of faux pas just now?

"I was assuming that you'd have a family with a human woman, but that's not necessarily going to be the case. There was the possibility that you'd have one with the Aberration Slayer. In that case—"

"Stop it. Talking about begetting a child with a little girl is enough to creep even me out."

"Fine, then we'll use my humble self as an example. Though it would be an instance of necrophilia."

"Come on, you should be using Hachikuji as the example here."

"Why would you be fine with me?!"

In any case, down the mountains we descended, loaded with unresolved anxieties—there was no sign of any town or village no matter how many hours we walked, even after dawn. But during one of our many breaks (I lost count of how many we took), we found ourselves blessed by a stroke of good luck: a single bar but a bar all the same of reception on my cell phone.

Of course, I knew that sometimes you could accidentally pick up some kind of signal when you were actually still out of service... I heard there were spots like that in the mountains, so while talking might be hard, I might at least manage to get out a text message if I tried enough times.

"You said we could get in touch with Kagenui by texting, right?"

"Yeah."

"I forget, Ononoki. Do you carry a cell phone?"

"No... I don't, just in case. I do remember her contact info, though."

"..."

Carrying a cell phone just in case would make sense, but I didn't quite understand why you wouldn't carry one just in case... In other words, was she wary of dropping her phone or having it stolen?

If so, Ononoki lived in an even harsher world than I'd imagined—she couldn't so much as walk around with a communication tool?

I wanted to continue down the line of thought if I could, but I didn't have room for it—I just punched the string of letters and numbers Ononoki gave into my cell and thought about what a cold, uncaring person I am.

"What should the message say?"

"Make sure it includes our secret phrase... Oh, and the cipher saying you'll wait for her reply. It's probably better if you don't include any specifics. She might not want to deal with us if she suspects that we're in too much trouble."

"Is she that hardhearted? If anything, I thought she was the type to come charging head-first into a dangerous situation."

"That's only when she's dealing with immortal aberrations..."

Other times, Sis is just a regular person for the most part, Ononoki said. "And actually, it'd be dangerous if she came charging head-first. If my sister is too excited when she arrives, you might end up getting exterminated, kind monster sir—oh, or maybe not. You're losing your power right now, aren't you..."

"In any case, I'd rather not make any more enemies than I already have..."

I know I shouldn't frame it this way, but while I was at it, I also sent messages to Senjogahara, Hanekawa, Karen, and Tsukihi to let them know that I was okay.

Though I wasn't in reality, they'd feel at ease knowing that I was in a situation where I could text them, at least.

I didn't want them to worry about me.

Heh. I'd become a considerate kind of guy.

Sending five texts in total took a bit of time, but I figured I'd think of it as a nice little break.

"Mister Araragi."

"What, Hachikuji?"

"I realize it's too late to be saying this, but the email you sent to Miss Hanekawa and the others read 'Dot worry.'"

"Yeah, it is too late! Why didn't you tell me earlier?!"

"I don't know if you want them to worry or not, but the normal reaction to a message written that poorly would be to worry..."

"..."

Hmm.

It's true that you'd be hard-pressed to call me an expert at using cell phones, but what an elementary blunder...

I turned off my phone, not to cut our conversation short or to avoid follow-up questions from Hanekawa and the others, but to preserve some of my valuable battery power. We then continued down the mountain, taking occasional breaks, and eventually reached the bottom the next morning.

August twenty-third, in other words.

Climbing down ended up taking more than a full day—and it was less like climbing all the way down the mountain and more like reaching a village within the mountains—in any case, we were wiped out.

It wasn't just my legs that felt stiff, but my whole body.

Was this how branches always felt? Must be tough.

Since we had been hiking unsure when the Darkness might show up out of nowhere, our level of mental exhaustion was incredible as well—it never did, fortunately, but the fact that it didn't meant that it might have appeared where Shinobu was, fomenting its own kind of anxiety.

"Well, kind monster sir, I guess the fact that we didn't run into a bear or anything that deep in the mountains should be reason enough for celebration... How's the reception on your cell phone?"

"I tried turning it on, but...hm, still not much. At least it's not out of service."

"I guess we got lucky earlier."

"I don't know about that. It looks like we haven't gotten a reply from Kagenui."

That I hadn't gotten any from Hanekawa or the other girls was weighing on my mind as well... Were they mad after all? Maybe they assumed I was dead already.

"Hmm... In that case, it might just be better to go ahead and call her. We can bother one of the homes around here and ask to use their phone. If cell reception is weak here, they must have land lines."

"Yeah…" I said, glancing at Hachikuji on my back—I was carrying her now after she'd run out of stamina and willpower halfway through.

Ononoki had her backpack on.

Now that I was back to normal, walking around with someone on my back was pretty tough, even if that someone was a ten-year-old girl… Actually, I doubt I'd have been able to carry anyone on my back down a mountain unless she was a ten-year-old girl.

What exactly about that was normal?

I was living dangerously.

"Will a direct call reach Kagenui if she's done with work by now?"

"Well, it will sometimes, and it won't at others… It's pretty random."

"What do you mean, random?"

"My sister always says that it's risky to fall into patterns as you go about your life."

"…"

Wondering about that, I walked down the unpaved path into the village—only a little bit further. In fact, I was just glad there was a path at all. We'd been walking on dirt and stones until just moments earlier.

"Now that you mention it, Oshino didn't establish any patterns in his life either—is that like some kind of shared rule amongst their old occult research club?"

Oshino and Kagenui had gone to college together where they belonged to the same club—it also counted Kaiki among its members.

How serious of a lineup could you get?

Of course, while they said they were researching the occult, it sounds like they just played Japanese chess all the time.

"But *shogi* seems to me like a game where established tactics are especially important… Maybe that's just a preconception of mine?"

"Izuko Gaen, too," Ononoki muttered. "Now that you mention it, she seems to have been a member as well."

"What? Really? So she knows Oshino, too—Oshino and Kaiki... That's kind of a strange connection."

"I think I heard she was their senior. From my sister... She said Izuko Gaen was a mean-spirited senior."

"She's mean-spirited?"

I couldn't believe it.

Wasn't there a single person in that club with a decent personality?

"Yeah. I heard her personality was worse than my sister's, worse than that Oshino guy's, and worse than Kaiki's."

"Can someone like that be allowed to exist? Are you sure she's not imaginary?"

If I was being honest, I didn't want to ask such a person for help, now that I'd heard about her... I wished I hadn't.

"Can we find a residential map? Probably not here. Where the heck am I?"

"You sound like Ryoga Hibiki saying that."

"Why do you even know."

"As weak as the signal is, you're getting something, right? In that case, can't you use your GPS to figure out where we are?"

"I don't really know how that kind of thing works... I just know how to use my phone as a phone."

"Yes, you do even mess up your texts. Dot worry."

"You'd better not turn that into a running joke..."

But now, I wanted them to worry.

I hadn't thought it would take this long to climb down the mountain... To be honest, I was starving for some Senjogahara, Hanekawa, and little sisters in my life.

Given our situation, I couldn't quite lose myself in cheerful banter with Hachikuji, either... My only hope was Ononoki now.

But Ononoki was cold.

Cold as a corpse.

She was a frightening tween girl whose most fundamental skill was her ability to ignore things.

"Which house should we go to for a phone?"

"A lot of these homes don't have door phones... Which is better, though, a home with a door phone, or knocking right on their front door... I guess you'd go with the latter if you were a salesman."

Which was exactly why I felt so guilty.

The fact that I was planning this out made it seem like I was doing something wrong. Well, wrong might be an overstatement, but something devious...

No, this was quite frankly no time to be prevaricating... It didn't matter who answered, I needed to sound sincere so they'd lend me their phone one way or another.

So I could be reunited with my partner.

My lifelong partner.

"Still, I'd prefer a home with a young girl, preferably in her teens... It'd make it easier to convince her."

"What a monstrosity of a line, kind monster sir. It seems that the monstrous parts of you are still alive and well. Bravo, well done."

We ended up picking a home more or less at random, one that kind of seemed like it had a nice entrance gate—I'd wanted to try the first home we reached, but we had to give up after their pet dog went wild barking at us.

The home didn't have a door phone, so I knocked on the front door.

"Excuse me. I'm a traveler. Please give me something to eat... Sorry, no, um, could you please let me borrow your phone—"

I explained what I was doing there, nearly spilling how I truly felt (It was easier for me to get hungry now that my vampiric nature was fading. I'd gnawed on twigs in the mountains to keep my hunger at bay, though).

I continued to knock.

"Excuse me, I'm a traveler—"

I continued to knock, thinking about just how suspicious my introduction sounded.

"I'll be right there-"

But no matter how suspicious my knocking, it couldn't have been anywhere close to the suspicion I felt at hearing the terribly aloof reply.

It was a very young voice compared to the home's appearance.

Very young, though not in its teens—but I wasn't tired enough to start thinking that I'd come across an opportunity or something.

"Thanks for waiting!" the voice said before the door opened.

It rattled to the side on unsteady rails.

Just as I expected, I guess—the person there was young.

A woman in her late twenties—and she had a youthful sense of fashion, too.

She wore a baseball cap turned to the side, baggy jeans, an XL, no, XXL-or-so-sized shirt, and accessories all over her body, necklaces, rings, et cetera—I was kind of surprised that she wasn't wearing sunglasses.

She didn't match the home's aged façade at all.

If you'll forgive me for sounding rude, she looked really fishy.

"Um..."

"Actually, while I said 'thanks for waiting,' I guess I was the one doing the waiting—nice to meet you," the peculiar woman remarked jokingly as she introduced herself with a smile. "I'm Izuko Gaen. The lady who knows everything."

028

The home obviously wasn't Gaen's registered domicile—coincidences that big don't happen.
 It was exactly like she said. Gaen had been...
 "Waiting."
 For whom? For us—of course.
 I think it goes without saying that her words made me think of Oshino.
 "It's amazing just how kind countryfolk are. When I told these people I was here waiting, they invited me in and said, 'Well, in that case, why don't you have something to eat?' I don't know what 'case' they were talking about—oh, it's enough to make you go soft. Not even Kaiki would try to defraud the people here—"
 "Where are we?" I inquired as we headed back towards the mountains—but in fact there was something else I wanted to ask her. What I needed to ask—was why she knew we'd knock on the door of that home.
 "Don't tell me you can't use an iPhone, Araragi. Here, just take a

look. We're right here, this dot. If you're curious, that means we're two prefectures away from your town."

"That's closer than I imagined..."

I wasn't sure how to feel.

Yes, I was relieved that I'd be able to take a train home... I was scared of airplanes since I'd never been on one, and I didn't have the money to travel by air in the first place.

"Want to check on an Android?" Gaen said, taking a second phone out of another pocket. "Oh, this one's out of service—too bad."

"How many cell phones do you have?"

"These are called smartphones. I have other cell phones, too. I guess five in total?"

"..."

While her words had just reminded me of Oshino, Gaen was very unlike him in that she was pretty tech-literate.

What was her deal?

Still, I did have to admit that she felt like his senior—except for the fact that she looked too young for that...

"Th-Then I guess you can instantly look up our way home using that smartphone, too?"

"Hmm, well. I guess it could do that, if everything works out right—yes, if everything does—"

For whatever reason, Gaen tried to dodge my wishful thinking.

"Um, Miss Gaen..."

"Oh, whatever. We can skip the greetings—it's not like we don't know each other."

She said this with a comforting smile, but she did know it was our first time meeting, right?

I couldn't know someone less.

"That's not true. You knowing about me is one thing, but I know about you—didn't I tell you already? I know everything—so I'd at least know every detail about you."

"..."

"Okay, let's talk around here," Gaen said, sitting down on an old bench that had been placed, who knows why, near the base of the mountain we'd just descended.

Almost as if she knew it'd be there—she sat down on this bench that blended into the scenery so well that I'd failed to notice it when I'd passed it by earlier.

"Sit down. What've you got to say? You want to talk to me, right?"

"Yes. But, well…"

I tried to say something but could only sit there, unable to voice any words or doubts.

It was a long bench, with plenty of space for Hachikuji to lie down beside me—Ononoki didn't sit.

She was standing as if she were on lookout duty, on guard. She might look cute, but her every mannerism nudged me to think of her as a true warrior.

"Come on, Yotsugi. What're you standing for? Get over here. It makes us feel awkward when you're standing there alone while we sit, okay? This is why I always say that aberrations can't read a room."

"…"

Yet her warrior bearing was futile in the face of Gaen.

"But Miss Gaen—"

"It's fine, just get over here."

Despite her valiant effort to mount a rebuttal, Ononoki was pulled over by Gaen's words, which left zero room for argument.

The only problem was that Hachikuji lying on the bench left no more room for Ononoki, who was forced to sit on Gaen's lap.

This seemed to be Ononoki's first time meeting Gaen, just like it was mine…but the lady was kinder to her than Kagenui ever was.

How do I explain it?

She had a personality that coerced you, fairly boorishly, into becoming friends with her—she stood in contrast to the others, whether that was Oshino, who spoke frankly with people in order to hold them at a distance, Kaiki, who never trusted a soul, and Kagenui, who only

233

ever seemed to think about fighting.

Actually, did those three have such difficult personalities precisely because of Gaen?

That was almost the impression I got.

"You know, Ononoki, if there's no place for you to sit, you could always sit on my lap. What're you thinking?"

"I should be asking you what you're thinking, kind monster sir," Ononoki shot back.

From atop Gaen's lap.

"Now, then—why don't you let this kind lady here explain this situation I'm sure you're very curious about. Izuko Gaen is someone who just loves to explain things. Kagenui was busy working when she got that text from you asking for help. She was in a tough spot, unfortunately, and the battle seems to be going long. That's why she ignored the message. Knowing her, she probably thought that Yotsugi would be more than enough to handle the situation. She believes in those she keeps as family, to the point where it becomes a form of violence—to the point where she's fine if one of those family members of hers dies as a result of her trust. But I knew—that this isn't a problem that you'd be able to handle on your own. I knew that an independent shikigami and a half-vampire whose link has been severed couldn't handle this problem on their own—which is why I came here to rescue you. Like I'm playing hero or something. In other words, really, I saved you some time and effort. A few day's worth," Gaen said in a single breath.

All I really got from this abrupt info dump was that she'd come to save us. When I thought about it some more, there were a lot of things that Izuko Gaen, someone who just loves to explain things, hadn't explained.

We asked Kagenui and no one else for help, and it should have been through a help-only hotline. So why did it not only get ignored by her but read by Gaen? It didn't make sense—and that text didn't have any specific details about our crisis, either... Maybe an expert could figure out the stuff about my link with Shinobu being severed by looking at my shadow, but still…

It felt like the more she explained, the more questions I had—but that meant she was sort of like the Darkness.

I didn't want to make the situation any more complicated.

"Hm? What's the matter, Koyomi? Was there something missing from my explanation? I'd be happy to add as much as you need if so."

"No…"

Now she was on a first name basis with me.

She was being so buddy-buddy with me even though we'd only known each other for an hour.

It was like she was walking straight into my home with her shoes on, tracking mud deeper and deeper inside—it didn't feel that bad because it was the ever-smiling Gaen doing it, but I couldn't conceal my confusion.

"Well, if I want you to explain anything, I guess it's why you knew we were here—we didn't even know what mountains these were—"

"It's because I know everything, Koyomin."

"Koyomin?!"

Now she was using a nickname?!

Who did she think she was, Senjogahara when she and I were all alone?!

"You could say it was my all-seeing eye—though in truth, I was clued in by the fact that a job I'd given to Yotsugi through a third party wasn't moving forward for some reason. I wondered why she wasn't showing up—and when I looked into it, I saw that you were involved, Koyomin… And I already knew all about Shinobu and Mayoi."

"…"

So, from the start, the job that Ononoki said she was putting off was connected to Gaen? No, that couldn't be it.

That was a little too much of a coincidence—it felt more right to assume that she had a hand in most such "jobs" to begin with.

Like she was some kind of boss.

Maybe Gaen was a major boss of some sort? She didn't look at all like it.

"Any other questions?"

"I have a lot of questions, but...no, I'll put them all off until later. So please, would you listen to...wait...I guess you already know, judging by the way you're talking? About the kind of situation we're in right now—and what we're facing?"

"Oh yes, I do. I have to admit it's something I wish I didn't know about, but I, unfortunately, even know about that. It's not easy being me."

"Then—"

"One sec," Gaen said. Just as I'd taken the bait, she held me back. "I understand how you feel. You want to know about this thing you call the Darkness as soon as possible—but don't get so worked up."

"Don't get so worked up... Easy for you to say—"

"It's fine—at least, you're not in danger at the moment."

"What?"

"*It's safe right now—I guarantee*," Gaen pronounced.

Now this was a pronunciation that lacked any explanation, any persuasive power, or any logic whatsoever—it almost sounded like she was only saying it to put us at ease.

But it was hard to refute her, too.

We didn't know a thing about the Darkness, after all—we didn't even know what we didn't know.

All we could do was rely on Gaen.

That was the situation we were in.

"You may be thinking that in your current situation, all you can do is rely on me. But Koyomin, that's not the case."

"..."

"Or rather—I'd like to move you out of that situation. I don't like it when all someone can do is rely on me—it makes for poor balance."

Gaen used the word: *balance*.

"So you're saying—I need to pay the appropriate compensation?"

"Hm? Compensation? Why, you almost sound like Mèmè—he

puts it that way because he's such a businessperson, but I'm not like that. Don't lump me in with someone as unprincipled as him. Listen, I just hate it when people rely on me unilaterally—which is why I want to rely on you too, Koyomin."

"You want to rely on me…"

"I'm saying we should become friends—for the time being, I have three requests for you before I dispense any useful information, Koyomin," Gaen said, holding up three fingers. "I want to ask you to do them for me as a friend."

"…"

"It's important to want to help out your friends, right? Heh, you know that unlike Mèmè, I don't believe in anything as cold as people just getting saved on their own. We live through saving each other, that's how we survive."

"Okay," I nodded. "Three things, right? I promise."

"Oh? Are you sure you want to say yes before you've heard me out, Koyomin?"

"You ought to heed a friend's request… And what's more," I could only say as I shrugged, not that I was trying to act cool or anything, "I'm in a situation where it doesn't matter what you ask of me. I'm going to have to do it, whether it's three things or a hundred—"

"Is that really how important she is to you? The former Kissshot Acerolaorion Heartunderblade?"

"Well, I mean."

It might have been hard for a third party to understand my relationship with Shinobu—and I didn't feel like explaining it at the moment, either. Gaen might already know without any explanation from me, of course.

But—even if she knew, I doubted she understood.

"And anyway, we don't have time. Even if you guarantee us our safety, you can't guarantee Shinobu's too, can you? If you have a request, please hurry up and say it—"

"Oh, that's what you're worried about? Shinobu must really be important to you if she's the first thing you're worried about."

"?"

What a strange way to put it.

If she's the first thing? She almost made it sound like there was a bigger issue elsewhere.

"*Maybe four hundred years ago*, but I doubt it'll happen now—though it might if the current situation persists. Okay, then I'll hurry up and get the words out. Before we go past a point of no return—so, request number one," Gaen began, holding up a finger. "There's someone I want you to introduce me to, and I'm in a bit of a rush—if you won't help me, my only choice will be to go to her directly, and she'd probably get a bad impression of me if I did. I want someone to be a middleman—and I think you'd serve best."

"I don't know who I could possibly introduce you to... I'm not what you'd call well-connected. Who're you talking about?"

"Suruga Gaen—though I guess she's Suruga Kanbaru now," Gaen said. "My niece."

"Oh."

Right, now I remembered.

I'd thought I'd heard the surname Gaen somewhere before—it was Kanbaru's mother's maiden name. She'd told me during the case involving her left arm.

They were aunt and niece.

Now that she said it, the resemblance between her and Kanbaru—didn't seem to be there at all.

They weren't at all alike.

"But why aren't you meeting her on your own if you're direct relatives?"

"Didn't I just tell you? Because she'd get a pretty bad impression of me if I did. The Gaen bloodline is tricky. I don't think she knows about my existence, either—I'd prefer to leave her alone myself, but I have my reasons. I guess you'd call them Gaen family reasons."

"An introduction... Well, I'll do it if that's what you want, but I'll need to get Kanbaru's permission first. Blood-related or not, if she says no...in other words, if she says she doesn't want to meet this 'aunt' of hers, I wouldn't be able to grant this request of yours."

"That's fine—I'll think of another way if she says she doesn't want to meet me. I don't want you to introduce me as her aunt, though. It'd be inconvenient."

"Inconvenient... Aren't you being a bit self-centered?"

"It isn't just for my convenience. In fact, it's out of consideration for Suruga's feelings—so, onto the second request," Gaen brusquely cut short the discussion of her first request to move onto the next. "This isn't a request so much as something for both of us—now that Yotsugi's gotten herself involved in this situation, there's been a bit of a problem with the job she's currently tasked with. It's still something that can be taken care of, but it'd be quite a bit of work—enough that it'd require the assistance of another expert."

"..."

Ononoki maintained a cool expression right there on her client's lap...but it seemed as though we'd caused Gaen a lot of trouble.

"So my second request is for you to maybe help out just a bit with that once this matter is all settled—you'd be useless as you are now, but I've heard you can be pretty handy when you're linked with the former Kissshot Acerolaorion Heartunderblade—so handy that Yozuru, of all people, praised you."

"..."

She'd praised me? After the way I'd fought?

It felt like she might have been joking...and even if she hadn't been, I wasn't gonna feel the least bit happy.

Well, it was only natural for me to help cover for whatever difficulties I'd tacked onto Ononoki's job, but given what Gaen was saying, it felt like—

"Is this something I'll be doing together with Kanbaru? Am I going to introduce you to her so that we can both help you out with your job?"

"Well, it's not my job—maybe you could call it our job. But you're right for the most part, I need Suruga's left hand right now. Of course," Gaen cut me off before I could get out any objection, "that too will be up to Suruga. If she says she doesn't want to help, I'll back down immediately. Just getting to talk to her will be help enough on its own—though your help will be absolutely vital, Koyomin."

"Okay. If you say so..."

I had no choice but to accept.

I'd need to choose my words carefully in bringing this up with Kanbaru, though—she showed a level of devotion to me that didn't even begin to make sense, so there was the risk of her agreeing to help out without so much as hearing the details first.

Yes, I got it, you don't need to say anything, you don't need to say another word, my dear senior! I'd accepted before you even asked me! or something like that.

No, she had a bigger vocabulary than that.

How exactly might I word it so that I'd be asking for her help but giving her the option to say no?

"Well, what's your third request?"

"Actually, you already brought it up. My third request was for you to ask Suruga if she'd help with the job, too—which you already said you would do, Koyomin, so now I can save you. Your big sis Gaen feels all better now. I'm so glad I can help you out."

"Is that so..."

Hearing that didn't make me feel any better, however—to be honest, I couldn't bear just sitting on that bench not even knowing what kind of predicament Shinobu was in.

"Um, excuse me, Miss Gaen? In that case, could we talk while we travel? I'm sure we could discuss this on a train—I'd like to hurry up and see Shinobu. I guess you could say I want to see her and make sure she's okay..."

"Your partnership brings a tear to my eye. I wish I could forge such a bond with someone." Gaen laughed, but she also didn't seem to be taking me seriously—and as proof of that, she wasn't even beginning to get up.

And not just because Ononoki was on her lap.

"Um, Miss Gaen—" Even I was getting a little annoyed, and I could tell that my tone was getting rough.

"Koyomin," Gaen interrupted in a pretty loud voice. It came off as somewhat stern, but she didn't sound all that serious because she was using a stupid nickname... "I'm telling you for your own good, you shouldn't leave this place—at least, not until you finish hearing what I have to say. I'm going to spell this out for you because it seems like I have to. Going back to that town is the worst possible choice you could make—it's the one thing you can't do."

"..."

"Yes, the one thing—at the very least, it'll ruin whatever equilibrium you've just barely maintained. Whatever decision you end up making *in the end*, you ought to stay here for the time being. You made the right decision to use the Disengagement Edition of Yotsugi's Unlimited Rulebook to come all the way out here to the middle of nowhere."

"But we got separated from Shinobu as a result."

"If it's that link you're worried about, I can restore it in no time at all. It'll be my way of thanking you for hearing out my requests, I promise you that much. And anyway, you wouldn't be able to help me with my job unless your link is repaired."

I've got a whole mountain of things I want Shinobu to do for me, too, Gaen added rather obtusely.

"Isn't it dangerous to let Shinobu act on her own, though? She's the one it's after—"

"Hmm. Maybe I ought to have started by correcting your misunderstanding that Shinobu is the one it's targeting—why exactly do you think so?"

"What?" I asked in turn—reflexively. "Um, well, because that's what she said? Of course, it's not like she was, uhh, that sure about it... Is she—not its target? But in her story about four hundred years ago—"

"That was the case four hundred years ago. I'm saying it's different this time—while it's only natural to take Shinobu's story as a reference point, Koyomin, your deductions are pretty sloppy if you think something's the case now because that's how it was before."

"..."

Hearing her spell it out, I had to agree, I'd been so desperate to figure out the mystery behind this unknown Darkness that I'd leapt to the easiest possible conclusion.

It was only based on experience.

That meant it was nothing more than a possibility.

If it was after Shinobu, why was it, anyway?

"Yeah... I guess that could have been random—maybe the Darkness doesn't care who its target is. Strictly speaking, we can't even be sure if it was Shinobu that thing was after back then—"

"Oh, no. I'm certain that phenomenon was after her four hundred years ago. That, *I know*—but I'm saying that this time and last time are different."

"You know..." I couldn't help but launch a jab at Gaen because she seemed to be giving me the slip, and throwing dust in my eyes, again and again. "You know everything—don't you?"

"Of course."

"Then you must also know who that phenomenon is targeting this time around."

"Of course."

I was sure she'd talk her way out of this one, too—so her affirmation took me by surprise. But I'd jumped the gun letting myself be surprised—because the real shock.

The true shock was still in store for me.

"It's that exhausted, napping girl over there the Darkness is after this time."

"...What?"

"In other words, Mayoi Hachikuji."

"What?"

029

"H-Hachikuji?"

"That's right. Which is why Shinobu is safe for the most part—your link being severed was like a random accident, but what amazing luck, there's a legendary vampire for you. And she might get even luckier. You could die and she'd go back to being at her full power."

I looked at Hachikuji.

Hachikuji, exhausted and sleeping—

The ghost of a girl I was best of friends with.

"I see," Ononoki interposed then. "Yes—I thought that might be the case."

"Really, Ononoki?"

"Well, like I said, I'd heard some things from my sister—but the possibility was there. Actually, it could even have been you, kind monster sir—anyone except me. I didn't want to create any confusion by throwing unnecessary info into the mix, though."

But.

Of all the possibilities, I thought it was most likely Miss Hachikuji,

Ononoki said, her face utterly expressionless.

I couldn't glean a single emotion—and it was her relentlessness that reminded me once again that she was an aberration.

Something decidedly different from a human.

Not something—I'd ever be able to understand.

"Don't look at me like I've done something wrong, kind monster sir—I did speak a little bit to Miss Hachikuji about this while you were passed out… We were only discussing possibilities, of course. If we're talking about probability, the likelihood didn't alter by so much as ten percent."

"What's going on, then? To be honest, I could kind of understand why it'd go after Shinobu—she's led a life so full of twists and turns that I could see anything happening to her. But not Hachikuji. She lived ten years as a human, then eleven years as a ghost—she's not in any position to be chased by that Darkness, even by accident—"

No.

Hold on a second.

It did feel—like the Darkness was moving toward Hachikuji earlier.

It went after her, engulfing the desks she was sleeping on—or so it seemed.

That was the feeling I got.

"Let me answer that question," Gaen cut me off just as I'd found myself grilling Ononoki. "It's not like Yotsugi really understands the situation. She only has secondhand information. I don't think even Yozuru saw what was actually going on—I don't believe her, she only seemed to be listening to half of my story. Maybe only a quarter."

"In that case," I said.

My tension ratcheted up—while it was good news that it wasn't after Shinobu, nothing changed in the end if it was going after Hachikuji.

No.

It only made things worse—if it was after Shinobu Oshino, a

former fighting vampire whether or not she's lost her powers, she had a better chance than if it was after Mayoi Hachikuji, your average ghost girl.

"I want you to tell me everything—not half of the story, but all of it. Tell me everything about the Darkness."

"Of course—that's why I'm here, after all."

But speaking from my outlook on life.

I think it's going to leave a bad taste in your mouth, warned Gaen.

While her words prefaced a story that clearly had a bad ending, just like Shinobu's before she recounted what happened four hundred years ago—this wasn't something I could afford not to hear.

Not now.

030

"I'm sure that Yotsugi and little Shinobu have already said this, and that you've felt it yourself, Koyomin, but that Darkness isn't an aberration. It's an existence that's something other than an aberration—a non-existence.

"Actually, you could say it's like a natural predator for aberrations.

"Or maybe the polar opposite of an aberration.

"While the Aberration Slayer and the Aberration Savior, the two blades Shinobu's first thrall wielded, also existed as aberrations' nemesis in a way, this is on another level—what's important here is that it's not an existence but a non-existence.

"It can't be defeated.

"It can't be killed, either.

"And eating it is out of the question—'running,' I guess you could say? 'Putting some distance' between it and you is really the most you can do.

"Though that's only temporary, of course—it's hard to always be running, a fact you should already know quite well.

"As you've encountered it two, even three times, Koyomin.

"Hm?

"What's that? Shinobu did get away from it once? Oh, well, I guess you can say that. If she's not its target now, it would appear as though she got away from the Darkness four hundred years ago—but that would be true in appearance only. It's far from the truth. I know very well just how far.

"She didn't get away from it.

"She succeeded in neutralizing the Darkness—by accident, though. She really does have incredible luck. It almost defies common sense.

"That's right.

"You can't defeat or kill or eat or run from the Darkness, but you can neutralize it.

"Yes, and I'm just about to tell you how to do that—but part of me is reluctant to, so forgive me for taking so long to get to it.

"At the very least, I'll have to start from the top.

"Its name?

"Yes, its name. All things need a name—every being has a name. But that's a nonbeing, not a being.

"No one can give that thing a name.

"Everyone calls *it* whatever they feel like, not just 'the Darkness'—everyone who sees or hears about *it*.

"For example, take the way they called the phenomenon being 'spirited away' four hundred years ago—others call it the Balancer or the Neutral or the Eraser...some even call it a Black Hole.

"Well, it does look like one. It's easy to get.

"You call it the Darkness—and there are some others who have called it that, too. It's such a straightforward description that it really doesn't express anything, but I like how simple and clean it is. I wouldn't say it's dull or mediocre.

"Personally, though, I don't think I'd give that non-existence a name. You give something a name to make it easier to understand—

but that thing isn't going to be any easier to understand no matter how you try to frame it.

"It won't get any easier to understand or more simple.

"There's no way to tie it down.

"It's unreasonable and absurd.

"That's what that non-existence is.

"A thing that doesn't exist—and a thing that erases existences.

"A thing that wipes out the existence of aberrations.

"Hm? Oh, yes, you're right. It does also wipe out humans with no mercy...but I guess that's just one method it uses to wipe out aberrations.

"Eliminating the witnesses, I suppose. If you want to make it sound like a modern-day crime, that is—I don't think that's its intention at all, of course.

"But you could say it's like a hired killer.

"Imagining a hitman comes closest to it. Though closer or not, it doesn't clear anything up. A hitman that wipes out aberrations—that's what's been targeting them. Shinobu four hundred years ago, and now Hachikuji.

"They're being targeted.

"Not that it's anything special—it's something that happens all over the world, you just never notice.

"You don't notice because this hitman does such a brilliant job—because normally you can't escape from that non-existence.

"Normally.

"There aren't many out there who can take action once that thing appears before them—and while Shinobu did get away, just about anyone, vampire or not, would die if three quarters of their body were consumed... And I'd say you were able to make the decision to immediately disengage thanks to your link to Shinobu, Koyomin. It was all thanks to your partner's experience.

"What's that? Your memories aren't linked?

"As long as your hearts are linked, it's enough.

"Oh, I'm being all doom and gloom? I could see how it might sound that way, but there's hope, too.

"You can relax. Relax.

"Even someone who knows everything like me can only tell you a little bit about what you call the Darkness, Koyomin—not because I'm missing information, though. There's nothing you can call information about the Darkness.

"You can't say you're missing something when it never existed in the first place, right?

"While I called it a natural predator for aberrations, you could also call it an anti-aberration, the way that anti-matter works on matter.

"Which is why you'll disappear if you collide with it—you see?

"You could also say it's not just the aberration, but also the non-existence, that disappears.

"You could, but they'd only be words.

"In any case, it's all over for you once you meet it. It's an all-powerful hitman—if you have a hard time understanding it as a hitman, then call it the Grim Reaper.

"No, I guess it'd be an aberration if you did—and once again, it's not an aberration.

"It's such a hard thing to represent, to talk about.

"You have to come at it from out around it.

"Not only that, you also have to talk about it exactly as it is.

"So, as for why a specific aberration gets targeted by this hitman. This part isn't unreasonable or absurd. I think you'll find yourself in agreement once I tell you.

"Maybe not in agreement, but at least you'll understand—for a fact about a non-existence, it's very easy to comprehend…or quite evident.

"You should be able to figure it out with some thought.

"In other words, you just have to think of something that Shinobu and Mayoi have in common. What do the two have in common, what's their common denominator?

"Come on, try giving it some thought.

"They're cute little girls?

"I'm so disappointed in you. Why would anyone or anything attack aberrations for such a borderline pedophilic reason? Well, that might be something you do, Koyomin, but *it*, at least, is different.

"They're being targeted for a reason. Though I've been saying it targets aberrations—if we're being more precise, what *it* targets are *aberrations that have strayed from the path of aberrations*.

"People who stray from the road of humanity get expelled from society, right? Likewise, aberrations that stray from the path of aberrations get expelled from the world—by way of a supernatural power. Yes, a supernatural power, one that some people might call fate. The inevitable force of fate.

"Fate. Do you like that word?

"I hate it. If you're in a situation where you're going to use such a word, I think it's better to go for something more childish, like 'supernatural' or 'power.' I'm the only one who needs to be talking like she knows everything—I know that Mèmè often sounds like he's seen through everything, but personally I'm not impressed by that.

"Of course, that's something that I don't like because it's *different* from me—still, I'll admit that this non-existence moves in ways that resemble fate.

"I hope you'll forgive me for putting it in a touchy-feely way.

"Hm? You're more confused by the idea of straying from the path of aberrations? I'd say that one is pretty straightforward... Okay, then try thinking specifically of what Shinobu did four hundred years ago.

"I'll tell you everything, Koyomin, but that doesn't mean you can quit thinking.

"Yes, that's right. Exactly.

"Four hundred years ago, Shinobu—*acted as a god.*

"She's a demon, but she acted as a god.

"That was the problem, and while it seems like she didn't realize it at all, she should never have done that.

"Listen, I understand what you want to say—Shinobu never called herself a god, it's just that the humans around her saw where her super jump landed and mistakenly thought of her as one. That's what you want to say, right, Koyomin?

"But you see—and this is the case for a lot more than aberrations, in fact you could say it about life in general—not making an effort to correct a misunderstanding is no different from lying.

"While it may seem uninhibited and respectable to say, 'Who cares what anyone thinks about me' and 'I don't mind what anyone thinks about me,' what you're really saying is no different from 'I'm going to fool everyone.' Especially in this case. It was like Shinobu intentionally didn't clear up the misunderstanding...I guess because she was enjoying her position as a god.

"On a whim, on a vacation.

"She put on a divine air.

"You wouldn't be able to criticize her if she became a god—aberrations turn into other aberrations all the time.

"But you shouldn't lie.

"Becoming a god is fine.

"It's tricking people into thinking you're a god—that's a problem.

"And that's why she was targeted for judgment—why that hitman went after her.

"And it went after more than just Shinobu—it went after everyone who 'witnessed' her as a god and not a demon—it corrected their mistake. Brutally, by force. Basically, this non-existence, the thing you call the Darkness, carried out its job of correcting mistakes—by making it so that none of it ever happened.

"By now you must see how Shinobu managed to 'escape' that non-existence. It should be clear. When she 'ran away' to the South Pole with her super jump—*she acted as a vampire.*

"She created a thrall.

"No, even before that, her absurd physical recovery—her super-regeneration, the expression of her immortality, might have been enough on its own.

"Because it exposed the lie that she was a god.

"That was all it took for the non-existence to no longer have a reason to act—I don't mean to dredge up something that happened four hundred years ago, but if Shinobu had eaten an aberration or given in to her vampiric impulses while she was playing at god, I doubt the people of that village, those fifty experts, and everyone else in the area would have disappeared—

"Oh, by the way. Those 'bad things' not gathering during the year that Shinobu lived as a god doesn't have any direct connection to the non-existence—it was just because she wasn't there as a vampire.

"No one witnessed Shinobu as a vampire, so she was able to escape those bad things' notice too—that's all.

"In fact, it'd have been good if 'they' had come—but in any case, that's it for my explanation.

"The witnesses were eliminated.

"No one was left to testify.

"And the culprit's lie was exposed—case closed.

"What's wrong with calling yourself a god? Is it really so bad that it warrants hundreds of people disappearing? How am I supposed to answer that?

"Those are just the rules.

"An aberration must never falsify itself.

"You sometimes hear about the characters in novels or manga starting 'to move on their own,' but what I'm saying is that doing so is against the rules in this case.

"I'm not sure what you think complaining about the rules is going to get you. It's not like I have the power to change them, I just know them.

"So in the end, Shinobu was judged.

"I personally think the punishment far outweighed the lie she told, considering how her life unfolded after that.

"No—it's true that she just barely avoided her punishment, or her judgment, before it was handed down, but it's also a kind of punishment and judgment to have every human around who's attached to you slaughtered. It's terrible enough to make you abandon your chastity.

"She pretended to be a god and so met divine punishment—his words might have sounded like spite, but they were true in the end.

"But that's all over now.

"It's in the past—and you're more interested in the present, right?

"There's no reason for Shinobu to be targeted now—while she's lost her vampiric nature and can't use much of her power, it's not because she's lying. That's her actual power level. She's not going to be targeted by the nonbeing.

"It's against the rules to falsify yourself, but it's fine to change. You can change your characterization.

"So she's safe.

"In that case you must know—who isn't safe?

"Mayoi Hachikuji.

"It's you—my little pretender.

"So why don't you start by getting up from your pretend nap!"

031

"Eek!" yelped Hachikuji.

She jumped awake at Gaen's sudden shout, which seemed to fill the air around us.

No—Hachikuji must have already been awake.

The whole time, just like Gaen said—or at least, at some point, she'd started to pretend that she hadn't awoken yet. Which would mean—

If she was only pretending to be asleep.

If she was pretending to be asleep, just like the time I put my hands all over her body—

"Oh, sorry to surprise you, Mayoi. I didn't mean to say that so loud. It's just that it'd have been a real issue if you kept pretending to be asleep like that."

"..."

Hachikuji paused for a moment, still looking surprised.

"Um—" she said. "Mister Araragi?"

"It's okay."

Stopping Hachikuji as she tried to say something, I grabbed her hand.

No—we held hands.

"Calm down. I don't know what's going on here, but I, at least, am on your side."

"Okay," Hachikuji nodded. I nearly wanted to put her on my lap and hug her the way Gaen was doing with Ononoki.

"Come on, you sound like you're making me out to be the bad guy or something. Cut me some slack, Koyomin, and you too, Mayoi. I'm on your side, too," a cheery Gaen assured.

While her honesty wasn't suspicious the way Oshino's was, my sense of friendship wasn't so feeble that I'd let someone get away with calling Hachikuji a liar to her face.

"What do you mean? What kind of lie are you accusing Hachikuji of telling?"

"I think you know."

"I don't know… Neither what you're saying now, nor what the hell situation we're in."

Now that she'd told me, I understood the utterly strange and mysterious phenomenon—the Darkness—though only tentatively. And yet—the situation hadn't improved one bit.

It was still full of things I didn't understand.

It all felt like a gigantic waste of time—if this was how it was going to be, I'd rather go straight back to my town to see Shinobu again instead of talking to Gaen.

I wanted to see Senjogahara and Hanekawa.

I wanted to see Karen and Tsukihi.

At the very least.

I didn't want to see—this truth of hers.

"Then I'll tell you, like some kind of famous detective who doesn't mind bringing about an awkward scene—*it's the lie of her being there right now.*"

"…"

"*You should have left this world to go on to the next by now.* Isn't that right, Mayoi?" Gaen said directly to Hachikuji over my head. Then, despite pulling her into the conversation, she continued before Hachikuji got a chance to speak. "And yet you continue to be there. *That is the lie you continue to tell.* The lie that you're right there. That's a pretty good reason to be upset. You wouldn't have to be a non-existence to tell you to knock it off."

"A lie? That's not what I intended..." Hachikuji said. She looked brave enough as she spoke to Gaen, not staring at the ground or getting choked up—yet Hachikuji couldn't meet her gaze.

She was looking away.

Just like she was looking away from the truth.

"It's not what I intended at all."

"Like I said, it's already a lie once you've caused a misunderstanding—Mayoi Hachikuji," Gaen pressed on with ruthless cheer. "It's as if you're a *ghost of a ghost* right now—and unfortunately, the world won't accept such meta-existences. Beings like that are fated to be swallowed up by nonbeings."

"A ghost—of a ghost."

Hachikuji repeated the words and seemed to gulp.

If I had to guess.

It was because they resonated so deeply—but I still had no idea what was going on.

"Miss Gaen? Could you please explain what you mean by that?"

"I thought I was done already—in fact, I'd like to go home if I may. But if you're requesting even more explanations from me, I'm happy to provide them. I do love to explain things."

"..."

"Mayoi Hachikuji is a ghost who died in a traffic accident eleven years ago—Mayoi Hachikuji is a snail aberration known as the Lost Cow, to be exact."

The Lost Cow.

An aberration that makes people lose their way.

An aberration that hinders you from finding your way home. An aberration—that keeps you lost, never able to reach your destination, only spinning around and around like some vortex.

"B-But that—"

"Yes. But that was something that you, your girlfriend, and that novice Mèmè resolved for her—the Lost Cow Mayoi no longer had to be lost," Gaen said. *"And yet—that child is still there.* What is that if not a lie?"

"…"

Well, sure.

Everyone thought there was something weird about that.

We wondered if that kind of thing really happened.

It wasn't as if we didn't have our questions about Hachikuji staying for so long in our town, on its streets, when she should have passed on to the next world—but we'd all put our doubts aside.

Actually, we didn't even see it as a problem.

We thought it was no problem at all and swallowed Hachikuji's explanation that she'd been promoted posthumously.

I mean, it wouldn't have been good for some people otherwise.

It seemed like a good thing, if anything—like fun.

I had fun chatting with Hachikuji when I met her on the street.

That's why—

"That's why it can't happen," Gaen declared. *"Do you really think the world is going to allow something that convenient?* What a ridiculous, happy end. Nearly hypocritical. I'll admit that there are red lies and white lies in the world. I know that very well. But you see, Koyomin—there's no such thing as an acceptable lie."

Not in face of the truth. Not in face of the rules, Gaen added.

"That child is telling a lie by existing and happily chatting away with all of you—and that's not acceptable."

"Why not…"

"I'm not saying that I find it unacceptable. The world does—sure, the rules might change one day, but that's how it is right now."

"..."

"Aberrations aren't allowed to stray much from their characterization—they can't act like another aberration or do something that would cause them to be mistaken for one."

Ultimately.

Ultimately, Mayoi Hachikuji is nothing but a Lost Cow.

"I'm sure everything would have been fine if she'd taken off that backpack and turned into a plain ghost, the way a shellfish can devolve out of its shell—but she needs to send people astray if she's a Lost Cow. She's not, though. Not since you saved her—"

I went to Senjogahara's home together with Hachikuji.

I never got lost when I was with Hachikuji.

In fact—she'd sometimes shown me the way.

That's why I thought that Hachikuji was no longer a Lost Cow—that's how I'd been seeing her.

That's how I'd been witnessing her.

It's how I'd been—deceived.

"Just look at how she fooled you—but really, that was nothing new. Didn't this child lie to you from the very beginning, Koyomin?"

"No. Hachikuji's—"

I gripped Hachikuji's hand. I held it tight.

"Hachikuji's never—lied to me. Not—once."

"Mister Araragi..." I could hear Hachikuji mutter behind me.

But I didn't turn around.

I continued to face Gaen.

"I guess so. You're right. My mistake," Gaen cooly retracted her previous statement—no, her question, in fact.

She was just asking—for my opinion.

"I guess it was to herself—that she lied."

"..."

"Whatever the case, the reasoning, the tale you tell yourself doesn't matter to a non-existence with no will or self-awareness of its own. So long as Mayoi has strayed from a Lost Cow's path, she's going to be judged and punished."

"Judged and punished—but that's…" I tried to push back.

I tried to contradict Gaen's words.

I was trying to prove something—that Gaen wasn't only mistaken about what she'd just said, but about everything.

"You don't have any proof of that—we don't know for sure that it's after Hachikuji."

"Sure, it's not like its rules are written out somewhere and its judgments are open to the public. If we're talking possibilities, there was of course the possibility that it was after you or Shinobu for so vaguely resembling vampires. Just like she'd said earlier." Gaen wrapped her arms around Ononoki, who sat on her lap, the way you might a stuffed animal.

Ononoki stayed expressionless.

I didn't have any idea what she was thinking.

"But, and while it might sound like I'm harping on this, that ambiguity is different from a lie. You and Shinobu have authentically changed into new kinds of aberrations. You transformed—you were altered. So while your story may sound unbelievable, it's not untrue. You two have been faithful to the characters you are. Which means the only liar here—is Mayoi."

"…"

"Well."

The truth had left me pale, and Gaen placed a hand on my shoulder. She had no reservations about doing this, as if we'd been friends for a decade.

"It's true that there's no physical evidence, but aren't there lots of circumstantial ones? The Darkness never came after you while Mayoi was passed out, did it?"

"Huh?"

My brain couldn't keep up with the point she was suddenly making.

But yes. Wasn't that true?

Right after it'd gone ahead of us to the other side of that turn at the light, right as Ononoki saved us with her Unlimited Rulebook—Hachikuji had passed out.

And as a result—the Darkness stopped.

It didn't come after us once we'd escaped using the Disengagement Edition—I wasn't sure about the accuracy of our conjecture that the Darkness is bad at dealing with vertical motion, but that wasn't what mattered—it simply couldn't follow us.

The "consciousness" known as Mayoi Hachikuji was gone for the time being.

"Yes, and as proof, didn't the Darkness show up even in that abandoned cram school as soon as she was awake?"

"Then what about when we were escaping through the mountains afterwards? Was it because she was tired and sleeping a lot? If it couldn't come after us, then—"

No, it didn't matter how often she slept... It wasn't like I'd carried her on my back the whole time...

We'd been walking together through the mountains, so deep that just standing in them wore you out—as we escaped downward, not knowing where to go—getting lost again and again—

"Oh."

"Right?" Gaen nodded at my realization. "Exactly. *You can't find your way right now*—regardless of Mayoi's intentions, you don't have any idea of how to get back home... So we could say Mayoi is fulfilling her duty as a Lost Cow in this situation. Which is why—the Darkness isn't appearing."

"..."

Gaen had said she could guarantee our safety—so that was why.

The Darkness wouldn't appear by Shinobu.

Nor would it appear by Hachikuji.

Of course—that was why, when Gaen bragged to us earlier about her smartphones, she wouldn't share our homeward route despite showing us our current location. Because the Darkness could appear at any moment unless I continued to be lost.

Now that I thought about it, I wasn't even sure if she was showing me where we really were at the moment—there was an extremely good chance she'd gone ahead and fed me false info to confuse me just in case I had asked someone in the village where we were...

Gaen was a way bigger liar than Hachikuji...

Not that I was going to criticize her.

Naturally, I wasn't going to criticize Hachikuji, either.

They hadn't done anything wrong.

No one had done anything wrong.

But—this wasn't about right or wrong.

What this probably was about—

"On the flip side, Koyomin... That means Mayoi would lose track of her role as an aberration again if you went back to your town and home—she'd be violating the rules and the Darkness would reactivate. While I mentioned earlier that Shinobu was really lucky, I've got to say all of you are pretty lucky, too. I hope it rubs off on me."

"So?" I asked Gaen, who was making it sound like the dust had settled and the curtain was about to fall. No—I hounded her. "So now, what am I supposed to do?"

"Huh?" She tilted her head, confused. She truly, genuinely looked like she didn't see why anyone would ever ask the question. "What are you supposed to do? What do you mean?"

"Well—okay, so I understand it's very likely that the Darkness is targeting Hachikuji."

"Um, we're kind of past talking in terms of possibilities here."

"So the question now is how to deal with it. Even if we're lucky enough to be avoiding the phenomenon because we've temporarily lost our way—that doesn't solve the basic problem, does it? I'm trying to ask you what I need to do to take care of this Darkness—"

"I already told you—well, maybe I didn't tell you, but you should be able to figure it out based on Shinobu's example. Right, Mayoi?"

Hachikuji replied with only more silence.

"Based on Shinobu's example? But I thought that in Shinobu's case..."

She escaped using everything she had.

And then she quit being a god.

She reprised her role as a vampire, and then—

"...Are you telling Hachikuji to go back to being a Lost Cow?"

That would be the only possible conclusion.

She just had to stop lying, and own up to it—she just needed to live an honest life.

As an aberration—

"If she keeps making people lose their way the way she used to—"

"I don't want to do that," Hachikuji responded.

Unambiguously, in her own words.

"I don't ever want to have to do that again."

"But Hachikuji—"

"I don't have to do that anymore thanks to you, Mister Araragi—I was able to visit my own home. That's why I'm never going to do that again. I made a decision to never do that again—to never tell those kinds of lies again."

"..."

Right.

I knew what Hachikuji's eleven years as a Lost Cow were like for her—so how could I ever tell her to go back to it?

It wasn't like being a vampire.

I wasn't a demon. I couldn't tell her that.

But in that case—we were stuck.

There was nothing we could do about the situation.

"M-Miss Gaen. Then what about a way to defeat the Darkness—"

"Like I said, that's not the kind of thing that you defeat. I've been going out of my way to use terms like phenomenon and non-existence, but if I'm being quite honest with you, that thing is something like a natural law. Like the way things fall downward—you might be able to float in the air for a moment by jumping, but you have to land eventually, yes? No matter where that may be—a lake, an ocean, or a mountain."

Inevitably, you'll land, Gaen said—and I had no reply.

I needed to argue back, but couldn't.

Nothing like this—had ever happened to me.

I'd never once been in a situation where there seemed to be so few courses of action—

"It's okay, Mister Araragi."

Hachikuji squeezed my hand back as she said that.

Almost like she was a big sister.

Just like the person I met that day—

She sounded strong and dependable.

"Then there's something we can do."

"There is? But what could we possibly do against that other-dimensional thing... She's saying it's like anti-matter to aberrations, even Shinobu at her peak couldn't take it on—even if I restored my link with her, heck, even if Oshino were here, what could we possibly—"

We were up against nothing less than a law of nature.

No matter what problems we faced or how ridiculous our situation seemed, we'd always dealt with it according to the laws of nature, whatever tricks we might've used.

We couldn't this time. And we certainly couldn't flout those laws.

"No, Mister Araragi, that's what I'm trying to say—we can do this like always. There's nothing special about this time, we just need to follow the rules and deal with this thing."

"What do you mean follow the rules," I practically parroted back, not understanding what Hachikuji was saying. "What specifically is that supposed to mean, Hachikuji?

"To be specific," she said, a smile spreading on her face. A satisfied smile that showed no sign of fear or anxiety. "I just have to disappear."

032

Gaen left without any fanfare.

She said she'd wait for us to contact her and gave me numbers for three of her five mobile devices—she said she couldn't give me all five for security reasons, but I don't really understand what she meant by that.

Of course I was going to keep my promise—I would contact Kanbaru, and I was going to help Gaen with her job. I wasn't going to lie there.

To lie…

"Ononoki… So why didn't you go back with her?" I asked the familiar, who'd gotten up from Gaen's lap to sit back down on the bench—looking as though nothing important had taken place, but still not standing up and leaving.

If she wanted to go home, surely she could have gone with Gaen—it would have been the most convenient for her, given her work.

"Well. I'm lost with you—I thought that if I went home now, the Darkness might activate."

"Oh. That's kind of you."

"Is it? Part of the reason is that the Darkness might come after me, as someone who 'witnessed' Miss Hachikuji. You might not be able to call it plain kindness. I don't know," Ononoki said, looking away.

I wasn't sure how serious she was being—but yes, that possibility did exist. No, but wait. The Lost Cow wouldn't lead astray anyone who walked away from it—so her concern might have been a little unnecessary.

Or it might have been an excuse.

"That's right, Mister Araragi, this problem is bigger than just me. I'm even going to be causing Miss Ononoki trouble—you understand, don't you?" Hachikuji said, sitting across from me.

Holding my hand.

No—Hachikuji wasn't holding my hand anymore.

I was just grabbing onto hers.

I'd grabbed it so she wouldn't go.

So she wouldn't disappear.

"After all—you know you're not the only one who's witnessed me, Mister Araragi. There aren't that many people who have seen me since I stopped being a Lost Cow, but a good few did—and the Darkness is going to go after those witnesses, too. To mention someone close to you, that includes Miss Hanekawa. I just spoke with her the other day."

"..."

"And there must be a lot of people who know about me, even if they haven't witnessed me. Right? Like Miss Kanbaru, Miss Sengoku, Miss Senjogahara, Miss Karen and Miss Tsukihi, Miss Shinobu, Mister Oshino—and Miss Ononoki, and even Miss Gaen, whom I met only today. You know that all of them could be swallowed up unless we do something."

"But they might not be."

"It's going to be too late once it happens, though—Mister Araragi. Do you want to make me feel the way Miss Shinobu felt four hundred years ago?"

So.
So please let go of my hand.

Hachikuji spoke the words quietly—like she was trying to reason with me.

"It's not fair for you," I objected, "to put it that way."

"But it's the truth—and it's the way things ought to be. You were supposed to have allowed me to move on to the next world in May, on Mother's Day—this is like overtime. No, not overtime—a bonus level, maybe?"

To put it another way.
A postponement—is what this has been.

"I didn't think this would last forever—it was going to end eventually. The end was more sudden than I expected, but well…that's just how it is."

When a child lies.
The lie usually comes to an abrupt end.

"I wonder if I lived a little too freely, doing things like going to your home and sleeping there, even if it was part of a lie. This case in particular didn't have any grave story or complicated reason behind it all—it's just that I kept on putting off going to the other side because I had such fun talking to you. I wanted to be able to enjoy those kinds of moments forever—or at least until your college exams were over, but, well, I guess nothing ever works out that neatly. I had fun this summer break, didn't you?"

"Wait… No, stop it. Don't try to wrap everything up. Don't start looking back. Nothing's going to end here—I'll figure it out. There has to be something, there's still time to turn this around—"

There had to be something, some way to save everyone.

Grave stories?

Complicated reasons?

Who needs them?

A girl, who had spent eleven years alone, just felt like playing for a while longer—is that something that deserved judgment, that deserved punishment?

A sentiment like that?

What about it broke the rules?

There had to be some kind of breakthrough we could make—because there was something wrong with the world if there wasn't.

"No, there's no breakthrough—in fact, hasn't the world been kind? Usually, you wouldn't get a few months like this, not when you're a ghost of a ghost—not when you're as preposterous as I am."

"No, but… But doing this, where we put all the blame on you in order to save everyone—"

"What are you talking about, Mister Araragi?" Hachikuji laughed. Like she was enjoying it. "Isn't that exactly what you've been doing all this time? You can't do that and then stop others from doing it themselves."

"Why?" I asked Hachikuji. Her attitude was nothing but cheerful, which almost made me angry. "Why are you able to stay so calm? Yes—it might look like that's how I've been doing things, but I've never once been able to stay calm. I've always been on the verge of tears—no, I've wept as I fought. How are you able to be that way, like you're not unsure or dissatisfied about a thing—"

"I would be lying if I said I'm not unsure… But I'm not dissatisfied. It was fun, after all. I'll just be in the sky watching over you from here on out, Mister Araragi."

"I'm telling you to stop saying that kind of thing—"

Listen to me.

I still haven't—talked to you.

I haven't talked to you enough.

There's still so much for us to talk about.

I want to talk to you more—I want to talk to you forever.

"Oh, I guess that was the problem. I shouldn't have said that I'm going to disappear. I'm going to go home, Mister Araragi. I'm going to go away—but it's not as if I'll have never been here."

"How's that any different… How are words going to make it any better—"

Even Hachikuji couldn't want this on the inside.

She had to be scared.

Just thinking back to the first time she encountered the Darkness—so desperate to escape it.

She couldn't be free of frustration and regret.

She couldn't be feeling fine—having to follow such an unreasonable rule, having to be judged by such an absurd law.

To be defeated by something that wasn't even an enemy.

To have to accomplish something that wasn't even a goal—it was all so senseless.

"Well, actually... Just like Miss Shinobu caused that incident four hundred years ago by pretending to be a god, I caused this one by pretending to be a wandering ghost—so I need to take responsibility."

"What responsibility..."

"Well—I suppose you'd want me to take responsibility for your bike first, Mister Araragi."

"Why would I care about..."

Okay, I did.

But that wasn't something I was going to force onto a ten year old.

"I'm not Miss Shinobu, but this happened because I wanted it to last just a little longer, and I need to settle this myself—"

"If you're going to say that, I'm just as guilty as you—I had fun talking to you, too. If you're responsible, then—"

So am I.

In fact, I was the one—who'd been entertained by Hachikuji.

And yet I couldn't do a thing now? How could I allow that?

I could never—so why wasn't I able to do a thing?

"Knock it off, kind monster sir—it's hard to tell which of you is the child here," Ononoki said by my side. Her expression as unconcerned and affectless as ever. "You need to learn when to give up—no, maybe in this case, you literally need to learn when to let things die. She's saying it's fine, isn't that good enough for you?"

"That's right, Mister Araragi—I'm saying it's fine."

"God, you just don't understand, do you?!" I raised my voice without meaning to.

Like I was lashing out.

"Stop talking about yourself for a second and try thinking about how I feel!"

This isn't about whether it's fine or not.

I don't want you going away!

"If it's the only alternative—then I'll just stay lost with you for the rest of my life."

"Mister—Araragi."

"Oh, right, there was always that—I guess that would solve everything, wouldn't it? Why didn't I think of such a simple solution? I just have to stay here and not go back to my town. All I have to do is stay lost with you for the rest of my life, whether it's in the mountains or in some unknown village. There'd be no problem then, because you'd be carrying out your role as a Lost Cow. The Darkness wouldn't attack Hanekawa or any of the others, either. I guess we'd be involving Shinobu, but she's always lived her life on the road. In fact, she might even enjoy going on that kind of a journey."

"Mister Araragi—"

"Yeah, that's it, that's what I'll do. Not a problem at all—I don't know how much longer I have left to live as a half-vampire—but I should be able to survive for at least another ten or twenty years. After that much overtime, that long of a bonus level, those eleven years of yours would finally be worth it and—"

"Mister Araragi!" she yelled.

It was the first time—Hachikuji yelled at me in this way.

"What are you talking about? You're going to waste twenty whole years for my sake? What about Miss Senjogahara? And Miss Hanekawa? And you have your little sisters, too. Even if you could involve Miss Shinobu, what about everyone else?"

"Well… I'd think about what to do for each of them…"

"Thinking isn't going to get you anywhere. You can't choose absolutely everyone."

You're not an Italian gentleman, Hachikuji tried to joke even in this situation. She was still the Hachikuji I'd always known.

"No… Even an Italian gentleman wouldn't be able to," I said. I was so useless.

I couldn't come up with any witty repartee or stage direction.

All I could do for her—was sit there and be sad.

Yes, even I realized that I was—just pretending not to know when to give up, just pretending to think, just pretending to agonize—just pretending to be at my wit's end.

But I understood. We'd already arrived at the conclusion.

Yes.

I—knew.

That ultimately, fate was something you couldn't change—I'd learned that from experience in a world eleven years prior to this one, hadn't I?

"It's fine, Mister Araragi. 'We might be apart, but we'll always be together,' or 'The memories in our hearts and minds will never fade,' or 'I'll always be near you,' or 'Our bond is eternal,' or 'I'll surely come back when you need me most'—please let yourself be persuaded by that sort of thing."

"How can I by anything as blithe as that?!"

Give me a break!

I brushed away Hachikuji's hand.

I stood from the bench at the same time—well, it looked like Hachikuji had successfully gotten me to let go of her hand.

Oh, fine.

I lose.

It wasn't like I was going to get in the last word against this girl—no matter how much we spoke, she was going to stay eloquent, and I couldn't even hope to argue it down to a draw.

So fine—it was fine now.

"Yes, Mister Araragi, it's fine," Hachikuji said.

I didn't turn to face her. My back was still to her.

"These last three months that I enjoyed talking to you are more than enough to make up for the eleven years I spent alone and lost on the street."

"..."

"So it's fine now. Thank you."

I heard a sound behind me.

Hachikuji must have gotten off the bench—maybe she was putting her backpack on again.

She was going to go already?

She wasn't dragging this out at all—and was actually satisfied?

Did she really need nothing more?

It wasn't my place to say anything if so—I don't believe that the only right thing for a ghost to do is to move onto the next world, but that's just what I think.

If our world's rules didn't think so—and more importantly, if Hachikuji didn't think so, I couldn't selfishly force my own house rules on them. That would make me no different from the Darkness.

What I needed to do here was probably to stop being stubborn, to turn around and see Hachikuji off with a smile—well, I could do it crying, too, but I was probably supposed to give her a proper sendoff.

That's how I needed to see her off.

At the very least, I wasn't supposed to be acting this obstinate and half-angry... I shouldn't be seriously angry at the Darkness, at Gaen, at Ononoki, at Hachikuji.

I'd probably regret parting with her like this.

I'd carry it around with me for the rest of my life.

I knew that but—I couldn't do it.

It made me feel like a petty human, even if I'd become a half-vampire and experienced all kinds of ghost stories—it made me see how small and empty a person I was.

It drove home that I'm just me.

I couldn't even humor one girl.

Ononoki was exactly right—I could barely tell which of us was the child here.

"Oh, that's right, Mister Araragi. Why don't we end by doing that thing we always do. You know the one."

"…"

Not that I had the mental fortitude to ignore Hachikuji when she called my name. After a pause, I still didn't turn around as some small form of resistance.

"What thing?" I said, keeping my reply short.

"You know, the routine that starts with me saying, 'A slip of the tongue.'"

"…Really?"

I wasn't able to smile, but nor could I stop this urge to smirk from welling up.

I couldn't believe it. Really, at a time like this?

Entertaining me.

Hachikuji was still entertaining me.

"So you were doing it on purpose after all."

"Of course I was. No tongue would ever slip like that," she smoothly admitted. "You know, Mister Araragi. Now that I think of it, we haven't done it a single time this story."

"…"

"Please, Mister Araragi. Think of it as your farewell gift to me."

"Fine, then."

I wondered if this was really a time for a slip of the tongue after all the times she'd spoken my name already—but in my current state, I didn't think I could give her a proper sendoff.

And I couldn't keep this up and give her a sulking sendoff, either—then at least, I might try a way that suited me.

Not soppily, but childishly, inappropriately.

We'd end our tale with a frivolous farewell.

The tale of a lost child and me.

273

Ah, geez.

Now I had a good excuse to turn around.

Ten-year-old girl or not, she really was like an older sister to me.

I wondered what was wrong with me, letting myself be the one getting humored—but while I say all this, to tell you the truth, a little part of me was looking forward to it.

Mayoi Hachikuji's once-in-a-lifetime, final slip of the tongue.

I wondered how it would slip.

To be honest, the bar was just getting higher and higher.

I'm sorry, but I wasn't going to quip back this time if it was a run-of-the-mill slip. I would just let it drop with a clunk. I'd simply reply, *Huh, what? Did you ask for me?*

That said, if she went for something too novel and a bit forced, I wasn't going to say anything. I'd just sit there "looking baffled."

Expecting so much from her might be cruel, but this was our last time.

I wanted her to rise at least that much to it.

I wanted at least that much license, too.

Okay.

With my mind made up, my feelings firm, and most of my nerves taut, I slowly turned to face Hachikuji, careful not to show any emotion.

"Smooch."

Hachikuji should have been behind me, but for some reason she was right next to me when I turned. Even more confusingly, her face was far higher up than where her height should have put it.

And she placed her lips on mine once I turned.

"………?!"

"Sm…oooo—oooch!"

After tasting my lips, while I was frozen in shock, for a few seconds, she moved back.

No, it technically wasn't Hachikuji who did the moving back. It was Ononoki, who had Hachikuji on her shoulders, who retreated.

Hachikuji matched my height by riding on Ononoki's shoulders—what had sounded like Hachikuji wearing her backpack was in fact the sound of the two of them getting ready.

Still in that position.

Mayoi Hachikuji said coyly:

"I'm sorry. A slip of the tongue."

Her cheeks were stained.

But not because she was blushing. She was crying, large tears dribbling down from her eyes.

Her cheeks, her eyes, it was all bright red.

But she was still smiling.

Hachikuji smiled until the very end.

"I loved you, Mister Araragi."

033

"So—what happened after that? What's the epilogue here, or the punch line, maybe?"

Ogi seemed eager to know more as we sat in the empty classroom after school, our desks facing each other.

"Nothing happened, really," I replied.

I'd grown languid in part because I was tired from all the talking, but my mood must also have grown a little dark after having to recall everything that had happened.

Dark?

No, that's not it. It wasn't getting dark.

Hachikuji arranged things—so that it wouldn't.

So that my mood would never grow dark, so that I'd never find myself in a bad mood when I remembered her or talked about her like this.

That capable producer had arranged things.

So I guess what I had now was fatigue from talking and just a bit of guilt over having spoken about her so casually.

It struck me as odd that I'd gone on and on about her—why was I telling this to a fresh transfer to our school, even if she was my junior?

Ogi Oshino.

Just because she shared a last name with that expert didn't mean she was worthy of my trust—in fact, it should have been a reason to view her with suspicion.

"After that, Hachikuji happily passed onto the next world, Ononoki and I returned to this town, and I helped Gaen with her work, just like I promised. As far as cases go, that was the bigger one by far... I never imagined I'd fight alongside Episode, of all people."

"What about Shinobu and Kanbaru?"

"Oh... I met up with Shinobu as soon as I got back to town and we restored our link. Actually, Gaen restored it for us—so she's still in my shadow. For her part, though, it does sound like she searched pretty hard for me. I don't really know. I feel bad for what I did to Kanbaru then—I mean, I did introduce her to Gaen, just like I promised, and she ended up getting pretty mixed up in the job I had to do..."

"Ah—that must have been tough. I can imagine," Ogi marveled in an exaggerated tone before beginning to clap for some reason.

It didn't feel like I'd told a story so moving that it deserved applause—if anything, it seemed ridiculous and more like some kind of funny story.

I didn't do a thing in the end.

I didn't do a thing, and I wasn't allowed to do anything.

It was one thing after another being done to me. I was being led from start to finish.

By Hachikuji—and by fate.

"But I still think—wasn't there something else we could have done? Some way to deal with the Darkness—if that thing wasn't an aberration, maybe there were different experts on things like it, the same way there are experts on aberrations. At the very least, I feel like Hachikuji made her decision too quickly. It couldn't have hurt to give it a little more thought before—"

"No, you just barely made it. Shinobu just barely made it in her story too, but you can't say the same about everyone around her. Compared to that, Mayoi did an incredible job reaching a decision as fast as she did. What wisdom, to decide to move onto the next world yourself before vanishing into the Darkness. I'd like to learn from her example. If you put the two side by side, probably because Shinobu is an immortal vampire, she took things a little too easy—oops! That was just a guess, of course."

"…? Uh huh."

Why had she rushed to add on that last part?

It wasn't like Ogi was there. Of course everything she said was just a guess or a simple conjecture…

"That's too bad, though," she lamented. "If only Hachikuji had the power to turn lies into truth like Hanekawa. You know, the kind of power to turn a cat into Black Hanekawa—heheh. I guess the world is a harsher place than that."

"Well, if I had to follow that story up with anything… It would be the way I ended up having to apologize naked on all fours to Senjogahara after I was unable to withstand my guilt over kissing a little girl, a young girl, and a tween girl over the space of a few days…"

"Er, um, that's actually a little too much information for me…"

"While I felt bad about burdening her with the responsibility of forgiving me, it ended up being an unfounded worry because she didn't forgive me… As my punishment, she forced me to watch a love scene between her and Hanekawa."

"Are you sure that wasn't a treat for all your hard work?"

In any case, I did get to hear a good story, Ogi said as she stood.

"Thank you very much."

"Oh, no, it's nothing worth thanking me for. I feel better too, having talked about it."

I still felt guilty over how casually I'd told the whole story, but now that I'd finally been able to talk about her like that, part of me might have been soothed.

Of course, it was kind of strange that the first person I'd told about Hachikuji no longer existing anywhere wasn't Senjogahara or Hanekawa or Kanbaru, but a high school girl I hadn't known for very long.

"Oh, no, at least allow me to thank you. Why, I nearly want to kiss you myself."

"I'm, uh, happy to hear that, but I'm going to have to ask you not to. Even if I wasn't going out with Senjogahara, I wouldn't be able to forgive myself if I kissed a girl who's over fifteen."

"That's the opposite of what a normal person's values would be. But thanks to you, now I know why things didn't work out. Both four hundred years ago and four months ago. Maybe what happened last month with Sengoku could have gone a little better if only we'd known why in advance."

"Last month? Sengoku—wait, you know about Sengoku?"

"Oh, uh, no, not at all. Umm, you know—she came up in your story just now. You said something about a girl who got in lots of trouble last month—"

"…"

Had I?

I'd said something about Sengoku? That, if anything, was something I shouldn't have been casual about.

The situation she was in right now was—

"Well, I think I have a good idea about what's going on in this town—Koyomi Araragi, Tsubasa Hanekawa, Hitagi Senjogahara, Suruga Kanbaru, Nadeko Sengoku, Karen Araragi, and Tsukihi Araragi—oops, and I guess there was Roka Numachi, too? Though you can take Mayoi Hachikuji off the list now—she really went away after that. She passed away."

"Did you just say something, Ogi?"

"Oh, no, Ogi didn't say anything—well, I have a lot of work to do, so that's it for me today."

For today.

She almost made it sound like our relationship was going to stretch far into the future as she began to leave the classroom—come to think of it, her nerves were a lot tougher than her slim figure might lead you to believe, given how she waltzed into a third-year classroom, empty or not, as a first-year student.

"Hey, Ogi. What do you mean by work?" I felt conflicted about stopping her as she tried to go, but I had to ask. I was curious because her words sounded so out of place coming from the mouth of a first-year who'd just transferred to our school. "Naoetsu High doesn't allow you to take part-time jobs, you know."

"Oh, I know I called it work, but I don't mean something like what a laborer would do—call it part of the family business. Maybe you could say it's a distinguished task that my family has carried out from generation to generation."

"So the same kind of job as Oshino? Working as what, an expert? As a balancer?"

"Oh, no, Uncle Mèmè is like the black sheep of the family—I do like him, but I'm a good girl who listens to her parents."

"Hm." True, I didn't imagine Oshino was adept at communicating with his parents and relatives and such. "So then what kind of work is it?"

"Just regular work. You could compare it to the overwhelming darkness that makes up the majority of space—the kind of work you can find anywhere. Righting what's wrong, ending what needs to be ended—if you really want to go there, I guess you could say it's punishing those who lie."

"…"

What was that supposed to mean?

Her explanation wasn't helping me out at all, no matter how far she went.

"Think of me as a herald of the end who allows no extensions—don't worry, you'll understand soon enough. I might even ask for your help in the future—bye, then!" Ogi said cheerfully before exiting the after-school classroom—leaving me all alone there.

"It kinda feels like everyone's disappearing and abandoning me. It's like I'm being deserted," I mumbled, but of course that wasn't the truth. My words were so sentimental that I wasn't even fooling myself.

I wasn't being deserted.

I—just wasn't moving forward.

It felt like I'd been stopped in my tracks at some point—I knew there were things I needed to do, but I wasn't moving my own life forward because I was so preoccupied with other people's lives.

I wasn't making great progress on my exam studies, either.

It always felt like I was failing to see something incredibly important, like I could never be at ease. Especially—since what happened with Sengoku. I couldn't focus on anything.

When I thought, I only thought about pointless things.

It felt like I'd given up on many things I shouldn't have given up on—and that even my sorrow over the fact was about to fade.

That's how it seemed to me.

It did seem that way to me.

"It's like there's so much I'm lacking—like someone's cleverly getting one over on me—like everything we worked together to gloss over and deal with, all of the little things we've agreed to ignore, are being pored over and examined with a fine-toothed comb and being thoroughly denounced—"

"Are ye aware?" a voice came from inside my shadow.

Right. I wasn't alone, was I?

She was there in my shadow.

She wasn't going to show herself at school, but I could hear her voice clearly.

"I assume ye are, but that woman—most likely is *something*."

"Well, yeah—she might be."

"Oh, so ye did know?"

"No—it's all a mystery to me."

I wish I knew. About all sorts of things, I said, standing up.

"For now, though, I want you to keep Hachikuji's disappearance a secret from everyone—let's see what happens if I only tell Ogi."

"Ah. And just when I thought thou were prattling on and on. Was this thy plan all along? Or did it come after the fact? So, for how long?"

"I dunno, until something happens—we'll need to keep Ononoki quiet, too. Hanekawa might figure it out right away, but let's keep pretending that Hachikuji still graces this town."

"Is that not out of thy lingering affections?" asked Shinobu. "Perhaps ye simply do not wish to admit that the girl has disappeared? Art thou certain this is not a wish to pretend that she continues to exist, the way one might count the age of a dead child?"

"..."

I didn't say anything, so Shinobu continued.

"Tell those kinds of lies—and the Darkness will swallow thee right up."

I snickered.

"Nah—"

Okay.

There was no reason for me to be sitting in the classroom forever—I needed to go back home already and study for my entrance exams. I had a laundry list of things to do, but that was at the top for now.

I wore my shoes and headed home.

I headed back home.

My way home, along which I would no longer be meeting anyone.

Oh, right, I thought.

Right, I never said that word to Hachikuji that day four months ago. What an idiot I was to notice only now.

It might be too late, but that wasn't a good reason. I needed to settle it in my heart.

I conjured the image of a young, pigtailed girl wearing a backpack, of that ever-energetic girl—of my little friend that I could still recall as

if she were right there—and spoke the word.
"Goodbye."
Mayoi Hachikuji.
I was fortunate to have encountered you.

Afterword

Come to think of it, I've written quite a number of afterwords, so many that I might even be able to make an entire book out of them, though I doubt I could get away with it ('course not). That being said, when I look back on everything that's led me to have this many pages written in afterwords alone, I see a lot that has and hasn't happened, but I also feel like those memories are pretty slapdash. Slapdash, or like a rush job on my memory's part. While this might come off the wrong way, "often never" might be more accurate than "has and hasn't" happened… It's not even a case of only remembering what's convenient for me and forgetting what isn't, I'll be depressed because something annoying happened to me when in reality that annoying thing never happened. It was all a dream I had the night before. If my memory serves me, I wrote this series to fight off an evil syndicate from outer space, but even memory, which should be serving me, can be rather unreliable. Beliefs and personalities, talents and abilities shift and change and end and begin, in which case I wonder what's certain at all in this world, only to realize, not a thing. As long as the world is held together by human perception, nothing is certain. On the other hand, if we recognize everything to be certain, the world will be filled with certainty, but does that seem deceptive to you? Just don't recognize the deception. I don't know.

Anyway, so many books in the series have come out that I'm not even sure which installment we're on, but this has been *ONIMO-NOGATARI*, probably the twelfth or so. The humanity's gone at this stage.* You could more or less say the same for the story, too. I feel like it was all about a half-vampire, Araragi, and some little girls... What kinda novel's that? As for the storyteller angle, the ones narrated by girls seem a little more serious, making Araragi seem somehow frivolous, which is a pretty big problem. I think he's being serious in his own way... Incidentally, I recall promising in a previous afterword that the truth behind the abandoned cram school burning down would come out, but it didn't have much to do with that case once I wrote it, huh? I do pray the memory is false. Anyway, this has been "Chapter Sneak: Shinobu Time," *ONIMONOGATARI*.

This is the second cover where we've gotten visuals of Shinobu Oshino, the last occasion being *KIZUMONOGATARI*. She really is gorgeous with her golden hair and golden eyes, isn't she? Thank you very much, VOFAN. I'm looking forward to you keeping this up for the last volume, *KOIMONOGATARI*.

I'd love to dedicate this tale to the beloved character who is Mayoi Hachikuji, but I know her. She wouldn't accept it.

* Prior to ONIMONOGATARI (with the exception of NEKOMONOGATARI) the Japanese title of every entry used a character with the radical for "person," イ (傷,化,偽,傾,花,囮).

NISIOISIN